WHICH WOULD YOU RATHER?

Published under licence by Brown Dog Books and
The Self-Publishing Partnership Ltd, 10b Greenway Farm, Bath Rd,
Wick, nr. Bath BS30 5RL

www.selfpublishingpartnership.co.uk

ISBN printed book: 978-1-83952-517-9
ISBN e-book: 978-1-83952-518-6

Cover design by Graeme Puckett
Internal design by Andrew Easton

Printed and bound in the UK

This book is printed on FSC certified paper

WHICH WOULD YOU RATHER?

GRAEME PUCKETT

BROWN
DOG
BOOKS

1

Friday 10 September 2021 – 5.32 p.m.

Brian Rayment turned the Honda Civic into the close and did a quick check to see how busy the road was. The road had an unusual arrangement but typical of the terraces built in the mid-1800s. The houses went from number 1 to number 38 up one side of the steep road and on the other side, each property had about 200 feet of land. Very quiet, just three other cars. Len and Rose, the old couple at number 21, had a far-too-big people carrier that their son Jonathan had given them and which they never used. A nondescript silver Euro hatchback with a wavy three-line scrape along the whole of the driver's side, was parked, rather irritatingly, outside his own house as it had been all week. Nobody knew whose it was. The burgundy Renault Clio, highly polished and gleaming as always, belonged to Brian's next-door neighbour Tony Bartlock. Tick one.

Tony spent a lot of time in his garage, not actually doing very much, other than not being with his soon-to-be-obese wife, Marlina. Tony and Marlina were a Donald McGill seaside postcard in the flesh, most of the flesh supplied by Marlina. He was downtrodden, skinny, with one of those for-God's-sake-shave-it-off moustaches that was never quite even. At some point in his career as a carpet fitter, he'd somehow come into a seemingly inexhaustible supply of red lead paint. Tony painted his garage, his shed, the fencing and any wooden fittings or fixtures in the garden with the red lead paint. The garage, where he spent most of his spare time – just about all of Tony's time was spare now that he'd retired – the garage had been painted twice in the last eighteen months. This was about average. Since the red lead paint made its inaugural appearance in the autumn of 1992, the garage had been painted forty-two times. Forty-one times in the red lead. Once, for a brief spell of five weeks during August/September 2012, it was green, the colour green that children paint grass, but it was soon back to its familiar red.

Marlina was fat and miserable. It was unclear whether she was miserable because she was fat or miserable despite being fat. It may have been that she was independently miserable. She was generous to a fault with her misery and made just about everyone she came into contact with miserable too. Her only pleasure in life appeared to be making Tony's life miserable. Tony was miserable now and so he was in his garage. Tick two.

Six weeks ago, carrying a large monkey wrench and a small clean screw-top jar, Brian had walked into Tony's open garage.

'Hiya, Tone – you there?'

The garage was empty as Brian had expected. He'd been watching it for about twenty minutes under the pretence of tidying the boot of his car. There'd been no movement or sound coming from the garage and Brian had assumed Tony had gone indoors. Once Brian was in the garage he quickly unscrewed the jar and crouched to the floor, which was heavily repaired cracked concrete. That was typical of Tony and typical of the things that irritated Brian about Tony. Why did he keep pointing in the cracks with piddly bits of concrete that wouldn't last the year, or using leftover mastic fillers and sealants? Why the hell didn't he just do the job properly and resurface the whole floor?

Brian could feel the startings of irritation about the floor but mentally shook himself out of it and got on with the task. He set the open jar down and then with his right hand he brushed together some of the concrete dust. Closing his hand around the small mound, squeezing tight, he lifted it in his clenched fist and like a human hourglass let the dust trickle into the jar. He screwed the lid back on, stood up and put the jar back in his pocket just as Tony entered the garage.

'What you doin' in 'ere?' asked Tony in his usual mumbled confrontational tone.

'Hiya, Tone,' said Brian brightly, ignoring the question. 'Here's that wrench I told you about. I've had it for years – got it at a boot sale – never needed it. You're much more likely to get some use from it.'

Tony looked around. *Almost as if he's checking to see if I've nicked anything* thought Brian. *Cheeky git.*

'Yeah OK – oright – ta,' Tony thanked him, somewhat reluctantly.

'You're welcome.' *I'll be getting it back soon enough … miserable git,* thought Brian.

'Anyway just popped in to give it to you. Thought I heard you in here so had a look. I haven't nicked anything too valuable.' Brian caught the fleeting look cross Tony's face that told him he'd been spot on about Tony sweeping the place for anything missing.

Turning and walking out of Tony's garage, Brian called out, 'Seeya, Tone,' waving his hand above his head but not looking back.

He could feel in his trouser pocket the weight of the jar containing the floor dust.

2

Brian had been running through his three-point checklist for over five weeks. He usually ticked two points – often Tony in the garage and the jar of garage floor dust. Three times he'd ticked off only two other cars, but on each of those occasions Tony hadn't been in the garage. One particularly frustrating day there were just three other cars, Tony was in his garage, but Brian was using his sister Sandie's car and didn't have the jar with him, as it was in the glove box of the Honda.

But today was the day – he had the jar with him.

Tick three.

As well as the screw-top jar of dust, Brian had brought a water vaporizer and a cast-iron waffle iron. The waffle iron had been the last item Brian had decided on. He'd played around with the idea of a brick – too awkward to hold in one hand; a cricket bat – too heavy and needs both hands; a piece of lead pipe and a hammer – both bad shapes that would leave tell-tale indentations. He needed a weighty, broad, flat surface with no distinguishing textures or marks, but also a means of holding or swinging it in one hand. The waffle iron was perfect. A heavy, square cast-iron slab on a slim steel shaft, with a comfortable wooden handle. The important thing with the waffle iron was making sure he knew which was the flat smooth back and which was the giveaway waffle-squared front.

Brian was fond of the cinema and films and television, the whole glamourous world of Hollywood and the movie business. He often imagined he was in a film and how he would be lit and from which angle he was being filmed. He pictured himself as the slightly tarnished hero of his life whom men would be fascinated and drawn to, and women would look at and desire from afar. He recalled the film *The Day of the Jackal* and the scene where the assassin is practising and adjusting the sights on his sniper's rifle. Edward Fox – the Jackal – has suspended a large watermelon from a tree and is using it as his target. This whole scene resonated with Brian. He'd pictured himself as Edward Fox when he'd bought six large watermelons at a Sunday market several weeks ago.

That Sunday afternoon he drove into the countryside to a spot in the New Forest he remembered going to with his grandparents. He put the first of the watermelons in a large, net vegetable bag and suspended it from a branch of a tree that he remembered climbing as a boy. He estimated Tony's height to be five feet six. The last time he'd spoken to Tony he spent the entire time working on and adjusting his estimate. He himself was five feet eight and if he looked square on at Tony he was looking straight at Tony's eyebrows. Five feet six was close enough.

Using an expanding tape measure – a roll of inches as a neighbour, a car-mechanic, always called it – he spent the next quarter of an hour adjusting the swinging melon until the top of it was exactly sixty-six inches from the ground.

Sixty-six, world cup, 4-2, Geoff Hurst hat trick.

He warmed up with a few arm exercises, swinging and rotating each arm in turn. Then with the waffle iron. It felt good and comfortable in his hand. Without any further preamble or psyching-up, he swung the iron round and down as hard as he could into the watermelon. It destroyed it. The net, the melon, the whole lot lay on the grass in a red pulp. The thing that had surprised Brian was how quick it all was. One second the melon had been hanging, still, dead weight from the tree branch – in the next instant it was a still, dead weight ruined in the grass. One swing of his arm. He imagined Tony there. He could picture the slow dissolve shot from a close-up of the melon into Tony's head and then a fast back zoom to see his whole body lying in the grass … and cut.

Over the next hour, Brian went through all the melons as he adjusted his technique, as Edward Fox would have done. By the third watermelon, he'd started working on a sideways smash in a sort of forearm volley approach. He concluded that he would need to connect with the back of the head, so had to work on a foolproof way to get Tony to turn to his left. By the sixth and final melon, he'd finalised the procedure. The strike would be a strong, sweeping sidewinder 'volley' from the right into the back of Tony's turning head.

3

Brian reached into the back seat of the Honda and picked up the now familiar-feeling waffle iron. Two weeks ago, he had wrapped the head of the iron with cling film, as it had remained, even through his daily fifteen-minute workouts swinging the waffle iron in powerful right to left sweeps. He checked that the cling film was still securely covering the head. He opened the glove box and took out the water spray and the small jar of dust.

With the car door open, concealing the whole midsection of his body, Brian held the items out of the car. He sprayed the cling filmed head of the waffle iron with water and then shook the dust from the jar all over it. He took one last long look up and down the road. Dead. Not a sign of life anywhere. Holding the iron down by side he shut the car door and walked towards Tony's garage.

As he approached the open garage doors, with his free hand he took out a £20 note from his back pocket.

He entered the garage and called out, 'Hiya, Tone. Whadja think of this? I reckon it's a fake – look at the queen's head.'

He breezed in, reached past Tony and held the note in the strong light of the chipped red Anglepoise lamp. Tony played his part well. He mumbled something, look displeased to be interrupted, adjusted his glasses and took the note, holding it up to study it – his back to Brian.

Brian adjusted his stance so that he was side on, left foot forward keeping his eyes on Tony as he raised the waffle iron to shoulder height. This was it. This was the moment he'd played out a thousand times. Sometimes in black and white – sometimes in colour. In slow motion, time-slice, close-up, with a dolly zoom and recently with an added soundtrack of a heavy, sustained piano discord. He imagined film students in years to come writing papers on this classic scene and debating whether this or the shower scene in *Psycho* was the best murder scene ever filmed.

This was it.

Brian called out in a sharp, alarmed voice, 'Oh my God, Tony! What's that on the door?'

As if in electrical shock, Tony jerked round to his left to look at the door. In the same instant, in a well-rehearsed action, Brian swung the waffle iron round hard into the back of Tony's head. Tony crashed into the tool cupboard then went straight down.

Once again Brian was struck by the speed with which it all happened. Seconds ago Tony had been a living, breathing, miserable man studying a £20 note. Now he lay prone and still on the concrete floor of his garage, his head bearing a remarkable resemblance to that first watermelon.

Brian's heart was thumping, not from the exertion but from the powerful adrenalin rush. He stood still for nearly a full minute, taking in the scene and running through what he needed to do now.

He took three latex gloves from his back pocket and stretched one over the bloodied end of the waffle iron. He put the remaining pair on. He went to the workbench and switched on the CD player and hit play. While the player was whirring in readiness, he lowered the volume right down. Once the CD was engaged he turned the volume up and heard the opening bars of 'Apache', the first track from *The Shadows 20 Golden Greats*. In thirty years the only music he'd ever heard coming from Tony's house or garage was the Shadows. Brian knew that when the film of this came out, 'Apache' would be the soundtrack to the 'waffle iron scene' as it would become known, the threatening beat of the opening Apache tom-tom starting at the point where Brian walked towards the garage.

Brian leant the covered waffle iron against the tool cupboard and crouched down to look at Tony. He gripped a handful of hair and lifted Tony's head, turning it slightly and repositioning it so the wound rested squarely on the concrete floor. He reached across the body and retrieved the £20 note. Having then turned up the volume of the CD to near maximum, he picked up the waffle iron and turned to leave.

'What the bleed'n ell's goin' on 'ere?' said Marlina, who stood in the doorway.

4

Brian's heart stopped. It stopped – then thumped back into action with a huge breathtaking beat. Act! Act now!

Marlina was looking at her unmoving husband and the blood around his head. She was taking a deep breath and preparing to scream. Act! Now!

Brian ran straight at her and threw his entire weight into her, cannoning her into the wall. She dropped, and sounded very much like a sack of wet sand as her head hit the concrete floor. She exhaled with a deep sigh and died.

Brian's first thought to himself was, 'In the last two minutes I've become a double murderer.' He then wondered if it was some sort of record. He pictured the Guinness Book of Records – fastest time to kill two human beings was two minutes and eighteen seconds by Brian Rayment on 10 September 2021. The victims were a husband and wife … No, it would have to be fastest time to kill two human beings in two separate killings. Brian reasoned that there would have been plenty of double simultaneous kills using bombs or a car for example.

What about a machine gun? He considered. A stream of separate bullets but so fast as to be almost as one.

He revised the Guinness Book of Records entry a second time. Fastest time to kill two human beings by two different methods. This was achieved in a unique incident by Brian Rayment on Friday 10 September 2021 in the astoundingly quick time of two minutes and eighteen seconds.

Having sorted the problem of his Guinness Book of Records entry, he realised he should turn his attention to the bigger problem of the two bodies. Marlina was a nuisance.

He felt with the weeks of planning and preparation, that 'Operation Tony' was all in hand. Marlina had just landed at his feet unannounced, unplanned and now very much unalive.

Brian had meticulously planned 'Operation Tony' so that he'd be found in his garage having fallen and cracked his head on the concrete floor. Oh dear – nasty accident – hard luck, Tony – neighbours all shocked – funeral in two weeks – lovely bloke – on with the show.

But a husband and wife both having an accident and each cracking their heads on the same little garage floor on the same day was a different kettle of fish, and a fairly fishy kettle of fish come to that.

Maybe Marlina came into the garage to call Tony for tea or something. Did they eat tea? She certainly did – she ate anything on offer. Maybe dinner? No, it would be tea for them, dinner's in the middle of the day. She came to call him for tea, saw him lying there, fainted, collapsed, or whatever it is large, overweight people do in these situations, and Bob's your uncle.

It could happen, thought Brian.

He wondered whether the idea of a suicide pact would fly, but he had to admit it didn't seem likely. Two middle-aged people deciding to kill themselves together by falling over onto the concrete floor in their garage.

In the interest of thoroughness, he briefly ran through some other options. He considered trying to move her, but quickly abandoned the idea due to a regularly recurring lower back strain. He pictured a night-time scene, probably filmed *nuit americaine* where he was halfway across the road dragging Marlina to his car. A close-up shot of Marlina's heels scuffing and breaking on the gravel road in the moonlight. His back gives out and he collapses in agony on top of Marlina. He can't move. Lights in the street start to wink on, curtains twitch … He shook the scene clear.

He wondered if he could dress the garage scene to look as if vandals had broken in. Tony kept lots of 'rattle' cans of spray paint, as well as the red lead. Brian had a sudden clear image of the garage having been turned over. The tool cupboard, tools, broken bottles and jars, screws, nails and unknown liquids covering the floor with Tony and Marlina in amongst it all. Aggressive sprayed slogans covered the walls.

Brian liked this idea, particularly the spraying of anti-Shadows slogans, but quickly rejected it when he realised it could get (a) quite long-winded and (b) quite noisy.

He stood there surveying the scene, thinking what a mysterious scene this would appear to whoever discovered it. He himself was feeling like a mysterious stranger in a dark thriller. He was having these thoughts just as 'Man of Mystery' started up on the CD – track 2 of 20 Golden Greats. This happy tie-in would be used to good effect in the film. He pictured a slow pan around the carnage on the garage floor, ending with a slow zoom into his furrowed brow and enigmatic expression. The volume increases on the opening bars of 'Man of Mystery'. The distorted first twang of Hank's Strat, followed by the four solid strums. He liked very much the idea that not everyone, in fact only a few, would pick up on the cultural reference. The problem was this soundtrack was turning into a Shadows soundtrack … No no no – can't have that. He mentally substituted 'Man of Mystery' with 'Dead Finks Don't Talk' by Brian Eno until he had time to give it more thought.

So, leave them where they are. Marlina came to call Tony in for his tea – collapsed when she saw him lying there.

For the second time, Brian turned to leave the garage. Tony gave a throaty groan.

5

Once again Brian stopped in his tracks. Tony was trying to move his head and continued to groan.

Right – simple choice. It was either finish him off or leave now and let's see how he gets on. Finishing him off seemed a bit heartless. It didn't feel right picking on a badly injured man. Maybe he could try and help him – make him comfortable, call an ambulance, be the hero. As much as the idea appealed, Brian could see nothing but problems with this. There'd be awkward questions and more to the point, awkward answers.

Although … he could say he arrived home and heard a loud crash coming from Tony's garage. He called out but there was no reply so he went in and saw the two of them on the floor. Marlina had bought it, but his good friend Tony was hanging on in there, so he did what anyone would have done and tried to help him.

'I just did what anyone would have done and tried to help him,' he would say.

Brian crouched down beside Tony. 'Can I get you anything, Tone?' he asked in a vaguely patronising way.

Tony moved his head slightly and opened his mouth.

'Tone?'

Tony closed his mouth.

'Tone, can I get you anything ... I said,' repeated Brian.

'Nnng,' replied Tony, after another two or three seconds.

'What's that?'

'Rrnnng.'

This wasn't shaping up well. Here he was trying to be a hero and help, and Tony was messing it up, not giving him a chance.

'What's "nnng" mean, Tone? What's rrnng? What're you talking about, Tone?'

'Nnrn.'

Typical, thought Brian, *thoughtless self-centred ...*

'Tone' as well. What sort of nickname was that? It didn't suit him at all. He had no body or muscle tone – certainly no musical tone, no real colour tone – well maybe some sort of mid-grey tone. Why, he wondered, did names always have to be shortened using just the first syllable? Tony was already an abbreviation of 'Anthony' he assumed. And another thing – what was that 'H' in the middle of 'Anthony' all about? How about using the first bit of Anthony – Ant. Would that work better?

'ANT! CAN I HELP YOU?'

Nothing. He pictured Dec sadly shaking his head.

'CAN – I – HELP – YOU – ANT? Oh forget it. You sort it out for yourself then, old son.' Talk about ungrateful.

Brian picked up the spanner and the waffle iron and stood looking at the two of them. Tony had quietened down again now.

He needed to give some serious thought to the best course of action. He'd go home, make a cup of tea and sit in his favourite chair. A bit of toast as well, two bits of toast, with butter ... sit in his favourite chair and get thinking. He left the CD player on – because Tony would have. He also left the red Anglepoise lamp on, with its yards and yards of twisted well-out-of-date paint-spattered cable. He hoped the CD and the lamp would create a convincing Tony's-still-alive atmosphere while he went home to consider the next step.

He turned and walked carefully towards the garage door, avoiding any of the blood, and the other unknown liquids that had been upset during the first three Shadows tracks.

Facing him, just inside the garage doorway, was a nervous-looking stranger in an ill-advised Hawaiian shirt. It was a size too small, or rather the stranger was a size too big. Why did people do this sort of thing? Doesn't he own a mirror? Doesn't he realise Hawaiian shirts are loose? How did he get to the age of whatever the hell he was without learning about stuff like that? And by the way – who the hell was he?

He looked with a frown at the nervous man, who was saying something about the car parked in front of Brian's house – the one that had been there all week – the one with the three scratches.

'It wouldn't start. Sorry to bother you. Wondered if you had any jump leads ...' He came to a halt with his explanation, apology and request as he finally took in the carnage lying all around. His eyes were wide open and he was preparing to scream, creating a face very, very similar to the one Marlina had made not six minutes earlier.

Brian thought, *I recognise that look – He's going to make a noise – He's going to scream – I have to stop him as quickly as I possibly can – Not just stop him, silence him – How can I silence him? – What's handy? – I could just barge him like I did Marlina – No it's not a clear run at him – I could throw something at him –*

Better be at his head – Better be a good shot – What can I throw? – What can I reach? – The CD player? – No – The spanner? – No, traceable back to me – The Anglepoise lamp? – Heavy base – Yes!

Brian thought all these things in one fully formed instantaneous understanding.

He reached forward, grabbed the top shade of the Anglepoise which was very hot and flung it in a well-practised side-winding arc at the nervous stranger. The lamp streamed across the room trailing the yards of twisted cable in the bright 60-watt light.

The heavy base of the lamp caught Mr Nervous heavily on the elbow while the hinged arm continued its journey and swung the hot metal lampshade into his cheek.

'Ow – Ow – Ow,' he shrieked.

'Shuddup! What's the matter with you?' said Brian in a shouted whisper. 'You don't go "Ow – Ow – Ow" when you've been hit with something. Can you imagine Robert Mitchum or Jason Statham or Tom Cruise going, "Ow – Ow – Ow"? … Well, maybe Tom Cruise,' he conceded. 'When you've been hit with something,' Brian explained, 'you either shake it off and come out swinging or else you drop like a sack-a-kack – either dead or unconscious. None of this "Ow – Ow – Ow" lark.'

Mr Nervous had stopped to listen to the lecture, but now he was desperately trying to pull the still-brightly-shining hot lamp off himself. The twisted cable wasn't making things very easy, however.

Brian realised he had to take control of the situation. He reached towards Mr Nervous ('Nervy' as he'd be called on screen), grabbed a handful of the cable and gave it a hard yank. He felt resistance and heard the 'Owing' start up again. He coiled one loop of the cable around his hand for better grip and pulled it violently as hard as he could.

In that instant, the lamp went out, leaving the garage in a dark late afternoon light. The heavy base, the hinged arm and the shade all clanged and clattered onto Marlina's legs.

The most striking effect though was 'Nervy', who just stood there juddering, wide-eyed and gripping the bared ends of the cable which had been pulled free of the lamp, smoke already starting to curl up from his clenched fist.

Brian just watched fascinated. After a full sixty seconds, Nervy finally played the part well and dropped dead to the floor like a hanged man cut down, his right hand burning now with an orange flame that flickered and lit the garage nicely.

6

Brian went over to the garage door and tried to shut it. Things inside the garage had reached the point where they needed to be kept from any more prying eyes … or potential victims … Brian added to the thought. The door wouldn't shut because Nervy's head and shoulders were sticking out of the garage and onto the forecourt of Tony and Marlina's driveway. There was an old grey boiler suit, spattered with years' worth of red lead paint, hanging on an angled nail in the door. Brian took the boiler suit down and threw it over Nervy's head and shoulders. From inside the garage, he tied the legs of the suit together around Nervy's neck. Now, still inside the garage, with his left hand he gripped the knotted legs of the boiler suit and hauled Nervy's head and shoulders up off the ground and just inside the garage in a kind of sitting position. With his right hand, he pulled the garage door shut, then let Nervy's head bang back against the door.

Brian considered his new record and revised entry in the Guinness Book of Records. The fastest recorded time to kill three human beings, by three different methods, was seven minutes and four seconds. He noted that since he first whacked Tony and switched on the CD player, the disc had only reached track 4 of *The Shadows 20 Golden Greats.*

The forthcoming film of today's events would be called, *To The Shadows* – no no, *Death in the Shadows* … no that's not right. Brian ran through several variations on this theme. *The Shadows of Death* – *The Shadows of Death in the Garage* – too long – *Murdering Shadows* – no that sounded like a documentary on wiping out Hank and the rest of the band one by one – *Murder in the Shadows* – that's not bad.

Murder in the Shadows starring Brian Rayment.

Murder in the Shadows starring world-record holder Brian Rayment.

Bri Rayment – Brian R – Brian 'Killer' Rayment – Brian K Rayment – what does the 'K' stand for, Brian?

He considered an anagram of his name – Barry N Inmate – Barnie Mantry – Barry Nitmane. Not good.

So. Introducing three-times-killer, world-record holder Brian K Rayment in, *Murder in the Shadows*.

Now that was clear in his mind he needed that tea and toast and time to think.

7

Brian sat down with his tea and toast, switched on the television and began the too-complicated and frankly boring procedure of scrolling through Netflix options. Seen it – seen it – seen it – don't wanna see it – seen it etc. He switched off Netflix and flicked from one tv channel to another. There was yet another cooking or baking programme on. *Cook Off*. It featured a soap opera star who'd been killed off last year and a comedian who should have been. He was showing himself to be every bit as inept at cooking as he was at comedy, just slightly funnier at the cooking. The two appeared to be having a competition to see who could ruin the most food in the shortest time. As far as Brian could see it was a close-run thing with the soap star just in the lead thanks to letting a bowl of whisked eggs slip to the floor.

The unpleasant bleached-blond presenter, a professional chef, was telling the comedian that he needed to 'fry it off'.

'FRY IT OFF?' shouted Brian at the tv. What happened to good old 'fry it'? What's the 'off' got to do with anything? Everything's off these days. Bake off, cook off, fry it off. You wouldn't have caught Fanny and Johnny frying anything off. Why did people feel the need to change perfectly reasonable words and phrases? Could you just add 'off' to any cooking situation?

'Hold on while I just grill this off.'

'So just boil off the eggs and check that the toast is cheesed off.' What if you were making pancakes?

'When they're golden brown just toss them off – be sure to wear gloves and an apron – be careful not to toss them off onto the floor.'

The professional chef was back, airing his forty-six-year-old views on the comedian's plums.

'COOK OFF,' shouted Brian as he changed channels.

"… one of the cleanest examples we've ever had on the show," said the new well-presented presenter in a salmon-pink suit which he'd almost exactly matched to his salmon-pink tan. His black shiny shirt gave him the overall impression of an enthusiastic liquorice all-sort. Brian could imagine the presenter tasting of sweet coconut, with that distinctive chewy liquorice kick in the middle. The coconut-flavoured presenter was holding and turning a heavy-looking lamp that resembled a tangle of Ivy branches.

'Three thousand quid,' shouted Brian, who was nothing if not interactive when it came to television.

'These are very scarce in this condition and …'

'Four thousand,' interjected Brian

'… certainly an extremely sought after design …'

'Five and a half grand and that's my final offer.'

'I'm sure you could reasonably hope to realise fifty or sixty pounds at auction,' the presenter was saying.

'I'll tell you what I've realised,' replied Brian as he switched off the television.

He'd realised he needed to get back to the more urgent consideration of what to do about or with the three bodies in Tony's garage. He'd earlier taken a clean sheet of A4 copier paper from his printer and folded it in half.

He took a pen from the table and wrote at the top of the folded sheet:

Possible solutions.

1) Leave them – let them be found.

2) Get rid of them – make sure they're not found.

3) Destroy the bodies – let that be found.

4) Move them – let them be found somewhere else.

5) Destroy everything within a thirty-yard radius – probably bomb or fire.

8

Number 1) Leave them and let them be found would undoubtedly be the easiest solution. The only trouble was there would be a lot of unknowns, anxiety and waiting and wondering, which didn't sound like a good recipe for relaxing life. There'd soon be a strong police presence. Tony's garage would be cordoned off and designated a crime scene. 'Forensics', as they called them in police dramas, would be crawling all over the place. There'd be door-to-door enquiries and he'd have to make tea for the two policemen – policemen or lady policemen – police people, possibly police people of colour or of no colour. Yes – most likely it would be two police people of no colour. Then there was the question of biscuits. Should he have a selection of biscuits or just one type? What about sandwiches? No, too much like a tea party – certainly not quite the thing for a mass murder inquiry. Might as well have a cake selection and sticky buns.

'Excuse me, Officer, could you pass the doughnuts.'

So just biscuits then. What would come across as a good honest biscuit?

Rich tea, ginger nuts, digestives, chocolate digestives? Rich tea, he thought, and half a dozen on a plate. Three each for the police people. Suddenly that seemed a lot of biscuits to be eating while you're trying to gather evidence in a murder investigation.

Brian made a sudden decision to scrap the number 1) idea of leaving them where they were, primarily due to the catering difficulties.

2) Get rid of them – make sure they're not found. Probably this would create the most work for him. Brian started on a train of thought involving incineration, butchery, baths of acid, midnight trips rowing out to sea, quick-drying cement. Just the thought of these was making him tired … and a bit peckish. He made two more rounds of toast and while he was buttering them he mentally discarded idea number 2).

He very much liked the idea of number 5) destroying everything within a thirty-yard radius. Now that could do the trick and could also be great fun but he knew nothing about explosives, except for some reason you needed weedkiller.

Brian found he could remember five incidents in his life where things had unexpectedly or spontaneously exploded. The first was an aerosol can of cellulose paint, that had accidentally been heaved into a bonfire. A full can of BMW arctic blue cellulose, heated to 100 degrees, blows with quite a fanfare if you know what I mean. There'd also been some large flat stones in a bonfire that had cracked and fired out red hot flinty shrapnel. Then there were chestnuts on a barbecue, an egg in a microwave, a shaken-up bottle of Cava. The trouble with most of these was that they were messy and would take a fair bit of cleaning rather than being destructive and causing total obliteration.

He briefly ran through a trial version of the explosion idea. He could gather up all the aerosol cans he could get his hands on: paint, deodorant, hairspray, furniture polish etc. He'd add to that five or six bottles of the cheapest fizzy plonk he could buy, some big stones, two dozen eggs and a big bag of chestnuts. Finally, a couple of large bags, sacks or tins of weedkiller of course. He'd also need to buy about four microwave ovens. In the dead of night, he would take all of these into Tony's garage and get the ovens plugged in. He'd then cram them with all the ingredients – set them all for two hours, then scarper. Even as he made plans Brian knew this idea was born of defeat and would probably end up making rather than solving problems.

The two ideas which involved him moving the bodies had been worrying him, niggling away in the back of his mind like long-awaited test results due from the doctor. One body – possibly. Two at a push, with a well-devised plan. Three was living in the realms of fantasy – that'll never do.

This left just idea number 3) Destroy the bodies but leave them to be found.

He quickly came to the conclusion that this was the route to take. Why hadn't he seen it immediately? Of course it was the best idea, combining, as it did, the fun of destroying the bodies with fire, aerosols, chestnuts, weedkiller or whatever, with no need for any heavy removals afterwards.

9

Saturday 1 September 2021

It would need a bit of rethinking, as it would be imperative that everything used in the destruction should belong to Tony and ideally already be in Tony's garage. Not things he'd brought with him. Brian decided on a middle-of-the-night trip to do some stock-taking of any potential self-destructive contents the garage had to offer.

At 2.35 in the morning, wearing latex surgical gloves and plastic bags held over his feet with elastic bands, he quietly slipped out of his front door, which he left very slightly ajar, stopped still and looked up and down the road. It was quiet and dark. No sounds – no lights of any sort. He stayed looking and listening for over three minutes, then walked cautiously down his front path and over the road to Tony's garage. In a black bin liner he carried another whole roll of heavy-duty bin liners, duct tape, a strong flashlight, notebook and pencil. He reached the doors and saw they were still in the 'fake locked' position as he'd left them. He quietly swung the padlock arm around and unhooked it from the two door handles. He opened the doors just enough so that he could squeeze in, and left the open padlock hooked over one of the handles ready for when he left.

The building was in darkness but for the moonlight through the single window and the red glowing dot of the CD player, now quiet and in standby mode.

The three bodies had a very different look about them in this light. This would be filmed from ground level, low angle with the bodies large and in the foreground, and him, the returning murderer, towering above them, legs apart, arms folded, silhouetted against the moonlight from the single window. He wondered if there was an appropriate threatening version of 'Moonlight Becomes You'. Chet Baker was as close as he'd get … or … how about the Beatles – 'Mr Moonlight'?

Yeah I'll do that, thought Brian, glad to have sorted out both the camera shot and soundtrack before he turned to the task in hand.

He took out the roll of heavy bin bags and tore off the first three, he also took out the tape. Stepping carefully between Mr Nervy and Marlina he made his way to the window and taped the overlapping bags to the frame, effectively creating a blackout. Hell's teeth it was dark in here now. He took out the torch, switched it on and held it between his knees. Taking the duct tape he tore off about two feet, immediately got it stuck to itself, and cursing he screwed it up in a ball. Now his hands weren't free. He thought a moment. He placed the tacky ball on top of his head and pressed down. It stayed there. He took the torch and placed it pointing forward on top of his head on top of the sticky duct tape ball. He pressed this down. This too just about stayed there. Much more carefully this time he tore off another couple of feet of tape. He attached one end to the top of the torch and pulled the tape down under his chin and back up the other side of his face to the torch again – pulling it as tightly as he could and finally securing it by pressing down again. He was impressed with this homemade Davy lamp.

He put the tape back in his carrying bin liner and took out the pencil and notepad. He put the bag on the floor.

'OH NO! Damn damn Billy Ugger damn,' said Brian as he realised he'd put the bag down in Tony's head. This was a bigger problem than just the initial grim realisation of settling his supplies in his neighbour's brain matter. He didn't want to leave his supplies here but he sure as merry hell didn't want to be taking bits of the inside of Tony's head back to his own house.

Brian started looking for any useful ingredients, accelerants or flammable aids.

Lots of red lead paint – probably useless. White spirit though, that was good, and some dirty old cellulose thinners in a jar labelled, somewhat unnecessarily, 'Dirty thinners'. Also, there were two jars of dirty turps: one jar of 'Dirty Turps' and another possessive jar of 'Dirty Turp's'.

And that's why I had to whack you, thought Brian.

There was a great deal of wood lying around and racked on some high supporting cross members of the garage. He systematically opened all the cupboard doors and found eighteen cans of well-out-of-date cellulose paint.

Two large coils of oily rope and a box of rags were in the next cupboard. Then, aiming the torch headlamp lower, Brian's heart bumped again as he saw two easily recognisable shapes under the bench. Please be full – please be full.

He remembered talking to Tony years ago when there'd been the petrol strike. Tony had proudly shown Brian the two army-surplus jerry cans he'd bought at a boot sale. He'd smugly boasted how he always kept them full for just such emergencies.

Brian reached under the bench and gently rocked one of the cans. It felt heavy and the weighty slop of liquid was audible. He repeated the rocking on the second can with the same result. He knew he should still do the final check. It would be just like Tony to fill up petrol cans with water or red lead paint or creosote or something. Brian had to drag one of the cans forward a bit to get access to the spring release cap. It was stiff but sprung open, releasing an immediate strong petrol vapour. He clipped the cap back and checked the second can. Perfect – forty litres of petrol. No more stock-taking needed, he decided, except for the taking stock of his bin liner with Tony's blood on. However risky it might be, it had to be a better decision to leave it here in the garage rather than take it home, he decided.

10

Still elated at discovering the petrol cache, Brian absentmindedly opened and closed the remaining three drawers which were in the workbench. He'd already started to close the third drawer when something finally registered and grabbed back his attention. He opened the drawer again – fully this time. Just as he'd thought he'd seen, about half a dozen brass gun shells were lying beside a green-labelled box marked '.38 COLT POLICE POSITIVE 50 Central fire smokeless cartridges'. Wedged behind the box was a bulky triangular package wrapped with a dirty cloth. It was very heavy as he slid it forward and removed it from the drawer. Brian had watched enough films and crime dramas to know what it was. He laid it on the bench and unwrapped the cloth – as he did so he caught the strong oily smell of the gun. It had an old fashioned, wartime look about it. Tilting his head so the torch shone directly on it he found the inscription COLT Police Positive .38 on the barrel.

Brian picked up the gun with a feeling of awe. He'd never seen a real gun in real life let alone hold one. The weight and feel had an alarming comfort about it. It felt made for his hand. He let it hang by his side, feeling the full heaviness. In the dark, he savoured the momentous occasion. Here he was, Brian Rayment, holding a genuine police revolver.

He couldn't quite get his head round the fact that it was Tony's. Questions tumbled into Brian's mind. What in the hell was Tony doing with a gun? Was it his? Had it been his dad's? Had his dad been a policeman? Were all policemen issued with guns? Had he ever used it? What did it feel like? Can I have a go?

Still standing with the gun at his side he knew he couldn't resist it much longer. Staring at a wall cupboard, he turned slightly side on and planted his feet evenly and firmly. He glared unblinking at the cupboard and set his mouth mean and straight. In one deft movement, he swung the gun up and hit a threatening pose at the cupboard.

'Are you talkin' to me? Are YOU talkin' to me?'

Take two. Arms hanging straight down, side on, the mean glare – the swift raise and pointing of the gun.

'Are you talkin' to ME?' … 'Well, I don't see anyone else here.'

Take three. 'Are you TALKIN' to …' BAANNG!

The noise was deafening in the small dark confined space at almost 3.00 in the morning of a very still, quiet night. The cupboard had splintered noisily and a jar of something inside had shattered, sending glass tinkling to the floor and liquid running all over the bench. Brian's heart was racing – the silence now in the garage seemed deafening. His ears and brain were switching from hearing complete silence to intense noise as the air reverberated with a shock wave from the accidental gunshot.

A fabulous smell hung in the air. A smoky, oily, burning, macho kind of smell like a smouldering peaked cap, thought Brian. He thought it would make a great aftershave – he'd definitely buy some. What would it be called? 'Smouldering Cap' he presumed.

'New – Smouldering Cap – The fragrance for men who live on the edge.'

'New – Smouldering Cap – The killer's choice.'

'Killer's Cap – For smouldering men.'

'Smoulder – The new killer aftershave for men.'

Brian switched off the torch on his head, made his way to the doors and opening one a bare inch he peered out into the street. No lights, no windows opening – it all seemed quiet. He reasoned that the noise probably did wake a few people, but given that it was over in an instant, they would have laid in bed listening for further commotion for a few seconds then gone back to sleep.

The finding of the gun and the shot fired were extra considerations now in his course of action. He needed to go home and reassess things. He'd return in an hour at 3.50 exactly and set in motion whatever plan he'd come up with.

He crossed the garage, reasonably carefully, back to the doors, stepping mainly between the bodies but once stepping on Marlina's fingers. When he got there he switched the torch off and slipped outside into the silent moonlit street. Having reset the padlock to its fake locked position he crossed the road, walked up his own front path and went indoors.

11

The gun was causing the most problem. Brian had already worked out a pretty foolproof plan of action, but the gun threw a spanner in the works.

There were two conflicting gun issues that Brian could see. Firstly, Brian wanted the gun. He'd always wanted a gun. This was a good gun as far as he was concerned, in that it was a vintage gun and looked like a proper gun should. It made a hell of a good noise and would make him look cool under just about any circumstances Brian could imagine.

On the other hand, the gun could be used to good effect to set up an alternative murder scene or at least muddy the waters nicely. This, however he thought it through, would entail leaving the gun at the scene and hence him not ending up with it.

Which would you rather, he thought, *own a real working vintage gun and a box of vintage ammo but have three dead bodies to deal with – or, give up any chance of having the gun but have a relatively easy escape route from the finger of accusation being pointed at me?*

There was the added niggle that Brian was proud of the fact that he'd never stolen anything in his entire life – even as a boy, not so much as a bar of chocolate. He was a law-abiding citizen – apart from the murders – and now here he was contemplating the theft of a gun. It bothered him.

All things considered, which of course was exactly the intention, it made sense to use the gun to misdirect any investigation.

He could still have some fun though, he reckoned. Maybe even get to fire the gun again.

He needed to shift the focus firmly onto someone else – one of the three on Tony's garage floor. What if Mr Nervy was a burglar and was in the process of doing over Tony's garage but was interrupted by Tony and Marlina? No that didn't ring true – a married couple in their 60s confronting an armed intruder.

How about Mr Nervy coming into the garage, Tony shooting him, Marlina arrives to see what the fuss is about and Tony shoots her as well, either by accident or taking advantage of the kerfuffle to get rid of her? Oh no, this was getting absurd – surreal even.

Surreal.

Yes, surreal.

It occurred to him: surrealism, that was the answer. It wasn't necessary to create a plausible sequence of events, in fact, the more implausible the better. If he could create a scene of as many inexplicable, unexpected and unrelated elements as possible it would make an investigation into motive, time scale and MO nearly impossible.

Brian set about gathering up all the things he could think of to use in his surrealist murder scene. By 3.45, he had four bin liners full of props and distractions as well as the necessary tools and matches. He had rigged up the very successful torch headlamp in an updated more sturdy version which he now had taped to his head. He put on a fresh pair of latex gloves. With the torch switched off, he quietly opened his front door and stepped into the cold night again. He clicked the door off the latch, pushed it closed silently, then made his way, for the last time ever, to Tony's garage.

12

Once inside the garage Brian found the one clear bit of floor space, at the end opposite the doors and in front of the workbench, and emptied the contents of the four bin liners. He had the first few steps planned but would then improvise.

First, he crossed the room to Mr Nervy and went through his pockets. A wallet and its contents revealed that he was Mr Stuart McGregor. Mr McGregor had £45 in his wallet, which Brian took.

While at home earlier, when thinking about stealing the gun, Brian had come to accept that there was no point in getting overly concerned about stealing. Murder trumped theft in the misdemeanour stakes, so any crime of a lesser nature than murder might as well be OK now. He put the wallet containing Stuart McGregor's credit cards and other personal items back in Stuart's pocket. Brian also trousered Stuart's car keys.

He was ready to start preparing the set. It took three short trips up and down the garage, in between the bodies, to carry the 10 lbs of baking potatoes he'd brought over to Mr McGregor. He crammed the potatoes under the man's shirt and down his trousers. He admired his work as he walked back to the heap of props to fetch the whiskey jar full of pennies. Tony, who had finally come to rest with his mouth open, was now the recipient of the pennies. When Brian could cram no more pennies in Tony's mouth he emptied more into Tony's shoes, down his socks and forced one into each of Tony's clenched fists.

It was going well. It was starting to become satisfyingly strange.

Brian opened a new 5 l. tin of red lead paint from one of the floor cupboards with a screwdriver he'd brought. He emptied the entire can of paint over Marlina and with the help of a sweeping brush from the tool cupboard, he painted Marlina from head to feet in the red lead paint. He forcibly jammed the empty paint can on her head and managed after quite a struggle to stretch the plastic handle under and in amongst her several chins. It resembled a sort of stovepipe hat – the kind worn by Isambard Kingdom Brunel in that photo of him by the big shipyard chains.

Pleased with his surrealistic start on the three corpses, Brian continued with the task by distributing the remaining food he'd brought: 4 lbs of carrots, a cauliflower, eight large onions, two past-their-best bananas, six frozen mackerel and a tin of treacle.

The various fruit and veg he put inside Tony's shirt and Stuart's trousers and down the front of Marlina's huge red-painted dress. He took three wire coat hangers and a pair of pliers from the pile and spent a few minutes opening each one out into a straightish length of wire. He forced one end of the first piece of hanger wire through two of the slightly thawing mackerel. With the mackerel threaded onto the wire, he brought the ends together and gripping both ends with the pliers, Brian twisted them to create a large mackerel necklace. He placed the necklace over the paint-tin hat, down and around Marlina's neck. He repeated the procedure until all three bodies had identical mackerel necklaces.

Having eased off the lid of the treacle, it was poured then finally drizzled over the heads of the two dead men. Brian wasn't entirely sure how much of his handiwork or larder contents would be recognisable or even detectable by the morning. However, in the event of any future forensic study of the scene, they were sure to be a very useful hindrance.

The next stage was the last he had planned and it was the riskiest. It would be noisy. Initially, he'd thought of working small, in the dark and being as quick as he could. But he subsequently revised this thinking. Hidden in plain sight and all that. He decided he would put the lights on – put the CD player on and use Tony's electric drill. As long as he didn't overdo the noise, people would assume it was Tony working late through the night – probably to get away from Marlina for just a bit longer. It would also cock-up any time-of-death estimates if anyone reported hearing Tony working in his garage at 3.50 in the morning.

Brian switched on the garage main lights and fired up the CD player. He ejected *The Shadows 20 Golden Greats* and inserted another disc next to the player, also the Shadows, entitled, *The Shadows*. Brian tutted and raised his eyebrows at Tony. The sudden starkly lit sight of Tony and the other two dead people, in all their culinary and artistic glory, made Brian's heart thump again.

'My heart missed a beat,' people say. But Brian remembered reading that these so-called missing beats were in all probability extra beats. He wondered how many missing/extra beats the human heart could stand. He reckoned he had shock-induced missing/extra beats about five or six times a year on average. At fifty-three years old he estimated that so far he'd had close to three hundred missing/extra beats in his life. He had a bet with himself that most people could stand well over a thousand. Then he got to questioning 'How much am I betting?' Brian felt very strongly about this. If you have a bet you have a bet and there has to be money or some stake of some value involved, or it wasn't a proper bet. Considering the likelihood that most people could withstand well over a thousand missing/extra heartbeats, he came up with a figure of £35 as his stake. *Evens. If I'm wrong, me number 1 pays me number 2 £35. Vice versa if I'm right.*

His mind continued wandering. How would he prove that he was right? Would he pay up and would money have to change hands? Left hand to right hand? Right hand to left hand? What if he welshed on the deal? Would he have to threaten himself – or even take himself to court? It would presumably have to be the small claims court. Rayment versus Rayment in the matter of an unpaid gambling debt.

The Shadows firing up with 'Shadoogie' snapped Brian back in the room.

He plugged in Tony's electric drill, undid the chuck and inserted a grinding bit from his own vintage OXO tin, in which he kept all his drill bits. He gave a short pull on the trigger and the drill briefly whined into life.

'Is it safe?' asked Brian.

Another slightly longer louder whine.

'Is it safe?' continued Brian, still channelling Laurence Olivier's Weiss Angel.

Leaving 'Marathon Man', before he was tempted to have a

go at Tony's front teeth, he moved to face the tool cupboard doors. He took the grinder to the cupboard and, pressing hard, swung the grinder round to gouge a circle in the closed doors. He stopped and listened for sounds outside. Nothing – he needed to crack on.

'I've started so I'll finish,' he said to himself in Magnus Magnuson's distinctive Irish lilt.

He continued with the grinder until he'd gouged a pentagon, or pentacle as he'd found out earlier on Google. A circle with a five-pointed star inside. In each of the five star points, he'd ground out a Greek letter. Beta, omega, mu, epsilon and delta.

Now he was working fast – on a roll. With the drill still running he moved to the garage doors. He redrew the pentacle and Greek letters in the doors and then released the trigger so the drill whirred to a stop.

13

Brian had now reached the moment he'd been waiting for. After all – how many people got to shoot someone? To shoot three people.

The whole aim of these shootings was going to be to create as much confusion as possible. Who fired which shots at whom, in what order and why?

The road still seemed quiet. Occasionally, the residents rolled back in the early hours after a celebration or night on the town, but by 2.00 at the latest everyone in the street was usually tucked up in bed. At 4.00 a.m., anyone being awoken would be more inclined to pull the covers over them and try to get back to sleep rather than getting up to investigate.

Brian turned the Shadows up a notch. The gun and box of shells were still on the bench. He picked up the gun, feeling and enjoying its reassuring heaviness once again. He pressed open the chamber that held six rounds, as most revolvers did. He was surprised to see that only one cartridge remained in the chamber. From his extensive knowledge of spy films, gangster films and cowboy films, Brian knew that in early model revolvers, the gun owner would often load just five of the chambers. The empty chamber would be lined up with the firing pin. This was because guns were prone to go off if the owner was riding a horse over rough terrain or in a bouncy jeep or leaping barbed wire fences on a motorcycle. The practice, though no longer necessary, had nevertheless remained, and many gunslingers still only loaded up with five rounds leaving the sixth free behind the firing pin. So, assuming five chambers to start with, then there was the accidental shot he demolished the cupboard with earlier, that left three unaccounted for. Had Tony fired three shots at some time – or perhaps more to the point – at someone?

Just the single cartridge then. The unlikelihood of the situation didn't escape Brian. Who'd have thought, just twenty-four hours ago, that he'd be standing here holding a six chamber revolver containing just a single bullet?

Russian roulette.

He checked the safety catch was on and pointing the gun away and squeezing his eyes almost closed he then pulled the trigger. It met the resistance he expected. The safety catch was engaged. He snapped the chamber shut and spun it round. When it stopped he held the gun to his temple and again squeezed the trigger until it resisted.

'Mau! Mau!' he shouted, then slapped his own face with his left hand, picturing the Vietcong captors forcing De Niro and Walken to play the game. He spun the chamber again.

'Mau!' slap 'Mau!' Again he squeezed the resisting trigger.

He had to know. He pushed open the chamber. There, lined up behind the hammer, was the single 9mm shell.

'There, but for the grace of the safety catch go I.'

He took the box of shells and tipped about half of them out onto the bench. Picking up five, one at a time, he loaded them into the five empty chambers. Ideally, he needed a silencer or baffle of some sort – the noise was a potential and not insignificant problem. Brian wasn't exactly sure where the noisiest part of a gun was. The obvious place, he reasoned, would be where the hammer strikes, but all the silencers he'd seen in films screwed over the barrel. That was good enough for Brian. He took the oily cloth that the gun had been wrapped in, shook it out then and folded it in half, then half again, then a third and fourth time.

Having wrapped the neatly folded cloth tightly around the barrel, he held it in place with a short length of duct tape.

He thought the best approach would be one of trying to lay most of the shooting on Tony. He moved around to Tony's prone, penny-filled body and stood with his feet astride Tony's head. Holding the gun at arm's length and aiming at Mr McGregor's chest, he held his breath for a second then squeezed the trigger.

Dammit – safety catch still on. He slid the catch backwards into the off position.

He adopted the same stance again, aiming at McGregor's chest but a little higher. He held his breath again for a second – then CRACK THUMP. A clear double sound. The decidedly muted sound of the shot followed almost instantaneously by the meaty thwack of the bullet entering a potato and out again into Mr McGregor.

Brian immediately got into the role – one he was born to play, he felt – and emptied the other five rounds into McGregor and his potatoes in quick succession. Now, picturing a final reel showdown, he leapt at the pile of shells and started reloading as fast as he could. Marlina would be reloading as well. Handheld camera, lots of blur and movement. A shot of his frantically moving hands then cut to Marlina's and back to his. No music for this sequence. The stark realism of a race to the death. He pushed the sixth bullet in, snapped the chamber shut, spun round.

CRACK CRACK CRACK CRACK CRACK CRACK THUMP.

All six shots in Marlina in under two seconds. Five were in her feet, the last one in her left leg. Not the best area for kill shots but Brian was very pleased with how he'd grouped his shots and besides, he told himself, he'd already killed her.

Over the next ten minutes, he loaded, fired and reloaded the police revolver several times until he'd fired all but four of the 9mm shells. He'd put plenty more in both McGregor and Marlina. Then he got more random, firing into the ceiling, the doors, cupboards and bench. The bench was a mistake. The bullet hit something hard and a ricochet zinged back and clipped his wrist, tearing the latex glove and bringing a free flow of blood.

Ignoring the wound and still with some shells left to fire, he moved over to McGregor and fired a couple into Tony. He didn't aim, he just fired in Tony's direction. The first shot caused a slight puff in Tony's shirt – that's all. The second shot kicked a small fountain of pennies in the air as it hit the large handful of coins that Brian had crammed into Tony's mouth.

14

With the shooting over it was time to set the gun up properly. There was an oil can on the workbench and Brian dropped some more oil onto the already oily cloth he'd used as a very effective silencer. He used the rag to thoroughly wipe the gun, leaving an oily sheen all over it. He took the revolver firstly to Marlina and prised open her fingers so that he could force it into her right hand. Once there, covering her painty hand with the rag, he gripped her hand hard, pressing her fingertips into the gun. He pulled the gun roughly, to free it from Marlina's rigor grip. He repeated the process with Tony to get a good set of his prints on the gun's handle. He had to replace the penny that he'd previously put in Tony's hand and which had dropped out during the taking of fingerprints.

Brian now took the gun to its final resting place – in McGregor's left hand. There was not a great deal of useful fingerprint left on his right hand. He made sure that McGregor had a good, firm, convincing grip of the gun and then turned and pulled his arm and hand so that the gun was pointing at Tony. Hopefully, this would lead any enquiry down the wrong path from the word go.

Ever since he made his initial recce of the place and discovered the forty litres of petrol, Brian had planned to finish the scene-setting by setting fire to the garage and all its contents.

Now he was here and pretty much at that point it didn't seem such a clever idea. The forty litres of fuel would catch quickly and burn ferociously. It would be a matter of minutes before the whole wooden garage would be a roaring conflagration, the road would be awake and the police and fire service would be on their way. If he set fire to the garage this instant Brian estimated that in an hour's time he would be answering some difficult questions from the police people.

'No no no that won't do at all. I'm not ready for that. Change of plan, change of plan – what is it they say? Plan B. That's it, time for Plan B.'

Did he have a Plan B? No he didn't.

'How about a Plan C?' he asked himself.

'Now now! Don't be silly, Brian,' he told himself.

It was a shame. Brian had been looking forward to spraying the petrol around over everything. He'd relished the idea of seeing everything get thoroughly soaked with the fuel before he finally put a match to it.

Thoroughly soaked.

That gave him an idea. He recalled that Tony had a ten-metre reel of garden hose hooked up outside the garage. It was always just a bit too short for any job of Tony's that required a hose – washing the car, hosing the path, watering the potted plants. You'd always see Tony pulling the hose taut at waist height, desperately trying to squeeze a few more inches out of it. Silly arse.

Brian switched off the main garage light and opened the door just enough to push himself through into the cool darkness. He was pleased to see that no house lights had come on – the street was still asleep. The Shadows still sounded plenty loud, but no one was bothered enough to complain.

Once his eyes had accustomed to the night he located the reel of hose tucked just to the side of the garage. He saw it was wound quite tightly and the tail end was typically stretched straight and under obvious tension. It was connected to a brass tap on a post. Brian turned the tap about an inch anticlockwise and heard the water coursing through the coiled hose. After a second or two the water slowly poured out of the free end of the hose tucked into the coiled reel. He turned the tap off. Untucking the free end he pulled it and found that it freely started to uncoil. He kept pulling as he fed it into the garage through the partially opened door. When at least half the hose was inside the garage he went over to the brass tap again and opened it up fully. He went back into the shed and closed the door. There was enough gap at the bottom of the door to completely shut it while gripping the hose underneath.

The hose had already delivered several gallons of water and was soaking into the clothing of the three on the floor. Brian let it run like this for several minutes until water was flowing under the garage door and outside.

He took hold of the hose and started spraying it all around the garage but being careful to leave the CD player completely dry. Brian continued pumping and spraying water over everything else for the next quarter-hour.

15

Sloshing around the garage, waves of water covering his feet, Brian reckoned the water-work was done and this had become his Plan B. He was particularly pleased with the idea of leaving just the CD player dry. He pulled open the door which was quite stiff due to the hose wedged under it. Once he was outside, he turned the water off and reeled in the hose. He was meticulous in this, replacing the reel exactly where it had stood to the side of the garage and tucking in the free end of the hose exactly as it had been. He returned to the garage and once again pulled the door shut.

It was nearly time to leave the garage for the final time. He had to keep on the ball with this. He couldn't afford to leave any giveaway item in the garage. He gathered up the waffle iron, spanner, bin liners, tape and all the other tools he'd used. He decided he'd keep the forty litres of petrol along with the two jerry cans and heaved them both from under the bench. He sprung the cap off one of the cans and lifted the can to the bench. The Shadows were in the middle of 'Sleepwalk' when Brian poured a liberal amount of petrol over them and the CD player. They continued singing on through the fuel.

Brian replaced the cap and took both cans to the shed door. With his hands full with the two heavy jerry cans and the bin liner full of tools he placed the sole of his right foot against the garage door and gave a hard push. Two of the lower door panels shot out and skidded across the path in front of the garage.

In the still of the night, the noise they made seemed a lot louder than it probably was.

I'm a thief, thought Brian. *I steal things and here I am kicking wood across the street in the middle of the night to advertise the fact, to anyone who may have missed it, that I'm stealing Tony's jerry cans full of petrol.*

It was interesting that the thieving seemed to be of greater concern to Brian than the multiple murder.

Brian looked at the door and saw there was now a gaping two-foot by one-foot hole where the panels had been. He went to retrieve the panels in order that he might fit them back in the door and scratched his hand on one of the protruding nails – ripping the latex glove still further. He lined up one of the panels using the old red lead brush marks and the original nail holes. As he was about to try and push it back, it occurred to him that here was a golden opportunity to create one final inexplicable situation. The ultimate head-scratcher.

Having worked out how the two panels needed to be lined up and refixed, he laid them on the ground, slightly to the side of the hole but correctly aligned and ready to fix back.

He unhooked the lock from the outside door handles and brought it inside. Once inside he pulled the door shut tight and locked himself in, the arm of the lock swung round into position and pressed home and securely locked. Brian wondered what his sister Sandra, Sandie (definitely not Sandy – sounds like a corgi – GET IN YOUR BASKET, SANDY!) would think of him locked in a small flooded garage with his three murder victims listening to the Shadows singing through unleaded petrol. He imagined telling the tale at a dinner party and was working out where he could get the most laughs, but then, thinking about it, surmised that it was probably an unlikely scenario – ill-advised at best.

All the things that needed to be out of the garage were out. Brian started to make his way towards the petrol-doused CD player, still pumping out Shadows obscurities. He was paddling in and around McGregor and Marlina – the plastic bags over his shoes were quite a hindrance. He took one last large step over Marlina, trod on her sausagey fingers and slipped very slightly backwards. He twisted in mid-fall to try and save himself and landed face to face on top of Marlina. She was slippy and painty and difficult to stand up from. At one point he was on all fours on top of her and gagging. He had a fleeting thought about being glad that no one was around to take photos and then post them on Facebook or Instagram or Snapchat. After some fairly ungainly manoeuvres and one final more gainly one he was upright again, but covered in a slime of watery red lead paint, in an offset printing sort of way.

He made a snap decision. He hated making snap decisions and preferred to take his time, think things through, sleep on them, but he made one now. He tore off his painty shirt and then having removed a box of matches from the back pocket, he took off his trousers, the suit trousers that he'd worn to work.

Bang goes that suit, he thought, *though I could always wear the jacket with some light-coloured summer chinos and an open-necked white shirt. Very 1930s sports look.* He was very pleased with his ability to think on his feet and quickly resolve these possible future sartorial difficulties.

He placed the two items over the CD player, which muffled the sound a bit. He reached under the trousers and turned the volume up. In the cupboard above the workbench, he remembered the jars he'd seen and took out both the 'Dirty Turps' and the possessive 'Dirty Turp's' jars. He emptied the contents of each over his shirt and trousers.

Being more careful now, and shivering, Brian stood there in underpants, the plastic bags on his feet and latex gloves. Again, the grateful feeling swept over him that no photos of him like this were ever likely to surface.

He opened the box of matches and took two out. In his experience, there was always a problem with the first one. Sure enough, as he struck the first match on the box, it broke as it lit, fell to the wet floor and fizzed out.

He moved closer to the turps-soaked clothes over the petrol-soaked CD player.

Holding the matchbox close to the pile, he struck the second match cleanly and touched his shirt.

WHUMP! The whole pile burst into flame and the Shadows played on.

16

Brian immediately felt warmer, cosy even as he stared at the roaring fire. But time to go. He switched the garage light off and made his way to the rectangular hole in the door, taking care not to slip or tread on the bodies. He had to bend low but he slipped through the hole more easily than he'd imagined. The night air hit his warm wet body and chilled him straight away. His teeth chattered involuntarily as he replaced the two door panels and pushed them hard. They wouldn't sit back entirely flush with just pushing. The nails had all found their original holes but he couldn't get them back fully without hammering them in some way. He sorted through the bin liner and found the waffle iron. He assessed the problem. Each panel had three rows of two nails. He reckoned with well-positioned blows he could do the job with six strikes – three per panel. It would certainly make a noise but recent experience had shown him that the radio, the electric grinder and kicked-out door panels had failed to rouse anyone. He weighed up the pros and cons of different approaches. He could just go for it – fast hard strikes with the iron – as many as were needed to get the panels back, undetectable, in their original position. This undoubtedly would be noisier, but would probably be all over in a matter of seconds. The original thought of just six hard accurate strikes could take a few minutes – even longer if he was wrong about the number of strikes. He was cold and needed to get home and in bed. Fast hard strikes then.

It went very smoothly. The waffle iron, still wrapped in plastic, a very good but unintentional silencer, turned out to be the perfect tool for replacing kicked-out door panels.

It's all silencers today, thought Brian. *I've gone for fifty-three years without the need for a silencer, and today I've used two.* But today Brian himself had been the most effective silencer, having silenced Tony, Marlina and Stuart McGregor.

He put the waffle iron back in the bin liner, which he took over the road and placed behind the low wall of his own front garden. He went back to the garage to collect the two jerry cans of fuel, admiring the completely normal-looking door panels. He returned with the cans and put them next to the bin liner.

Finished. It was over. Nothing more to be done in the garage. He stood on the edge of the road outside his house listening to the Shadows, who amazingly were still going strong.

'Hiya, Brian. What are you up to?'

Brian's heart did another thump – missed beat/extra beat. At this rate, he was going to use up his allotted missed/extra beats in a few months. He spun round to see a tall, pale, smiling young man holding a heavy-looking grip. It was Jonathan, Len and Rose's son.

Attempting to gather his wits, Brian said, 'Oh I've just been for a bit of a run – I often do if I can't sleep. What about you, Jonathan? What are you doing out and about at this time in the morning?'

'I've come down from Birmingham to visit Mum 'n' Dad for a few days – and they're not in, or not awake or not all there or something. I can't get an answer. They're both a bit deaf – probably been soundo since about eight o'clock. I left my key back home. I've been asleep in the car for about three hours until some noisy bugger woke me up. Dunno what the hell they were doing, drilling, hammering, chopping wood – sounded like a rifle range or something at one stage. Anyway, what's with the pants and plastic bags?' asked Jonathan, not unreasonably.

'Oh, it's supposed to be good for you. According to some doctor in the paper,' added Brian, improvising. 'You strip down to your pants and as long as you keep your hands and feet covered in plastic – or latex – you'll be perfectly warm,' said Brian, himself warming to the theme if not the cold night air.

'Sounds brilliant,' said Jonathan. 'Have you finished for the night then?'

'No I might just do one more lap,' replied Brian, anxious to escape any more quizzing.

'What do you call a lap?'

'Up the road here – first right – first right – first right – second right and you're back here.'

'I'll come with you. I've got some plastic bags in me bag,' said Jonathan, removing his clothes.

'Oh it's probably a bit late for you to start now – I'm already warmed up,' shivered Brian.

'No it's fine – I could do with a bit of a stretch.' Jonathan finished fastening some bright orange Sainsbury's bags over his feet by ripping the handles and tying them in a knot around each ankle.

'Quick selfie 'fore we go.' FLASH.

Before Brian could refuse or resist, it was done. There for posterity.

'I'll just put me kit in the car,' said Jonathan and set off down the road. He was back in less than a minute.

'Off you go then, Brian. You lead the way.'

The two set off in the dark and cold. As they approached the first right turn Jonathan called out, 'What do you do with your keys?'

'In me pants,' replied Brian

'Me too,' said Jonathan as they disappeared around the corner. 'Front or back?' continued Jonathan.

'Well – sort of front,' said Brian.

'Me too.'

17

THE SECOND DAY
Saturday 11 September 2021 – 5.30 a.m.

Brian finally got to sleep at 5.30 in the morning. When he and Jonathan returned from their unscheduled late-night run, Jonathan had gone back to his car to sleep. Brian had taken the bin liner of tools and the jerry cans through his house and out into the back yard. He burnt the bin liner, and the plastic used to cover the waffle iron, in a small incinerator and wiped all the tools and the jerry cans clean. After a long hot shower, he drank a very large brandy – it was too much really – and went to bed.

He had some extremely unusual dreams featuring cameos from Hank Marvin shooting at tins of red paint and Isambard Kingdom Brunel standing in a full bath of potatoes in front of his big chains.

Brian awoke on the bright warm Saturday morning at 11.45.

He lay relaxed in his bed with the sun streaming in through the big sash window, going over the eventful day before. All in all a very successful day with a probable world record to boot.

He smiled to himself as he pictured the discovery of three sodden bodies all apparently having shot each other, many, many times, and all with the same six-shot revolver, in amongst the ingredients for a large vegetable soup and each with a mackerel necklace. Evidence of the occult or a black magic ritual, along with the localised charred remains of clothing and CD player, would cause a fair bit of extra discussion and investigation. And what would they make of the red-painted lady and her husband full of pennies? Once they'd sorted all this out there would be just the small matter that all this took place in a garage locked from the inside.

Brian realised that the next day or so could be fairly nerve-wracking as he waited for the inevitable discovery. He was very glad that events had conspired to line up a Friday as the big day. His work at the pharmacy had finished for the week and he was grateful to have the weekend free as usual.

It seemed sensible to conduct his Saturday as normally as possible. He dressed in his Saturday lounging-about clothes, jeans, T-shirt and deck shoes. After his usual breakfast of homemade coleslaw on toast, he gathered together his car keys, phone, bags, windcheater and wallet, locked the front door and went out to his car. Brian always went into town on a Saturday afternoon. As he walked towards the Civic he looked closely across the road at Tony's garage. The bottom of the wooden garage was soaked and the concrete base and surrounding path were still very wet. A faint burnt smell lingered in the air but all was quiet and still.

The irritating silver hatchback that hadn't moved for eight days now was still there and still irritating. Stuart McGregor wouldn't be needing it any more, that was for damned sure. Following this line of thought, Brian realised that Tony and Marlina wouldn't be needing their gleaming Renault either. The Renault immediately became as irritating as McGregor's silver hatchback. He made a mental note to deal with both cars soon and drove into town.

Later that afternoon, when he arrived back at the house, he noticed straight away the letter wedged in the letterbox.

'Mr Rayment – by hand'. It said.

He opened the envelope and read,

'Hey, Mr Rayment! Great fun last night. We must do it again. What do you think of my new Facebook profile pic? Here's a link. Laters – Jonathan.'

Brian felt a familiar ball of worry welling up in his chest. He was both keen to see and dreading to see the picture. He went to his pc, switched it on and booted it up. He hated, absolutely hated that stupid expression. 'Booting up' was what you did on a Sunday morning to play football for Larkhall Old Boys.

The 'laters' in Jonathan's note also rankled. While the computer took its usual four or five minutes to boot up, Brian mentally started to list all the modernisms that annoyed him.

Haitch – yay – besties – selfies.

The screen had now settled to show his desktop – 'desktop' – *there's another one,* he thought.

Brian typed in the long hypertext link – got it wrong, so typed it again more slowly. To his horror, the long landscape-formatted profile pic filled the screen. A stark flash-lit shot of two white-bodied, half-naked men against the night sky, one middle-aged, the other in his late teens, the younger man's arm around the older man's shoulders and both of them in their underpants.

'Oh, Good Quentin Crisp above!' breathed Brian. It was his go-to response to anything in his opinion overtly and inappropriately camp.

A second wave of horror washed over him and he right-clicked the picture- properties – time and date – Saturday 11 September 4.14 a.m.

He looked more closely at the picture. In the background was the clear silhouette of the garage opposite. The flashlight had reflected in the wet surrounding concrete and there was the faint fire glow strip shining under the door.

So, within twenty-four hours of the crime, a photograph, placing him squarely at the scene of the crime at the time of the crime, was now on an international social media site with 2.9 billion users.

18

Brian spent the evening and the rest of the weekend trying to get involved in other things, but his mind wouldn't allow him that luxury.

He hardly slept on Saturday night and was up making hot drinks, watching telly and reading throughout the dark hours in an attempt to exhaust himself. He was, however, already physically very tired but his brain was in a loop, replaying and adjusting the previous day's events and running through the many possible futures he had to look forward to.

Finally, it caught up with him mid-evening on Sunday when he dropped off during 'Thunderbolt and Lightfoot' at the point where Clint puts his dislocated shoulder back using two belts linked and wrapped around a tree.

'You ain't no country preacher, preacher.' He slept in the chair for four hours straight and then grabbed another six in bed. On Monday morning he went to work at the Lloyds pharmacy as what was a pretty fair impression of normal.

As the week progressed, Brian relaxed more and settled into his regular routines at work. The cold-sweat flashbacks became fewer and shorter, and on Thursday he even caught himself wondering if it had all happened. Every so often, though, he wondered exactly when the police would come knocking, as deep down he knew they would. If he was honest with himself, he was surprised there'd been no sign of them already. He didn't have too long to wait.

The following day, Brian arrived home from work at 5.46. He put the kettle on and made a cup of tea as he always did. Sitting in his favourite armchair with it, he started thinking how different things were at this time last week.

There was a knock at the door. Brian exhaled loudly. Why did that always happen? They've had all day to knock and they knock as soon as I've knocked off. Brian answered the door. The two police officers stood there looking very smart and with expressionless faces.

'Good evening, sir. I'm Detective Chief Inspector Webster and this is Detective Sergeant Higgs. Mister Brian Rayment, is it sir?'

'Yes it is.' Brian was surprised how short DCI Webster was – he was even more surprised that DCI Lucy Webster was a woman.

'Would you mind if we asked you a few questions, sir?'

'I haven't got any biscuits.'

'Beg pardon, sir?'

'I haven't got any biscuits or cake or sandwiches or anything. I didn't know when you'd be coming.'

He noticed a brief look pass between the two officers.

'When we'd be coming, sir?'

'IF,' tried Brian. 'If you'd be coming.' That didn't sound much better. 'THAT – I mean. I didn't know THAT you'd be coming … So I didn't get any biscuits … obviously.'

'Well never mind about the tea party, sir. Just a few questions, if that's alright. Shouldn't take too long.'

'Yes of course, Chief Detective Inspector – Inspector-ess,' he added trying to remember her correct title and be politically correct. 'We don't get many lady policemen around here,' he explained. Another look passed between them.

'Sorry, lady police people I should say – or – lady police people of colour to be perfectly correct.'

Brian noticed the definite turn to catch each other's eye and the micro-expressions of raised eyebrows.

'Think we could come in please, sir?'

'Yes, I think you could.' Brian made no move.

'Shall we?' prompted DCI Webster.

Brian showed them into his front room and on the way kicked over his cup of tea which he'd put on the floor when they'd knocked on the door. The tea covered quite a distance and left a violent-looking splash mark on the oatmeal carpet. He now had one of those instant decisions to make. Either leave the police people on their own while he tried to sponge it out, or leave it until later when it would have soaked in more. He decided to leave it and made no mention of it.

Both the police officers stared at the broken teacup for a second and then in unison back at Brian to see his response.

'Anyway, what's this all about?' Brian asked convincingly.

'It's about your neighbours at number twenty-one, sir.'

'You mean number twenty-five?'

'Twenty-five, sir? What makes you say that?'

'Oh I just thought it would be them next door at number twenty-five.'

'Why, sir? Why would you think that?'

'Oh I don't know,' Brian stalled, 'because he's always being a nuisance, being irritating, making a din playing Shadows.'

'Playing shadows, sir? How does he play shadows? What is he – children's entertainer? Some sort of mime artist? Doesn't sound like playing shadows would be particularly noisy.'

Brian wondered what was the matter with the woman. She was talking like a simpleton.

And she's supposed to be a chief inspector detective-ess, he thought. *Well she's gonna need to detect a lot better than that.*

Brian felt he needed to take control of this meeting, which was already going too far down a wrong and dangerous avenue.

'So, it's about Len and Rose at twenty-one is it?' he asked.

'That's right, sir. Know them well did you?'

He picked up on the past tense.

'Yes I did – I do – I know them pretty well.'

'When did you last see them, sir, to talk to?'

'Must've been about a week and a half ago.'

'Could you be more specific?'

'If you like,' said Brian. 'How about 2.35 p.m. on Wednesday, eighth of September 2021.'

'How can you be so specific?' asked DCI Webster.

Brian was genuinely puzzled.

'Because you just asked me to be?' replied Brian, turning it into a question.

Webster tried another tack.

'As accurately as possible, when was the last time you saw them to talk to?'

'Must've been about a week and a half ago,' repeated Brian. 'I waved to them in their garden and asked how they were.'

'And how were they?'

They were in the present tense for a start off, thought Brian.

'Oh alive and kicking,' he replied jovially.

'That's a strange way to answer if you don't mind me saying, sir. Why do you say "alive"?'

Why indeed? thought Brian. *Because I'm nervous and I've got dead neighbours on my mind and my conscience and I've just booted a nearly full cup of tea across my living room and don't appear to be concerned about it,* he wanted to answer.

'Oh – just a manner of speaking. They were laughing and joking and looking like they always do,' he improvised. 'I saw their son Jonathan a week ago. He came to visit them and was sleeping in the car'

'Wouldn't they let him sleep in the house?'

'Jonathan said they're deaf.'

'Don't deaf people allow their sons to sleep in their houses?' These the first words from Detective Sergeant Higgs.

Brian wondered where they were getting policemen, police people, from these days. These two were a pair of idiots.

'Don't deaf people allow their sons to sleep in their houses?' I mean you just wouldn't get a question like that in *Prime Suspect* or *Call of Duty*.

Brian had had suspicions about Detective Sergeant Higgs from the start, mainly because he looked startlingly similar to Danish actor Lars Mikkelsen, who specialised in untrustworthy men-in-authority roles. The likeness was so strong that from the moment Higgs uttered his first question Brian decided that he wouldn't trust him.

Taking the initiative once again, Brian asked, 'Was there anything more you needed to know about Len and Rose?'

'Do you know anyone else who's seen them recently?'

'Yes I probably know everyone who's seen them recently.'

'Who would that be, sir?'

'Well I don't know, do I? I'm at work during the day I don't keep a track of people who see Len and Rose. That's a daft question,' he added and then immediately wished he hadn't.

'Sorry if our questions aren't up to scratch, sir, we're just trying to investigate a serious crime so any help in answering our questions, however daft they may seem, would be very much appreciated.'

'Yes, I'm very sorry, your honour – I mean, sir – sorry I mean ma'am. I'll try to be more helpful,' said Brian.

'Do you know anyone who had a grievance or an argument with the couple recently?'

'Almost certainly. I'd know anyone who had a grievance or argument with them,' he replied. He appeared to be considering something more. 'If you don't mind me trying to help … I think a better question would be, "Do you know IF anyone had a grievance or argument, and if so who?"'

'OK. Thank you very much, sir. And what would the answer to that question be?'

'No,' said Brian. 'You mentioned a serious crime – what happened?'

DCI Webster seemed to weigh up how or whether to answer. She glanced at Higgs, who gave an almost imperceptible nod. She faced Brian and waited a couple of seconds before speaking.

'It appears they've been murdered. Nothing confirmed yet, that's what we're investigating, but they're both dead and we don't know how or why. Would you have any information at all, however insignificant it may seem, that may help us with our enquiries, sir?'

'No – not about them I haven't,' said Brian, placing rather too much emphasis on the 'them'.

There was that look again between the two police people-why did they keep doing that? Were they an 'item'?

Brian didn't think that police people of different ranks should be flirting like this while they were questioning him over the murder of his neighbours – albeit the wrong ones.

DCI Webster stood up and Higgs followed suit.

'I think that's about all for the moment, thank you, sir. We may well need to speak to you again at some point,' said Webster.

'Yes fine, any time,' lied Brian

'Oh just one more thing, sir.'

'Columbo,' shouted Brian.

'Beg pardon, sir?'

'Peter Falk – Columbo. He used to say that. "Just one more ting". Just when the perp thinks he's got away with it – Peter Falk – Columbo would say "Oh, just one more ting, sir" and he'd ask the one question that would prove the perp guilty of murder.'

'Well I wasn't expecting to prove you, or any perps, guilty of murder with my last question, whatever this Columbus did.'

'BO – BO – ColumBO,' said Brian, irritated that this silly woman, who hadn't a clue who Columbo was, had made it to the rank of DCI or DIC or CID or whatever the hell the initials were. Brian disliked initials and by association, he disliked people who used initials.

'I was going to ask if you happened to know if your neighbours at number twenty-five – you know, the noisy ones who play with shadows – have gone on holiday or are away anywhere? We haven't been able to make contact with them at all.'

'No I haven't seen either of them for a week now,' Brian answered truthfully. 'I know they were talking of taking a year off to tour the British Isles by train. I think they may have already left,' he added less truthfully.

'Travelling by train for a year?' Higgs spoke for a second time.

'Well I don't think it was just one long train journey,' said Brian. 'I think they were getting on and off and that. You know – have a ride, see somewhere, stay somewhere, have another ride. You know, to get away from it all, so no one would know where they were.' As Brian was making all this up the idea was quickly becoming very appealing to him.

'OK well thank you very much for that, sir, we'll follow it up. And thank you for helping us with our enquiries. We'll be in touch.'

Brian showed the two of them out, thinking to himself the whole time, *I've helped the police with their enquiries – I'm an adult – I talk to the police – I help the police to catch criminals – I'm a stool pigeon – a stoolie – I'm a grass – a narc – yes I'm a copper's narc – yes – that's what I am – a copper's narc.*

Eamonn Andrews was introducing him, 'So tonight, Brian Rayment, pharmacist, triple-murder world-record holder, actor, gunslinger, thief and copper's narc, THIS – IS YER LIFE.'

So that was funny then, he thought. *The police come round to question me as I knew they would, but not about Tony and Marlina as I thought they would.*

Brian wasn't sure if he was more surprised that Len and Rose had been found murdered, or that Tony and Marlina hadn't.

This was a turn up for the books though. Fate had dealt him a good hand for once. At the exact point in his life where he was trying to shift the focus away from himself and Tony's garage, a double murder crops up a few doors away to do exactly that. Len and Rose should certainly keep the police people busy for quite a while. He considered how long it might be before the goings-on in Tony's garage were discovered. Was there anything he could do to delay that inevitable moment? The stink was going to be the problem. Number 25 had already acquired a distinct unsavoury air about it, which paradoxically was getting more savoury by the day. Brian wondered if he could somehow manage to get hold of a large amount of neutralising pleasant-smelling stuff – aftershave or talcum powder or air freshener for example. He was quickly concerned that this could get expensive until he remembered that he was now a thief.

'Once a thief always a thief,' he said to himself out loud. 'That's what my old mum always used to say,' he said, still out loud.

Then he realised she never said anything of the sort.

19

Saturday 18 September 2021

Following up on the pleasant-smelling-stuff idea, just after midnight Brian drove out to the local pharmacy where he regularly worked. He was a locum and worked shifts at half a dozen local pharmacies as and when required. The one he was unlocking at the moment was the one he most frequently worked at and for which he carried a key.

He knew the place intimately so there was no need to put any lights on. He was in quickly and he shut the door silently behind him. Taking a bin liner, his bag of choice, from his dark windcheater pocket, he swept the shelves of all the aftershaves and colognes he could see. There were a lot. He collected twenty-eight bottles of David Beckham Instinct eau de toilette. It had been on a promotional offer but nobody had been interested. They'd shifted just one bottle to a young girl who had a credit note. He added a mix of Old Spice, Boss, Davidoff Hot, Calvin Klein CK1, Turbo, Lynx, Ted Baker and Joop.

It was quite a struggle to lift the bag. He worked out a three journey plan. Firstly he opened the door as quietly as he could, into the street and opened the boot of his car and the driver's door. He went back to the shop, leaving the door but collecting the bin liner full of bottles which he took straight to the car and into the boot. Finally back to the pharmacy where he locked the door, returned to the car, shut the boot, got in and drove home.

As he drove home Brian weighed up his options for how to best use the aftershaves and colognes. He considered emptying the whole lot into a watering can and then liberally watering the garage with it. The problem with this was one of having a suspiciously similar-smelling watering can to deal with. He decided that emptying one bottle at a time would be the best approach. This way he could test the efficacy as he went.

When he arrived home it was 1.50 in the morning. There were two lights on in the street. One upstairs light at number 18 and Tony and Marlina's twenty-watt security light in their hall that would go off in exactly ten minutes. The only message this dim light gave was: 'We're out.'

Brian sat in his car for the ten minutes to see the light go out.

Reaching in the boot he withdrew two bottles of David Beckham's Instinct eau de toilette and walked over to Tony's garage. Now he was closer he got the full impact of the smell. It was truly noxious and far worse than he'd realised. Holding his breath he unscrewed the top of each bottle and taking one in each hand shook the contents all over the front of the garage.

The first unexpected thing was that flies in their hundreds left the garage doors and flew everywhere, awakened from their night-time stupor by the sting and pungency of the shaken cologne. In the dark Brian hadn't even been aware of them, so the sudden frenzy and buzz of wings was as much a shock to him as the aftershave was to them.

The second surprise was the instant change in the

overall atmosphere around the garage. It was still extremely unpleasant in a way that made you screw up your nose and mouth involuntarily. Reminiscent of Eric Haines, the stinky boy at school, who had third-degree BO but who just used deodorant on top of the BO rather than consider washing himself. Reminiscent, but an extreme version of it.

Brian brought the empty bottles back home, had a shower but still reeked of the David Beckham Instinct eau de toilette.

He slept well and was still asleep when there was a knock at the front door at 9.45 on Saturday morning. He got out of bed, looked out of his upstairs window and down onto the two police people. They knocked again.

He'd been sleeping in underpants which, to be honest, had seen better days. There was a split in the centre seam which had never bothered him until now. He looked for trousers to pull on but there were none. He'd done a big wash yesterday and hadn't sorted any of it out yet. The only vaguely trousery item was a pair of Sandie's leggings over the radiator. Leggings trumped split underpants – and surely they'd just look like narrow trousers. Everyone wore narrow trousers these days. So he tried, for the first time in his life, to don a pair of leggings.

Knock knock knock – again downstairs.

Good God above! How did women get these things on? He struggled, approaching the task as if the leggings were trousers, sitting on the edge of the bed, both legs at once then pulling them up. He got them to his knees, twisted, then they just seemed to seize up. He stood up holding the top, pulling hard and jumping up and down shouting, 'Just a minute, just coming.'

The leggings were now sort of up around his thighs with the split pants still on show. The worst of both worlds, he thought.

He still had a bare chest so grabbed the suit jacket he wore for work. He ran slipping and stumbling downstairs, taking the last four on his heels, painfully juddering his tail bone. Before he got to the front door he caught a brief glimpse of himself in the hall mirror – he was Max Wall. A sort of x-rated Max Wall with split pants and bollocks all part of the ensemble. He forced his tongue under his top lip as Max used to do to create a kind of ape face, hunching his shoulders to let his arms swing long like a gorilla. He opened the door to the police officers.

He lumbered around in front of them in full gorilla mode, beat his chest then dropped to the floor on hands and knees, walking on his knuckles. All this sudden early morning action, the nerves and this new all-fours position had taken its toll on Brian's nervous system. He could feel it brewing. *What the hell,* he thought, and let out a long, loud, all-on-one-note fart. Still in character, he stared straight ahead, sniffing for some moments, then very slowly turned his head to look at the police officers.

'Goot efening, laties and gentlemen,' he said in a very reasonable stab at a Max Wall impression. 'May I help you?'

It was DCI Webster and another officer Brian hadn't seen.

'Should we come back in a bit, sir? Say twenty minutes. Give you time to – ah – give you a bit of time?' asked a bewildered Webster.

'Yes that would be lovely,' said Brian relieved at the twenty-minute curfew.

'Appreciated, I mean,' he corrected.

He shut the door and went to the back of the house to sort out some sensible clothing.

What the hell was the matter with him? It was all very well these flights of fantasy that he liked to indulge in. True, his friends and workmates loved it and said they could put him on telly, but these were officers of the law – the Long Arm, the filth – they could put him in prison. He needed to present the illusion of a calm, normal, law-abiding citizen, keen and eager to help the police but keen to get back to the daily routines of his calm and normal life. On current form, he appeared to be a lunatic.

Surrealism, oddness and strange behavioural juxtapositions were a very good idea when executing and staging a triple murder, but quite the wrong thing when trying to avoid being implicated in one.

20

When the officers returned, Brian was dressed neatly and soberly and on his best behaviour.

'Good morning again, officers – do come in.' He ushered them into the front room. DCI Webster, being a good detective, detected the tea stain, now dried, from the day before.

'I'm sorry for the strange start earlier,' said Brian. 'I'm appearing on stage in a local comedy and I was putting in some rehearsal.'

'That's very interesting, sir. I'm Sergeant Dew by the way. I believe you've already met my boss, DCI Webster. So what's the name of this play?'

'King Kong. It's a comedy version of King Kong. I can get you some tickets if you'd like,' said Brian rather rashly, torn between a desperate desire to please and an irresistible urge to lie his way out of and into trouble.

'King Kong? What, on stage?' asked Sergeant Dew incredulously. 'Will you have to break wind like that on …'

'I think as time is of the essence we should return to matters in hand,' interrupted Webster, keen to haul things back on course. 'We need to ask you a few more questions regarding the Bartlocks.'

'The who?' The Bartlocks. sounded like a group of Doctor

Who's arch enemies. The Daleks, the Cybermen, the Zarbie, the Bartlocks.

'Your neighbours, the shadow boxers who are touring the country by train,' Webster prompted. 'Please think very carefully, sir, when exactly did you hear them talk about this trip, and what did they say – exactly?'

'It was a week last Friday and Tony said they'd probably have to make a quick getaway in about a week.'

'Did Tony use those exact words – "make a quick getaway"?'

'Yes,' said Brian gaining in confidence. 'He said he had one very important job to take care of and then they'd be making a quick getaway. He told me they were going to get away from it all and no one would be able to find them or track them down.'

Dew was writing furiously and DCI Webster was checking he was getting it all down.

'Right! Now, this is very important, Mr Rayment – can you recall hearing, at any time, Tony mentioning that he had a gun? Did he ever show you a gun or tell you his father had a gun?'

Brian wondered how to play this card. The truth was that Brian did know Tony had a gun but Tony had never told him of it or shown it to him. The truth was also that Brian only discovered the gun having killed Tony and Marlina.

Brian shied away from telling the truth whenever possible, unless it was unavoidable. The truth, in his experience, invariably got him into trouble. Lies also got him into trouble but they bought him a bit of time and created an element of doubt. Unfortunately, Brian's brand of lying, as well as creating an element of doubt, also created an element of surprise, which was usually what got him into trouble.

'Oh yes, he had a gun alright.'

'Had a gun? Has he disposed of it? What makes you say "had"?'

'Oh no no – he's still got it, he cleans it and plays with it.'

'How does he play with it?'

'He sort of points it people and goes "kpwow kpwow" or if he wants it to sound like it's got a silencer he goes "thwoop thwoop".'

'Have you seen him do this?'

'Uum, yes,' Brian decided.

'Did he ever point it at you – in a threatening way?' asked Sergeant Dew.

'Yes,' said Brian, thinking whatever he asks me next I'm going to say, 'No'.

'Did he ever discharge it in your presence, sir?'

'No.' Next answer would be 'yes' and then he'd continue alternating 'no' and 'yes', he planned.

'Did he ever threaten to shoot you or kill you?'

Oh, dear.

'Yes,' answered Brian, sticking to the game plan.

'Did you take the threat seriously?' DCI Webster took over.

'No.'

'Why was that sir?'

'Yes,' answered Brian, now not listening to the questions.

'Yes what?' asked DCI Webster puzzled.

'Yes please,' replied Brian quickly, reminded by Webster's tone of the prompts for politeness when he was a child.

'Why didn't you take the death threat seriously?' Webster tried again.

'Because he was drinking a cup of tea at the time and it made him look homely.'

'Because he was drinking a cup of tea at the time and it

made him look homely,' Webster repeated verbatim.

This wrong-footed Brian. Repeating word for word what he'd just said certainly came from left field and he wasn't sure where CID Webster was taking this. He decided to follow suit.

'Because he was drinking a cup of tea at the time and it made him look homely.' *Your turn,* thought Brian.

The DCI decided Brian had won that round and that it was time to wind up the interview. Not expecting an answer she asked, 'Can you think of any last thing, regarding a firearm that may help us, sir?'

Brian couldn't remember if he was on 'yes' or 'no'. He hedged his bets. 'No – but he did do Russian roulette at me once.'

'He did do Russian roulette at you once?'

Brian did not like this repetition.

'Yes, he loaded the gun, spun the middle bit round (that was a nice touch pretending not to know that the middle bit was called the chamber), put the barrel down his trousers and pulled the trigger. It just clicked.'

'You say he put the barrel down his trousers – isn't it normal to put the barrel to your temple?'

'If you say so, ma'am. Personally, I don't think there's anything very normal in putting a gun barrel to your temple.'

'Did Mr Bartlock say why, in this instance, he put the barrel of a possibly loaded gun down his trousers?'

Improv time again.

'Yes. He said it was a variation of Russian roulette called Japanese game-show roulette. It could still do a lot of damage and was still nice and stressful but not likely to be fatal.'

'Thank you for your time, Mr Rayment, you've been very helpful.' The two officers got up to leave.

'Good luck with King Kong, sir,' said Sergeant Dew. 'Don't forget the tickets.' DCI Webster glared at him.

'Oh, just one more thing,' said Brian

'You're not going to prove us guilty of murder are you?' asked Webster.

'I'm sorry?'

'Isn't that what your Peter Falk, Columbo, used to say? – "Just one more ting". Then he'd ask a question and prove the suspect guilty of murder.'

Brian was impressed. Very impressed. CDI Webster had given the impression that she hadn't a clue what he was talking about when he first mentioned Columbo. Now she was accurately recalling the actor, the character, his signature line and the weekly outcome of his detecting expertise. She'd either known all this all along or she'd remembered it perfectly. Either way, Brian was impressed and starting to quite like DIC Webster. He made a mental note to try and learn the correct order of her initials.

'Yes very good,' he said, 'you're right. No, what I was going to say, if you don't mind me doing so, was I'm very glad you got rid of Higgsy – I didn't trust him.'

'Nor did I,' said DCI Webster surprisingly. 'Too shifty – too much like Lars Mikkelsen for my liking.'

Brian felt suddenly quite attracted to the detective chief inspector, and hoped that she'd be calling again tomorrow.

21

All day Sunday and for a fair bit of Monday at the pharmacy, Brian spent a good deal of his time going over Saturday's events and conversations. It was clear the police were onto Tony and had him marked as their prime suspect for Len and Rose's murders. They would doubtless be around again tomorrow in a renewed attempt to determine Tony's whereabouts. Brian was hopeful of an opportunity to get to know DCI Webster a little better, but he'd need to play it cool. Once the officers got no reply, they would almost certainly break into Tony and Marlina's house. It would only be a short step then before the bodies were discovered in the garage. This meant Brian had only tonight to take care of any further business. He reminded himself that he was now a bona fide thief with Stuart's car keys and £45 and Tony's jerry cans and 40 litres of petrol already stashed away – his first honest to goodness haul. Might as well be hanged for a sheep as a lamb he thought.

That lunchtime he took a trip into town where he made a quick tour of all the charity shops. He was very pleased to have picked up a decent trench coat mac for £8. Far too large but an excellent traditional style. He'd been hoping to find a fedora but being a realist knew this was very unlikely. He had, however, got a woman's brown floppy felt hat with a wide brim for fifty pence. With a bit of steam and manipulation, he was sure he could work the hat into an acceptable approximation. Brian had never smoked in his life but this lunchtime he bought a packet of cigarettes and a box of matches.

It was dark by 8.05 that evening and most of the road was settled indoors and watching the box. Brian quickly nipped over the back fence from his backyard into Tony's. Once there he couldn't be seen and could take his time. He tried the handle on their new plastic back door. The door opened. Of course it did. When Marlina left the house eight days ago she had a reasonable expectation of returning. Brian tried to imagine her thinking to herself – 'I suppose I better lock the back door, in case Tony and I both get killed and the house gets left wide open to burglars.'

As he entered the Bartlock's house he could see himself spending a couple of hours here, going through everything and helping himself to anything he wanted – valuables, books, records, clothes, appliances, fittings and fixtures. The reality soon became apparent. There was nothing of value, no books or records of interest, clothes he wouldn't be seen dead in, and old fashioned out-of-date appliances and fixtures. In short, it was all rubbish and of no use or interest to Brian whatsoever. On realising this he was suddenly overcome with a wave of sadness for these two wasted lives of disappointment, misery and failure, represented here by this houseful of junk.

The two things he did need were Tony's car keys, which he found on a hook in the hall and some large sheets – three of them – which he found in the airing cupboard. He was back in the comfort of his own house within twenty-five minutes, once he'd locked the Bartlock's back door and dropped the key down their drain.

He was lucky in how the cars were lined up in the road. Rose and Len's huge people carrier was parked slightly up towards number 23 rather than directly outside their own house. Tony's Clio was if anything outside number 24. No car was between them at the moment. Now outside and using Tony's key he opened the Clio door and got in. Having switched the ignition to first position to free the steering wheel, he released the handbrake and allowed Tony's car to roll back so that it almost touched Len and Rose's people carrier. He sat in the car for a minute to make sure there was no inquisitive or curious street action. He got out and shut the door in a controlled quiet way and walked up to Stuart McGregor's car, the next in line. He took Stuart's car keys from his pocket and went through a similar procedure. Entering the car, turning the ignition to first position to free the steering wheel and releasing the handbrake. He allowed the car to coast backwards as before, until it was nearly resting on the Clio's bumper. The last of the three cars to complete this stage of the operation. As he walked up the hill towards his house, he wondered why this walking to and from these vehicles was making him feel nauseous. It was, of course, the smell coming from Tony's garage that was causing the problem. The foul reek was saturating the whole surrounding atmosphere of this section of the road. Over the last week, Brian, along with all the other surviving neighbours who had no clue to its cause, had begun to accept the increasingly sickening stench as an unpleasant new resident of the close.

He went indoors to rest and to prepare things for several hours later when he would complete section two of the operation.

22

Brian spent a little bit too much time steaming and manipulating the women's felt hat into a just-about-acceptable version of a fedora. He was scowling at himself in the full-length mirror of his bedroom. It was not enough Humphrey Bogart and too much Margaret Rutherford for his liking. He put on the unisex trench coat mac. It buttoned both ways. With the Margaret Rutherford hat on people would start to think he buttoned both ways. The mac was huge and ill-fitting, but with a lot of cinching of the belt in at the waist and turning the collar up, it greatly improved the Bogart/Rutherford ratio.

Before he had started work on the hat, Brian had gone over into Tony's back yard again to bring back their green plastic watering can. It was this he was now filling in his own back yard with the remaining forty-three bottles of aftershaves and colognes. Even outside in the still evening air, it gave off a strong sickly scent that was pretending to be pleasant. When he'd emptied all the bottles, he carried the now surprisingly heavy watering can carefully through his house and into the small front garden. He then went through to the back again to fetch the two jerry cans of fuel, which he also brought through the house to the front garden.

He put on the trench coat and felt hat – he could fine-tune

the appearance later. In his pocket, he checked for the two sets of car keys, the cigarettes and the matches. He checked his watch, an expensive vintage 1948 Omega Sea master – £285 on eBay last month – it was 12.46. Just nineteen minutes to go. Brian had set the time of the operation at 1.05 a.m. There was nothing magic or special about 1.05 a.m., but he thought it all added to the tension and suspense of the scene to be working to a specific time.

Time to set up the last stage. He packed the folded sheets under one arm, picked up the two full jerry cans and took them down to the three cars. The two cars he'd moved earlier he had left unlocked. He opened the front door of each and put the respective keys in the ignition. He made the final adjustment to their positions by rolling each one back until it rested on the car behind. Finally, he opened the bonnet and boot of each car and threaded and draped the sheets through and over all three cars, effectively joining them together in a chain.

Time check – 12.57.

Should be perfect timing. He went back to his own front garden and got the heavy watering can. He turned to get several lungfuls of the cleanest possible air, inhaled deeply one last time and held his breath. He crossed to the garage as quickly as he could. It took him just over half a minute to shower the garage, almost completely, with the contents of the watering can. Still holding his breath against the absurd contrast of the two competing, dreadful smells, Brian ran back to Tony's car, threw the watering can into the back seat and finally exhaled.

Time check – 12.59 … No – 1.00.

Five minutes. He took out the packet of cigarettes, opened them and for the first time in his fifty-three years put a cigarette in his mouth. He attempted to light it as Bogie would have done. He burnt his fingers and dropped the match. Time was running out and it dawned on him, rather late in the day, that he had not a clue how to light a cigarette. He knew what it looked like and how you shielded it all from any breeze with your cupped hands, and how you had to shake the match afterwards and then say a sentence that started, 'C'm'ere, shweedheart'.

He rested the cigarette on the low front garden wall with the front end overhanging. He lit a second match and held it under the end, gently blowing on it. That worked a treat, the cigarette glowed and it saved him the bother of getting smoke in his mouth. Where exactly was the pleasure of having smoke in your mouth? He left the glowing cigarette out of harm's way on the wall, ready for time zero.

Time check – 1.02 – three minutes.

He rolled up the sleeves of the trench coat, which was starting to become more of a nuisance than the classy piece of film noir wardrobe he had envisaged. He sprung the cap of the first jerry can and got going straight away dousing and soaking the sheets, the car interiors, the paintwork, under the bonnets and in the boots. The job was done pretty thoroughly with the first twenty litres but he had a second twenty litres in the other can so …

Time check – 1.04 and ten seconds.

Time to get ready for the shot. He pulled in the belt of the mac tight and tucked the end in over the main belt. He pulled the collar up high and pinched the front of the hat and pulled it down, snapping the brim. The glowing cigarette he picked up and placed between his lips. He found that by blowing he could make it glow brightly and still avoid any inhalation.

Time check – fifteen seconds to go.

Brian removed the cigarette and, holding it between his thumb and forefinger, prepared to flick it at the petrol-soaked chain of cars. This would be filmed from four different angles, all starting with a black screen. The intro would be the slo-mo close-up shot of the rotating cigarette arcing in the air. As the cigarette approached the cars the speed would slow further, almost a frame-by-frame motion. At the exact moment the cigarette hit the car, normal speed would resume and the sound would kick in loudly with the roar of the petrol igniting. Brian K Rayment would be rim-lit with orange firelight. At this point, the rhythmic intro drumbeat of Brian Eno's 'Baby's on Fire' would kick in.

Six seconds – Five – Lights! – Four – Three – Camera! – Two – Action! – One!

As well as never having smoked a cigarette in his life, neither had he flicked a lit cigarette in his life.

Right on cue, Brian flicked it and it spun off course vertically leaving a trail of glowing sparks. It was not going to hit the cars. Brian watched it spiralling upwards, heard the small 'whump' of ignition and saw, and felt at the same time, that his trench coat was on fire.

23

In a panic, he left Humphrey Bogart and slapped furiously at his trench coat sleeve only to notice that the glowing cigarette had now landed on him. It had found some other petrol splashes. His mac was now also alight and on fire on the other folded-back cuff and the bottom hem. His left arm in agony he scrabbled and tore at the belt and buttons in an effort to remove the coat. He was concerned that pretty soon neighbours would start getting interested, so he had no desire to draw unnecessary attention to himself. He was finding out, however, that setting himself on fire was quite difficult to do quietly and unobtrusively.

He got the trench coat off and saw to his terror that his shirt and trousers were both smouldering. He ripped them both off too before the fire could take a hold and threw them on the burning mac. At that instant, a stray spark caught the car chain and the road lit up with a roar. Standing in the street once again in his underpants he was this time quite warm and had never been so artistically lit.

He looked at his arm – it was bad, very bad and looking at it seemed to remind him he was in excruciating pain. He had to get to the hospital, ASAP.

His car keys were on a shelf in the hallway. He ran in, got

the keys and shut the front door on his way out. It was a shame, he thought. He would have loved to stay and watch the fire, which was spreading rapidly and already immense. He'd have loved to stay and chat with the other residents who were nearly all out on the street filming the event on their phones or calling friends and relatives to come and watch. Someone had even called the emergency services.

Brian was already in his car and making the three-and-a-half-mile journey to the hospital. He was doing his best to ignore the intense burning pain in his left arm. 'Thank God I'm still alive,' he breathed out loud to himself. He started questioning, 'What had God to do with all this?' What was he thanking God for?

'Thank you, God, for not letting this extra-large second-hand trench coat burn me up alive while I'm trying to set fire to three neighbours' cars using stolen petrol.'

He might as well thank Jimmy Edwards or Nat King Cole. A multi-named 'thankee' doesn't work he decided. How about Madonna – no still a bit religious-sounding. Thank Sting – better. Someone famous who you'd know by just their surname. Thank Brando. Thank Presley. Thank Sinatra. Yes. Now that worked. Thank Sinatra, had a good natural familiar ring to it. Thank Sinatra.

He arrived at the hospital and pulled up outside the main entrance. As he got out someone in a cap called out, 'You can't leave it there, madam.'

Annoyed by the 'madam' despite the pain he was in, Brian lobbed the keys over to the capped individual and called, 'Put it where you want,' and went into A&E.

It was surprisingly empty for a Sunday night and having

registered at reception he sat in one of the thirty-six red plastic seats – three rows of twelve. There were just four other patients, all fairly evenly spaced out and none of them in the mood to socialise. All of them stared at him. He was soon called into the next free triage assessment cubicle.

'Good morning, sir. Brian Rayment, is that right?'

'Yes. It's my arm – it's very badly burnt.'

'We'll get straight on to it, Brian. Let me get you a gown, you must be freezing dressed like that.' Brian had forgotten he was just in his underpants. It was happening so frequently that it was beginning to feel quite normal. Nurse Terras came back with the gown for him.

'Do you want to take that lovely hat off, Brian, or keep it on? Up to you.'

'Hat? 'Oh, Good Quentin Crisp above!' Ladies' hat and underpants – not a good look under almost any circumstances. The hat was something else he'd forgotten – in the heat of the moment, so to speak.

'I caught fire, you see,' explained Brian as if it were spontaneous combustion. 'I was burning, so I stopped thinking about my hat.' He immediately wished he hadn't said 'my hat'. It made it sound like a treasured possession. 'I didn't have my hat on my mind, just on my head,' he finished lamely.

'OK – we'll leave it there, for now, we need to have a good look at that arm,' continued Nurse Terras. 'Can you just confirm your date of birth, first line of your address and your postcode?'

'Yes of course,' said Brian, 'can you hurry, though, I'm afraid I'm suffering here.'

'Whenever you're ready then,' said the nurse.

'Yes ready when you are,' replied Brian.

'So if you can start by confirming your date of birth then, Brian.'

'OK I'm ready,' said Brian a little more testily. The nurse looked slightly puzzled. It was an expression that Brian saw on a fairly regular daily basis. Now he was slightly puzzled and returned the expression.

'Are you going to tell me your date of birth then, Brian?'

'Yes of course if that's how you want to do it now. Second of the twelfth, '68.'

'Great – now if you could just confirm address and postcode.'

'Back to that way is it? OK ready,' said Brian. Nurse Terras finally saw the problem.

'Could you tell me your address and postcode please, Brian?'

Brian told her.

'Thank you, Brian. Now let's look at this arm of yours. Ooh, that is nasty. You were quite lucky though, a few seconds longer and that that could have been a lot worse.'

'Yes. Thank Sinatra,' he tried out for the first time.

'Oh yes, what about him?' said Nurse Terras.

'I was just thanking him,' said Brian.

'Did he help you then?'

'No not really,' said Brian. 'I think he's dead'

Nurse Terras took a pen from her tunic pocket and wrote in the top corner of Brian's notes 'OTS' (on the spectrum).

24

Tuesday 21 September 2021

After an hour and twenty-five minutes, Brian left the A&E wing of the hospital wearing borrowed pyjamas, a coat and a heavily bandaged left arm in a sling.

He was back in under five minutes when he could see neither his car nor the capped individual he'd thrown his keys to.

'Car?' said the receptionist. 'I don't think you'll be driving with your arm in a sling. If you wait over there one of the ambulances will be taking a few patients home in a while.'

'In a while?' *What did that mean?* thought Brian. 'Any idea how long that could be?' he asked.

'Any time within the next two or three hours,' replied the receptionist.

It had been a long day, he was full of painkillers, he was tired, his arm throbbed and he wanted to be in bed. Brian decided to walk the three-and-a-half miles. If he stepped on it he could do that in an hour.

For the second time, he walked out of the A&E unit and headed off home.

After walking for just over a mile and for twenty minutes, he spotted his car. More accurately he spotted the blue flashing lights of the police cars, a few police people in yellow high-vis jackets, the cones and the blue police signs saying 'POLICE – ROAD CLOSED' and 'POLICE – ACCIDENT'. His car was slewed, partially on the road, partially on the pavement with the driver's door open. The front end looked specially panel beaten to fit snugly round the street-light post.

He started to walk towards the gathering to explain that it was his car, and then thought better of it. Already the machinations and wheels of his brain were turning and working out ways in which this could be turned to his advantage. He carried on walking home and turned the corner into his street at ten to five in the morning. He expected to find the fire fully extinguished by now, which it was. What he hadn't expected was to see the road completely shut off with scene-of-crime tape. There were several police cars, all with blue lights flashing and making their presence felt. All the police were wearing the same yellow high-vis jackets as the officers at the site of his crashed car. Some were questioning those residents who'd made a night of it and were still out on the street filming and phoning. Two other officers were employed to check the occasional car or pedestrian trying to enter or leave the street. As he walked down the few yards before he reached the tape and the two officers at the checkpoint, he noticed that Tony's garage doors were now slightly open and there was a knot of heavily masked officers in white chemical coveralls.

'Can we help you, sir?'

'Yes I live at number twenty-six and I just want to get home to bed,' said Brian. *I ought to be acting a bit more surprised*, he thought. 'So what on earth's going on here, officer? Is there a bomb or something?' he said, more alert and with a nice mix of incredulity and annoyance. Oh, that was good, that was very good.

'No not a bomb, sir, as far as we know, but the SOCO officers are checking it all out now.'

'Don't you mean SOC officers?'

'No, SOCO, sir – it stands for scene of crime officers'

'That's what I mean. If you say SOCO officers, surely that's like saying scene of crime officers officers, Officer?'

Silence for a bit, then, 'Yes, sir. Do you have any proof of identification and your address please, sir?'

'No I'm wearing someone else's pyjamas. But my name is Brian Rayment and I live in this road at number twenty-six.'

'Ah, next door!' said PC Major.

'No! Actually in number twenty-six. I don't live next door.'

PC Major, a skinny boy who'd only qualified as a police officer four weeks ago, couldn't recall anything in his training or exams that covered dealing with such members of the general public.

'Just ask CDM Webster, she knows me.' *CDM?* he thought. *Oh good God above, that's Cadbury's Dairy Milk.* He had to get to grips with these initials.

'DCI Webster? corrected PC Major. 'You know her?'

'Yeah yeah – her and Dewy and Higgsy. Just ask any of them. Dewy's coming to see me be King Kong.' One of life's recurring problems for Brian was his tendency to confuse his fantasy world of lies and imagination with reality. He genuinely was starting to look forward to his comedy King Kong performance at a local theatre and had even made a mental note to get the tickets for Dewy.

Major turned and walked with a bit of pace to the group of

officers around the completely burnt-out cars.

He was back shortly and told Brian, 'DCI Webster has confirmed that she's "had the pleasure of your company on several occasions", to use her own words. You're free to go on home to bed, sir.' He pulled back the tape to allow Brian through. Brian went home to bed and soon fell asleep dreaming of the lovely IDC Webster saying, 'Yes I've had the pleasure of his company on several wonderful occasions.'

25

Tired though he was, Brian didn't get much sleep that night. An unnecessarily loud knock at the door came sharp at 9:30. He was expecting it, just not quite this early. When you go to bed at 5:30, being woken at 9:30 seems very early. Bleary-eyed and still in the foreign pyjamas, he shuffled drunkenly downstairs and answered the door. Two new police people stood there. One was a lady policeman – Warmed caramel, No. 376 – and one was a male policeman – Faded Bazooka Joe, No. 224.

Like a lot of words, phrases and initials, the phrase 'people of colour' bothered Brian. He didn't understand it or how to use it. It made no sense to him. 'Colour of people' seemed a fairer and more sensible phrase to use in the interests of equality, accuracy, correctness and an all-inclusive diversity. Everybody was a colour. He imagined a kind of Farrow and Ball detailed colour chart showing the complete range of human hues and tones. Everything from pasty whites through pinks, creams, fawns, yellows, reds and a whole range of browns, all named, numbered and ready for easy reference. He estimated that the complete set would be a beautiful range of about 480 subtle variations. It would certainly be a worthwhile future project. Brian's thinking was due to a combination of his art college training and the influence of a captivating physics teacher, who Brian loved and whose every word he hung on. Words were important to Brian, but colour was more important. His final year thesis at art college had been on the psychology of colour. If there was one thing he knew about it was colour. Remembering his physics teacher – Mr 'Force-equals-mass-times-acceleration' – delivering a particularly interesting lecture on light, Brian recalled that, scientifically, white is the presence of all colour, whereas black is the absence of all colour. So to be artistically and scientifically correct, as well as politically correct, Brian concluded that for the perfect combination of equality and accuracy everyone should be referred to as a person of colour. Being more specific about the colour could only help, and could be easily achieved, by using his new 'Colour of People' chart. Hence his thoughts about the new arrivals.

'Good evening,' said Brian, for it still felt like evening to him.

'Good morning, sir,' they each responded, one after the other. 'We didn't get to speak to you last night – I gather you came home in the early hours, sir?'

'Yes, quite recently. Just now really,' said Brian.

'We're making enquiries into several incidents in the road. Primarily we want to ask you about the burnt cars. Did you see anything suspicious? Did you see anyone near the cars? Can you give us any information that may help?'

Brian acted well the role of a man deep in thought. His subtle range of facial expressions conveyed that he was trying hard to remember an important elusive detail. Beneath the surface of this award-winning little cameo, Brian's mind was racing.

'Yes I did see something suspicious,' he started, not entirely sure how he was going to continue. 'There was a huge woman in a huge trench coat wearing a funny sort of felt fedora, only it was a lady's hat,' said Brian telling it how he saw it. 'She was like a huge female Humphrey Bogart and ...' he left it hanging, unsure where this was going.

'... And?'

'... And she had a box of matches and ...' *Stop saying 'and'*, he told himself. 'And she was hanging round by the cars whistling. No hang on – no she wasn't. What I meant to say is, I saw her throw a match at the cars and then her coat caught fire so she took it off.'

'We need to get all this down, sir. This is all extremely helpful. Do you mind if we come in please?'

'No of course not,' said Brian, very pleased to be 'a witness said'. They all went indoors and got up to speed with Brian's testimony so far, omitting the hanging round and whistling bit.

'I've got biscuits this time if you'd like,' he said.

'No thank you – very kind but no thanks.'

'Or a slice of quiche?'

'No definitely not, sir. Thank you. Anything else you can add, sir?'

'I've got a bit of Tesco's apple pie left?' he offered.

'No, I mean anything else you can add to your testimony – anything more you can think of?'

'No, I can't think of anything,' which was, of course, exactly the situation. 'Oh yes, I can. I've thought up something – thought of something. After this Lady Bogart woman had taken her coat off, she rushed into my house – the front door was open for obvious reasons – stole my car keys and drove off in my car. Oh yes, and she dropped her hat on the way so I put it on to keep warm.' Running over what he'd just said, Brian realised the 'putting the hat on to keep warm' sounded strange. 'I was quite chilly by then because I'd taken my shirt and trousers off,' he added for clarification.

'Why had you taken your shirt and trousers off?'

'They were smouldering.' He could tell by the looks on their faces they needed more. 'Uum – some sparks flew at me from when Bogie took his coat off. Her coat.'

Once again – revised and in full.

'Some sparks flew at my trousers when Bogie took her coat off.'

There's a sentence I probably won't be using again, thought Brian.

He spent another five minutes helping the two officers out with a few more details. Of course, he was able to be very precise with the time, knowing that the fire started at exactly 1:05 the previous night, albeit with the trench coat rather than the cars.

'Did you report your car missing, sir? So we can tie in the times and of course for your insurance purposes?'

'Yes I reported it missing.'

'When was this, sir?'

Brian stared at her. Was she for real?

'About a minute ago – to you,' he added.

'No I meant did you make an official report?'

'Aren't you official? I thought all police people had to be official. Can you have unofficial police people?'

'No, you have to report it to get a crime reference number so you can quote this to the insurance people. You'll just have to confirm your name, date of birth …' *Oh don't you start,* thought Brian, '… first line of your address and postcode. Don't worry, sir, I'll make a note to sort you out a CRN.'

CRN? More initials.

'Thank you for sorting the CRM, Officer. Much appreciated.'

'No, thank YOU very much, sir. You've been very helpful. We'll get this typed up and be back later on today for a signature, if that's OK. I'll bring the CRN for you when we return. See you later, sir, and thanks again,' said the very polite PC Shauna Moon.

There was a lot of activity all day long in the street. The rest of the morning was taken up with the three burnt car shells being loaded on trailers and taken away. Neighbours gathered together in a rare communal spirit to sweep up the debris left by the blaze.

SOCO were busy all day in and around the garage. There were a lot of them and they appeared to be doing shift work. Every item in the garage was photographed, bagged, tagged and removed. In all, four full vanloads of bagged items were taken back for forensic analysis. At around 9.30 that evening, an ambulance finally arrived to remove the three bodies, now zipped up in gas-proof rubber body bags. Even in the darkness, with the garage completely emptied, the flashlight photography continued for nearly another hour. At 10.40 it appeared that everything was finished when the SOCO team all left in one police transit van. The road was suddenly peaceful and quiet after twenty-one hours of non-stop, noisy, bright activity. It remained peaceful and quiet for a good ten minutes before another van arrived to take the place of the SOCO van. On the side of the van was written POLICE BIOREMEDIATION SPECIALISTS – the forensic clean-up team.

Unlike the SOCO, they were very quick. They reversed the van up close to the garage and jumped out of the back – four of them. All still kitted out in the white hooded hazmat suits and masks with dual cartridge respirators, they worked as a well-practised team. A large heavy-looking, flexible hose was reeled out and fed into the garage. A loud low-humming motor was switched on and remained running for a good five minutes. There was a rushing sound as a thick fast jet of white foam shot into the empty garage. Under the intense pressure of the jet, coils of the foam were forced through gaps in the wooden sides of the garage like thin white snakes making their escape. When the garage was full of foam the rushing jet was cut off and the motor switched off. New SCENE OF CRIME tape was placed around the garage on free-standing supports. The forensic team left and the road was finally quiet.

26

For the next four days, three separate teams of investigators were knocking on doors up and down the road interviewing residents. From the two interviews he'd had so far, Brian had managed to glean several interesting bits of information about the investigations. Firstly the police believed that all three crimes were in some way linked. They further believed that whoever killed Len and Rose was also involved with the garage murders. They were working on the assumption that it was the killer who returned to burn the three cars in an attempt to destroy evidence. The prime suspect was thought to be a very large woman approximately six foot three or four and weighing about fourteen stone. Brian's car was now in forensics being thoroughly dusted in the hope that any prints other than Brian's would lead the police to the prime suspect. And finally, that the police were referring to the garage murders as the Dali Murders. This really did annoy Brian. They had picked up on the surrealism but had stupidly tagged it as Dali, being the go-to surrealist. Surely anyone could see it was nothing like the work or style of Salvador Dali.

'It would be like … like …' Brian struggled for a suitable analogy. 'It would be like a restaurant that had sunflowers everywhere and all the chairs were little homemade wicker chairs with a pipe on them and the perspective of the restaurant was a bit out of whack and then calling the restaurant Warhol's.'

All along Brian had Luis Buñuel very much in mind as he was 'surrealising' the scene. It's true that Dali worked on the script with Buñuel on several of his films – but the look and the feel of the films were all Buñuel's. Dali had co-written the scripts for *Un Chien Andalou* and also *L'age D'or*.

L'age D'or was the film from which Brian took his inspiration. *The L'age D'or Murders* had a much better and relevant ring to it.

If they wanted to get clever and punny they could've used the G'rage Door Murders – that would've at least had a vague tie-in.

The problem was solved for everyone the following day when most of the daily national papers went with 'The Garage Murders'.

At about five on Thursday evening there was a familiar knock at the door. Brian instinctively knew it was CID Webster. As he'd had this thought – about the knock being familiar – he tried to work out why this was even possible. He came to the conclusion that, as the knocker hasn't changed and the door hasn't changed, any differences causing familiarity or unfamiliarity could have only occurred through the way the knocker was knocked. This could be sub-divided into four categories: volume, rhythm, timing of the gaps between the knocks, the number of knocks.

At times Brian was truly amazed at the depth and speed of his thinking. As he made his way to the front door he allowed his mind to ramble on along with his knocking theories. With just a few steps to the front door, Brian smiled to himself as his mind relayed for him:

'With his sterling work, analysis and research into the personalization and individuality of door knockers and the knocking process for purposes of detection and security, this year's Nobel Physics Prize goes to Brian Rayment. Brian Rayment MBE – what the hell, Sir Brian Rayment.'

Before he could revise Eamonn Andrews' introduction of him for 'This Is Your Life' he reached the front door.

He opened the door with a smile, saying, 'Afternoon, ma'am,' before he could even see her. PC Shauna Moon was openly pleased with the happy greeting, but Brian blew it immediately by saying, 'Sorry I didn't know it was you.' PC Moon did well to hang on to her smile but couldn't quite think of an appropriate response to this.

Brian realised that this may have come across as a bit rude so he tried to neutralise it with, 'I couldn't see what exact colour you are. I couldn't see that you're Warmed caramel – No. 376. I couldn't even see that you're a lady policeman, whatever colour you are.' *That ought to do it,* thought Brian.

PC Roger Snook – Giraffe breath – No. 202, stepped in to help out his colleague. Snook was tall, gingery blonde and pale with a tall, gingery blonde, pale face and no discernible facial features.

'Mr Rayment, sir, you're aware of our three ongoing enquiries. It appears you are the only person to actually get a look at our prime suspect.' Brian had a mental image of Helen Mirren in various stages of undress every time anyone said 'prime suspect'. He was now learning that he was the only one to get a look at her. This kicked off another interesting fantasy of him and Helen Mirren alone in a room with her getting changed into her police outfit. No. 'Outfit' was wrong –

children have 'outfits'. Getting changed into her police uniform. Yes, that's more like it.

'We were hoping you could work with our police artist to recreate a picture of the suspect, sir.'

Brian briefly imagined describing a half-naked Helen Mirren to the police artist, even to the point of asking if he could keep the drawing. Then, snapping back to reality, 'Yes yes, of course. Only too pleased '

'We'd have to go down to the station, sir. The artist is there now. We were hoping that, between the two of you, you could make up a decent likeness of the suspect'.

'Oh yes, I could definitely make up a likeness,' said Brian, eager to get started.

27

Having been introduced, Brian sat in interview room two with two police officers and the police artist – Detective Sergeant Clinton Hodder. DS Hodder was a smiley chap with a small inch-long curved scar from the corner of his mouth and up his cheek. It gave him a kind of permanent smirk. Brian thought the scar was one of the best he'd ever seen and would have given – what? £200? £300? – to have one like it. He imagined himself with a scar like that and how cool it would look. He imagined friends asking him how he got it and being able to tell them awesome tails of fights, bravery, duels and adventures. DS Hodder was explaining how the process of producing a portrait would work. Brian was half-listening but the other half was more interested in working out the best and least painful way of acquiring a scar like DS Hodder's.

Brian hated pain and with his arm still bandaged and acting as a reminder, avoiding too much of it was uppermost in his planning. He could always get something from the pharmacy, some sort of anaesthetic, though he was doubtful that they'd have anything strong enough over the counter. There were a variety of so-called 'numbing creams' – tattooists used them – lidocaine ointment or Emla numbing cream, but he was not convinced they'd do the job. He decided ice would be best. If he iced his mouth and cheek to numbness, he ought to be able to withstand the necessary self-surgery. He had a scalpel and a pack of new blades somewhere indoors. He'd use them. There could be a lot of blood so it would probably be best if he could arrange to do it near the hospital. He had to go back to A&E on Monday to have the burn dressing changed, so maybe he could combine the two. Not having a car, though, was going to cramp his style severely. He could catch the bus, or possibly splash out on a taxi, but he'd have to take the ice, the scalpel, some towels and a mirror. Quite a cumbersome mix. In his mind's-eye he saw himself on the grassy bank outside the A&E entrance, trying to set up the mirror, hold the ice in place and then cut his face with a scalpel. All this, while a steady stream of doctors, nurses and other patients were walking in and out of the A&E block.

No. No no no! No good at all.

The toilets!

Of course. Perfect. He could dispense with the mirror for a start. And the towels. It would be warm, dry and he wouldn't be disturbed. When it was all done, he could rush out of the toilet and straight up to reception, where he'd get seen immediately as soon as they saw his face.

'So, if we could start with the shape of the face,' said DS Hodder, unknowingly creating a perfect segue from Brian's plans to scar himself to the artist's impression.

'The shape of my face?' asked Brian wondering what sort of police officer this DS Hodder was. How could he have possibly known that Brian had been thinking about his face?

'Not your face, sir, not your face, the face of the person you saw setting fire to the cars.'

111

'Oh yes of course – Bogie,' said Brian finally back on track. 'WEELLL,' exhaled Brian slowly, as if to indicate the start of a long and detailed account. 'I didn't see her for very long, but I had a good close, clear view of her face for about five full seconds. It was a horrible face, I'll never forget it as long as I live.' Brian was a lot happier now that he was in the full flow of improvisation, which was where he liked to be.

'I just happened to be coming out of my front door, which I left open for her to steal my car when I saw her arsonising the three cars.' Brian liked the 'arsonising' and thought it sounded very much like a police officer giving formal evidence in court. 'The accused proceeded along the road in a suspicious manner before arsonising the aforementioned vehicles, m'lud. After she finished her arsonisation, her huge coat caught fire and we looked at each other, eye to eye, for five seconds in the bright light of the fire.'

'Eye to eye, you say, sir?' said the tall gingery blond PC Roger Snook. 'I believe you reported earlier that she was approximately six foot four. Forgive me, sir, but I can see you fall a little short of that. What are you? Five foot eight? Five foot nine?'

'Yes five foot eight,' said Brian. No point lying about that. Trust this tall gingery plod to get all high and mighty about the height.

'Can you recall how were you aligned so that you were looking eye to eye, sir?'

Oh, just shuddup, thought Brian. 'Yes, she was crouching.'

'Why was she crouching?'

'So she could look me in the eye.'

'But why did she want to be looking you in the eye?'

'Well I don't think she wanted to exactly – she didn't really have any choice.'

'Oh? Why do you say that, sir?'

'Because, as I said, she was crouching.'

Stalemate.

'Anyway,' DS Hodder took over. 'Let's progress shall we, Brian? The shape of the face?'

'Sort of oblongy, like a man's – like Humphrey Bogart's'

Brian was extremely disappointed to see that DS Hodder wasn't going to be drawing this on paper with charcoal or pencil. Instead, he had opened up 'Identi-Kit 7HD', a piece of software designed for just such purposes. There were six pages of face shapes. Rectangular, square, round, oval, heart-shaped, pear-shaped.

'The first task for you, Brian, is to decide which of these six shapes is closest to the face shape of the woman suspect.'

Suspect woman would be more accurate, thought Brian, seeing as she doesn't exist. He chose the rectangular shape. DS Hodder clicked on the rectangular shape, which opened up six more pages of rectangular variations. 'See anything you fancy?' asked DS Hodder after ten seconds of silence. *Anything I fancy?* It was like his mum taking him shopping for new school shoes.

'WELL,' started Brian, again with that same ominous threat of a long rambling answer, 'I fancy that the second one in on the fifth row is very much like our prime suspect, that's what I fancy.' Again a picture of Helen Mirren in a white bra flashed fleetingly into his mind. Brian thought that the use of the phrase 'our prime suspect' was a very shrewd move. He was one of them! They were all in it together! Brian and the detectives, all on the tail of a mass-murdering giantess arsonist. Brian's mental detour took yet another wrong turning as he started to consider that Brian and the Detectives sounded like a 1960s pop band.

''Ow's about that then, all you guys and gals – especially all you little girls out there. Goodnessss gracious! We now have, for your pleasure and delectation, as it 'appens, a brand new single – Lady Killer – straight in at number 3 from Brian K Rayment and The Detectives.'

Having clicked on the second outline in the fifth row DS Hodder had revealed another page of outlines for even further fine-tuning.

Brian could already feel this fast becoming boring, and needed a method of making quicker selections. He decided to fall back on an old favourite of his, using his phone number 07535 453422. He planned to create a new app that would doubtless make him a fortune. The principle was using the numbers of an easily remembered number – in his case his mobile number – to randomly help with decision making. Brian had called this system Phone Originated Random Number Options, or PORNO as the app would be called. The number 0 meant no selection at all – stick where you are. Using this method, he'd next select seventh line down fifth image in, followed by third line down fifth image in. For the next half hour, this method worked extremely effectively and streamlined the whole process. The only hiccup occurred when trying to decide on the style of glasses the suspect had been wearing. Brian's PORNO system had inadvertently selected her as having eyewear, and Brian and DS Hodder found themselves looking now at the randomly created face wearing a black eye patch. Brian was sweating. This wasn't working out as well as he had hoped.

'I'm very sorry to be wasting your time, Officers. I'm afraid I'm just not very good at this,' explained Brian. 'Can't I just tell you that she looked very much like a female Humphrey Bogart?'

'Oh yes, that could certainly help. Thanks, Brian,' said DS Hodder surprisingly. 'Now, did she look like anyone else as well? Did she remind you of anyone else?'

'Yes. Strange you should ask that. I did think there was a bit of Margaret Rutherford about her. Do you know who I mean?' asked Brian unhopefully.

DS Hodder surprised him again.

'Yes yes, I do know her. Used to play headmistresses or rich eccentric widows in 1950s black and white movies. The thing is,' explained DS Hodder, 'if we have two lookalikes to work with, we can use a morphing program to blend the two of them and create a variety of composites. First thing we need,' said Hodder excitedly, 'is good pictures of both Bogart and Rutherford – preferably with similar lighting and from the same angle.'

On a second computer, he opened up two Google Image pages – a Bogart page and a Rutherford page. *Now this is really good fun,* thought Brian, *this is what it's all about. Time well spent.*

After a happy fifteen minutes for both DS Hodder and Brian, they'd come up with two good pictures of the film stars in their prime to use in the morph. Having scanned both portraits into the morphing program the detective sergeant plotted the key points of each face. The width and height of the eyes, nose and mouth – the angle and shape of the eyebrows – the positions of the chin, jawline, temple and top of the head. He also plotted the width and height of Bogie's fedora with the comparable measurements of Rutherford's Miss Marple Style Hat.

'Right! Look at this,' said DS Hodder. He was more excited than Brian. 'This is the good bit.' Hodder clicked on the image of Humphrey Bogart on the screen. Imperceptibly over the next twenty seconds, the image of Bogie gradually absorbed elements of the old lady until after twenty seconds it had become an image of Margaret Rutherford. He handed the mouse to Brian.

'Move the slider to change the ratio of one image to another until it looks right.'

Brian played with it for a few minutes, trying quick and slow runs of the slider. He seemed to be veering towards a little more than halfway. Brian finally stopped moving the slider.

'That's her,' he exclaimed, the slider having stopped at a point that was fifty-four per cent Rutherford and forty-six per cent Bogart. Strangely, the thing that convinced him to stop the slider here was the hat. The morphing of Bogart's trademark Fedora with Rutherford's headmistress-at-a-wedding hat had perfectly created the felt hat he'd worn at the arsonisation.

The four of them looked at the two computer screens. Brian and Hodder were seated, the other two officers stood behind them. Nobody spoke for quite a while as they each tried to make sense of the two screen faces. Two faces that were, in fact, about as un-alike as it was possible to be.

The face on the right was of a strong, determined-looking, intelligent woman with the slight suggestion of a scheming smirk playing around the mouth. A vague sinister air, caused by the unusual rakish hat, completed a very plausible looking suspect. The face on the left, the one entirely randomly created from Brian's PORNO system, was very long and thin with a huge bubble of blonde curls. The mouth hung open showing gappy, slightly protruding teeth. The turned-up nose, by pure random accident, was the smallest nose on the nine pages of variations and in the long face seemed almost non-existent. The right eye was heavy with mascara – the left eye had a pirate style black patch over it.

Bizarre is not the word, thought Brian as he stared at the scary and basically unbelievable face. He quickly revised his thinking, however. *Bizarre is exactly the word.*

28

The group of four in interview room two decided unanimously, after some discussion, to go with the image on the right. They referred to her alternately as Margaret Bogart and Humphrey Rutherford. The composite face appeared in print for the first time, in the local paper, the following day, Friday 24 September, under the headline:

HERE'S LOOKING FOR YOU, KID

Below is an artist's digital impression of the UK's current most wanted criminal, said by the only known eyewitness to bear more than a passing resemblance to the film star Humphrey Bogart. The suspect is thought to be a female about fifty years old, well built and very tall, approximately six foot four inches. She is wanted in connection with up to five murders, including the so-called Garage Murders, as well as a possibly related arson incident.

The notorious Garage Murders have been tagged 'the most surreal and inexplicable capital crime ever committed', with evidence of the occult, shootings, cooking, marinating, flooding, beating, electrocution and body painting occurring in the three murders, all of which apparently took place in the garage. The biggest obstacle to police enquiries has been the fact that the three bodies were found inside the garage, which had been locked from the inside.

Two other murders have been attributed to the suspect – a married couple who lived in the same street, a few doors away from the Garage Murders. The couple in their sixties were discovered forty-five miles away in a McDonald's car park.

Anyone spotting the suspect has been advised not to approach them but to report the sighting as soon as possible to the police. If anyone recognises, or has any further information on the suspect pictured, please contact the police immediately.

Brian was excited to see his picture, as he thought of it, in print. He was also very pleased, elated in fact, to read the report which contained a lot of reassuring information. 'The most inexplicable capital crime'. In terms of things to read, that was a murderer's dream. And what great news to hear that the locked doors were stumping them. For the first time since that eventful Friday evening (two weeks?) ago, Brian had the very real feeling that he may possibly get away with it all. Reading this short report he was aware of his shoulders dropping, of a weight lifting, of a welling of relief flood through him. The long-awaited medical results had come back – all clear.

The one new piece of information that he'd known nothing about was that of Len and Rose being found in a car park forty-five miles away. Then he realised that of course he knew nothing about it, he had nothing to do with it.

At the pharmacy, working a half-day Saturday, he was overly jolly, joking with colleagues and customers alike. As always with Brian, whatever his current mood or frame of mind, it was always cranked up about ten per cent more than the expected norm. Brian of course didn't see this, it was just those around him who had the benefits and challenges of the extra percentage.

The first customer in that day was Mrs Hackett. She and her husband Marc had been coming to this pharmacy for twelve years for repeat prescriptions for their many and varied medications.

'How are things today, Mrs Hackett? You're looking well,' said Brian, full of unusual beans.

'Well, I've been a bit run down with a nasty code all week – and yesterday I was ever so upset cos lost a ode brooch of my mum's.'

'Oh dear oh dear! That is upsetting isn't it?' said Brian. 'Was it valuable?'

'Yes it was pure gode – not rode gode but pure 18-carat gode.'

'Have you tode the police?' asked Brian unable to resist mimicking Mrs Hackett's Twerton accent.

'No, they don't do no good.'

Brian had now abandoned any sympathetic responses and was mentally focused on the more important issue of constructing a sentence that would make the fullest use of the strong Bath dialect.

'You coulda tode 'em that you'd bin hoding it tight while you was foding the newspaper the man just sode you and lo and behode the wind bode you over and took the gode brooch right out of your ode hand.'

Mrs Hackett frowned at him, not understanding, or maybe understanding only too well.

'Now! What can I do you for?' said Brian getting things back on course.

And so the morning continued.

That evening, Brian had looked out several waterproof

plastic food bags, the scalpel and a new blade. Earlier in the day, he filled the ice tray and several other small containers with water. Although his left arm still had a burn dressing and was bandaged, yesterday at the pharmacy, along with the daily quota of medications he dispensed, he also dispensed with the sling. It was slowing down everything he did and his arm was no longer painful so it seemed a sensible move towards the normality of Brian's far-from-normal life.

His elation rose still further that evening when, due to intense public pressure, DCI Webster was forced to give an updated announcement on the progress of the case. The announcement was made outside the Somerset Police Headquarters to a deep sea of reporters through a fence of microphones. It took place at a delayed 6.30 and appeared on all the national television news programmes. It was short and to the point and far more optimistic than was the case. She said, 'Due to some exceptionally good eyewitness report and description, we have a strong likeness of our prime suspect in the so-called "Garage Murders" and related crimes. The investigation is well advanced and we expect to be making an arrest imminently. Thank you.'

The usual request for any further information regarding sightings, or even the identity of the suspect was made with a voice-over, as well as on the displayed banner running at the bottom of the screen.

Brian smiled to himself and allowed himself a small air punch and a 'Yeessss!'

It wasn't the sort of thing he normally did but he was here at home on his own and he deserved it. The lovely CND Webster had called him an exceptionally good witness. What did she mean by 'good' exactly? Intelligent maybe – attractive? He spent the next few minutes running through possible intended meanings, and because of the brief reference to the Prime Suspect, he included a short mental cameo of Detective Inspector Jane Tennison taking off her police uniform – except the hat – and getting ready for a bath.

29

Monday 27 September 2021

It was going to be a big day for Brian. He was having the dressing on his arm changed and he was about to acquire a brand new scar, identical to the one he so admired on DS Hodder's face. He'd packed a rucksack containing all he'd need for the procedure. In a separate side pocket, he'd put the scalpel with a newly attached blade, and stuck it into a cork for safety. In the main bag he had folded up a soft white hand towel and on top of that, he'd rested a plastic bag full of ice cubes. Yesterday he had a change of plan. He was not going to catch a bus or a taxi, but intended to walk the three-and-a-half miles once again to the hospital. This allowed him maximum freedom of flexibility for the different stages of the operation.

His appointment for the dressing change was for 11.30 so he set off in good time at 10.00. He had drawn in Biro, as a template for the incision, a curved line from the corner of his mouth up into his cheek. Somehow the Biro line made it more real – he was going to get a nice new scar. When he was about twenty minutes away, he stopped, removed the bag of ice from the rucksack and pressed it to his mouth and cheek. He folded the white hand towel in three and covered the ice pack with it. He pressed the whole package hard into his face and continued walking to A&E looking like a man with severe toothache.

The advantage of this strategy was two-fold. Firstly he would arrive at the hospital with a fully numbed face, and ready to go. Secondly, it would save a lot of time.

When the A&E block came into view Brian stopped briefly to take the scalpel out of the side pocket. He continued walking until he arrived at the doors still holding the ice pack to his cheek.

He took a few moments outside, breathing deeply and getting himself focused for the job at hand. He knew there was a block of three toilets on the left-hand side of the corridor facing you as you went in. The first one was the disabled toilet and would undoubtedly be the best choice if he got lucky.

He went up to the double doors and, shielding his eyes, looked into the A&E reception area. It was fairly empty – just three or four people sitting down and another three or four walking around – but fairly open and empty.

Brian opened the doors and entered. With the towel and ice pack held against his face, he walked directly to the disabled toilet and went in.

He set things up ready in this, his personal operating theatre. The scalpel with the cork removed he placed on the sink. He flushed the ice away and draped the towel around his neck. He put on his +2.5 reading glasses and stood up close to the large mirror. The toilet cubicle was clean but had that bottomy smell that a lot of disabled toilets have. Brian thought it was as if about a dozen trouserless men were all bending over in there. Not breaking wind but just all bottomless and all bending over in the fairly warm confined space. He refined this so that rather than just random bendings over, the twelve bottomless men would all be in a circle and facing outwards – bottoms inwards – and he would be in the middle of the circle in this warm room with the twelve bottoms facing him. He could tell that he was already starting to extend this thought to find a way to test the accuracy of this theory. He snapped himself back to the surgery.

He looked at his face, which was livid and frozen. What would you call that colour? Brian decided to call it 'pale beetroot'. He had never seen his face that colour before. He thought if you took a beetroot, a cooked beetroot, and a large heaped tablespoon of mashed potato, and mashed the two together, you'd get a pretty close match to the colour of his cheek. He considered the problem a bit longer and decided a dash of brown sauce may be needed to knock the pink colour back a bit. He'd have to be careful with the brown sauce – it would be very easy to overdo that. Maybe mustard or French mustard might work better. He made a mental note to try this out when he got home.

When Brian was seventeen he left grammar school and started at the local art college. He completed a foundation year there, the most enjoyable and eye-opening year of his life to that point. He won a place at Bath Academy of Art where he spent the following three years on a BA degree course. This three-year period jumped into first place, where it stayed, as the best period of Brian's life.

During his four years at art college Brian's heart and mind were opened up to the many things that shaped who he was today. One of the recurring themes in the many aspects and applications of art that Brian learnt about, was the juxtaposition and contrast of different elements to create a pleasing or arresting effect. It was the unusual, the unpredictable – a break away from the norm – something unexpected to achieve something different or new, something to make an impact. It was the essence of both comedy and surrealism. In pet shop terms there is nothing unusual in a pet shop owner selling a parrot. A pet shop owner selling a dead, non-existent breed of parrot, the Norwegian Blue, and then trying to argue the case for its still being alive, is funny – or at least it was in 1969. A piano with a vase of flowers on it is nothing out of the ordinary – a piano with a rotting donkey on it gets your attention. Buñuel and Brian both realised this. In the past, on many occasions, Brian had used this idea of unexpected juxtaposition and contrast to help himself and give himself an edge in potentially difficult or tricky situations. On one occasion he had been dreading a forthcoming meeting with his bank manager. The meeting was to discuss his overdraft and to hopefully arrange a large loan. Brian was not in the least confident about a successful outcome of the meeting. His first thought was to wear his best suit to show respect and also to try and create the illusion of being a reliable and trustworthy customer. He put the suit on and he did indeed look smart reliable and trustworthy. He made his way to the bank but stopped just around the corner to add the finishing touches. He took out a bright red lipstick which he scribbled over both his ears. He massaged both ears for some time working and blending the lipstick well in then using the same procedure gave them a second coat. He wiped his fingers clean and walked into the bank without ever checking in a mirror the final result. The reaction of both customers and bank staff alike gave him a much better indication of the effectiveness of his red ears. The bank receptionist, who never once looked him in the eye, advised him to take a seat outside the manager's office and that would be called in soon. He was called in soon. The bank manager gave a small but visible start, his well-practised smile slipping momentarily. Having asked Brian to take a seat, and then how could he help him, he stared straight into Brian's eyes almost unblinking. For the duration of the whole short meeting, the manager stared straight ahead into Brian's eyes for fear of showing any sideways glance at the ears. Brian told him what he was after and the bank manager gave it to him. Brian was convinced he got the loan he was after because his ears were bright red.

One of the other things that made a great impact on Brian during his time at art college was colour in general, and the use of colour in particular. He learnt very early on how colour could influence a person's emotional reaction to a painting, a person's clothing and hence that person or an item for sale in a shop. You will never find a washing powder or toothpaste with yellow packaging. Anything for sale in a garden centre is likely to be green or brown. A photograph of your family that has faded to greys and blues won't give you as happy a memory as that same photo in warm bright colours.

Brian was still standing close to the mirror as felt his face. The only sensation was one of his fingers touching a block of ice. He could clearly make out the Biro template he'd drawn. Taking the scalpel he moved in even closer so that his reflected image, as well as the scalpel, was razor-sharp. He placed the scalpel against the start of the Biro line and, pressing very lightly, he followed the line up his cheek. It was about three-quarters of an inch long. He felt nothing at all. He was surprised to see little red tears emerge slowly from the line. He ran over the line of second time with the scalpel pressing slightly harder and still feeling nothing at all. A small solid red curtain ran down his cheek this time and started to drip off his chin. He could see that it was a very clean cut and he wondered whether this was yet enough to create the scar he desired or would it simply heal to invisibility. Now he'd had two practice goes he was getting used to the feel of it all – he decided to make one last cut. Moving in close to the mirror once again he followed the short curved line with the new blade. For the first time, he felt a twinge of pain and winced. He ran his tongue along the inside of his cheek and his tongue burst right through, splitting his cheek and widening his mouth by a third.

'Thloody 'ell,' he just about said, as a lot of blood made its presence felt. Brian started moving a bit faster now. He pressed the towel to his still frozen face and ran out to reception with more muffled and bubbling. 'Thloody 'ells.'

30

The nurse in reception was very quick off the mark and had already called for assistance. Within a very short time, Brian found himself on a stretcher and being wheeled into the same triage cubicle that he was in a week ago.

'We need to confirm a few details, sir,' said one of the nurses. Brian fumbled in his pocket and was able to hand her the original paperwork from when his burn was treated. All the details that needed confirming were on the sheet of course. Brian was very pleased that this avoided another of those, 'we-need-to-confirm' cycles. One of the nurses studied the sheet while a young male doctor spoke to Brian.

'Are you able to tell us what happened, Brian?' he asked. 'Try not to move your mouth too much,' he added unnecessarily.

'Try not to nake ne yawn then,' said Brian with his teeth clamped together.

As an eleven-year old schoolboy Brian had amazed his school chums by being able to talk without moving his lips. It was one of those things that came to him straight away without too much hard work or practice. He tried it and could do it – his friends tried it and couldn't. The trick was keeping your teeth firmly shut together. Brian appeared to have been born knowing this. The skill came into its own, primarily during history lessons. Mr Milford, a teacher with halitosis and dirty pullovers, bored class after class, day after day, year after year. One day Brian discovered he could stare directly at Mr Milford and talk loudly at him without moving his lips, and consequently without getting into trouble. His classmates loved him for it and he gave lessons in the lunch hour for various schoolboy favours and tips. Mr Milford tolerated this for two terms. Finally, it occurred to him to use the old army trick of threatening to punish everyone if the culprit wasn't named. Under the threat of half an hour's detention, the class fat boy, David Parsons, snitched on him.

'Please, sir, it was Rayment, sir. He can talk without opening his gob, sir.'

'Shuddup Snosrap, you fat git.'

'Yeah, shuddup, fatty Snosrap, ya git!'

'I'm not a git.'

'Quiet all of you!'

'Sir, am I a git, sir?'

'I don't know, now BE QUIET!'

Brian still recalled this exchange verbatim after all these years. It still struck him as odd that Milford was prepared to say in front of a class of eleven-year-old boys that he didn't know if David Parsons was a git or not. David Parsons was a boy who had a 'victim' mentality and was consequently victimised. Schoolboys in the main have an inbuilt homing device on victims and quickly learn that they are either a victim or a victimiser. This doesn't mean that a large number of schoolboys actively become persecutors or tyrannical, more that they learn to side with the victimiser camp, if only by association, merely to avoid being picked on themselves.

'Victims' tend not to understand this. Parsons had large fleshy ears with extremely long fleshy lobes. The other boys found this funny at first but then funny turned to irritating and the cruel nicknames began, starting with the obvious 'Big Ears'. They moved onto 'Arsons Parsons' – then just 'Arsons'. Still not finding this satisfying enough for them or annoying enough for Parsons, they went with the old schoolboy standby of using the name backwards, and from that day, until his last day at school, David Parsons became 'Snosrap'. Brian met David Parsons forty-one years later a purely chance meeting on platform two of Bath Spa Railway Station waiting for the same train. Rather than sit on the train together for what could possibly be a long and awkward journey, they arranged to meet a week later for a drink two hours before their train was due. David Parsons, now a public health inspector, had lost a lot of weight since their first form grammar school days. This meant that he weighed about the same now as he did then. After the drink, Brian was able to state categorically that David Parsons was indeed a git.

'I thas attacked,' said Brian through his clenched teeth.

'Are you able to tell us exactly what happened?'

'Yes. The Hunthree Dogart lady attacked ne thith a knithe.' Brian was wheeled into a small theatre and prepped for some stitches. During this time he was alternately asked questions and told to try not to move his mouth. Although his face was still very cold he was given a local anaesthetic. The six external stitches were very quickly and neatly completed. The five inside his mouth took another hour and not inconsiderable discomfort to complete. The worst aspect, from Brian's point of view, was his mouth had to be cranked and clamped wide open to give the doctor maximum access. When the procedure was finished, Brian was left with a surprisingly small white plaster pad on his cheek. He was advised, fairly obviously he thought, not to chew food on that side of his mouth for a week or two. Now it was all over, so to speak, Brian was keen to know just how good his new scar was going to be. He thought he should present the question in a positive way and with a smile.

'So – I expect this will leave quite a noticeable scar?' he asked hopefully.

'You were very lucky indeed that it was such a clean cut. It will be quite sore and swollen for a few weeks but in a couple of months, you won't know anything happened. No one will notice it.'

Stunned and quiet, Brian was wheeled away to wait for his scheduled dressing change. Because of the emergency repair on his cheek, he was now nearly two hours late for his appointment and so had been put to the back of the queue. He was finally seen at 5.30 having slept most of the afternoon in an uncomfortable plastic chair in the hot A&E waiting room.

31

While Brian had been preparing for his scarification, back at the serious incident room, DCI Webster had called her daily meeting of the entire murder squad working on the five current unsolved murders. It was assumed that the arson attack on the three cars was related, involving as it did only vehicles belonging to the five murder victims.

'We all know that the arsonist is the key to this whole fiasco,' she was saying. 'It's been seventeen days now and we're none the wiser. Mike, have we heard back from forensics on Rayment's stolen car? They must have got something from it.'

'Yes, guv. Plenty of Rayment's prints with quite a few of Andrew Harrington's on top of them. We've got his address in Bathford. He's got plenty of form but all just twocking and breaking and entering.'

'Bring him in,' said Webster.

'We tried to, guv, but he's on holiday.'

'What do you mean, he's on holiday? On holiday where?'

'Travelling around camping apparently, guv. His wife didn't know where he was.'

'No, and we don't know where he is, do we? Camping? In September? Without his wife?'

'That's what his wife said, guv. She didn't say the bit about not being with him but we sort of came to that conclusion by the fact that she was at home talking to us.'

'Oh, excellent detection, Detective! Right, get onto all the campsites in the UK and see if any Andrew Harringtons have booked in.'

'Guv, there's over seven thousand campsites in the UK.'

'Better get cracking then,' said Webster. 'Did you get his bank details from the wife?'

'Two card accounts. One with Nationwide – one with NatWest. We've got a trace on both of them. Last time he used a card for a purchase was two days before the car theft and at the local Sainsbury's. However, he withdrew £500 from each account the day after the car theft and another £500 from each the day after that – that was the day he went camping.'

'So he's gone camping with £2000 in his pocket.'

'May not be in his pocket, guv, it may be in …' Webster halted Sergeant Collings with a glare.

'Do you all realise the magnitude of the situation?' The room mumbled and nodded consents. 'This is our prime suspect in two separate killing sprees and a dangerous arson attack. The press is making us look incompetent, and more importantly, we are making ourselves look incompetent. Finding this man Harrington is our top priority. Mike, you and Terry get more from the wife. She must have more she can give us. Where they went on holiday. Have they been camping before? If so, where did they go? What clothes has he taken with him? Which outdoor coats has he got? Where in the country does he have friends or relatives? If we can narrow down the area he's likely to be in, we can see if other cars have been stolen and check the campsites as well as B&Bs, hostels, and hotels in that area. The two Peters, you two check out local train stations, bus stations taxi cabs. Show his photograph and see if anybody remembers him buying a ticket or booking a ride. It's a long shot, I know, but you never know. We have to bring him in as soon as possible.'

The issue concerning DCI Webster, and the one she didn't mention at this stage, was the fact that apparently they had two prime suspects. There was Andrew Harrington, an unhappy man of five foot nine with an undernourished, weasely appearance according to his file sheet, which was last updated eleven years ago. Harrington's fingerprints were all over Brian Rayment's stolen car. Then there was the six foot four inch Humphrey Bogart lady whom Brian Rayment had witnessed stealing his car. The thing that linked the two suspects was Brian Rayment's stolen car – ergo Brian Rayment. DCI Webster thought the word 'ergo'. She used it once in front of the whole squad room and it led to frowns and sniggers. She liked the word but hadn't used it since.

In an interesting moment of synchronicity, just as DCI Webster's thoughts had come around to Brian Rayment, there was a phone call for her concerning Brian Rayment.

'Oh hello, is that DCI Webster? I understand it's you I need to speak to. This is Michelle from the reception at A&E. As you know, we always report to you any incident of crime or violence that ends up here at A&E. We had a man in here yesterday, a Mr Brian Rayment, who I believe you've already met. He was the victim of a vicious knife attack. He was trying to tell us who attacked him but we don't have many details as communication with Mr Rayment was a little difficult yesterday.'

Get away! thought Webster. 'Thank you for that, Michelle,' she said. 'Do you happen to have a time logged for the incident?'

'Yes, it was strange, it was at exactly eleven-thirty – he had an appointment.'

'I don't understand?' said Webster, making it a question. 'He'd made an appointment because he knew he was going to be attacked?'

'It is an odd coincidence, isn't it? He had an appointment for a change of dressing at eleven-thirty. It appears he was attacked near the hospital, on the way to that appointment.' DCI Webster went silent, processing this new strange development.

'Do you think he knew he was going to be attacked?' asked Webster after a moment.

'I couldn't say, but he did seem to know who it was who'd attacked him.'

Time to pay Mr Brian Rayment another visit.

32

Tuesday 28 September 2021

Dosed up with painkillers and antibiotics, Brian slept deeply that night. He'd taken the day off so took the opportunity to sleep on until 9.30. He sat on the edge of his bed rotating his feet and ankles fifty times each then rotating his neck, right to left fifty times. He ran through a set of five exercises every day. As well as the ankle and neck rotations he did fifty squats, fifty sit-ups, and fifty press-ups. He loathed these last three, particularly the sit-ups. He frequently resolved to himself that early in the morning he would get the difficult ones out of the way first – get them over with – get them in the bank as it were. This would mean the ankle and neck rotations would be a doddle by comparison and could almost be treated as a cooling-down session. It was a much easier mental resolution than physical resolution. In reality, most mornings Brian started with the neck and ankle rotations telling himself that if he thought it through logically it made far more sense to treat them as warm-up exercises rather than cooling-down exercises. When he started his fitness regime about nine months ago, he made a mental pact with God to complete all five exercises every day. If he failed to complete any of the exercises, then God was allowed to do something nasty to him. After a few days, he revised this to – God was allowed to do something a bit irritating to him. It didn't seem right or fair that God should give him a fatal disease or a nasty car accident, just because he didn't complete his exercises. Brian fully accepted that he needed to be punished, so the threat of say, stubbing his toe, or his car not starting, or kicking a cup of tea over, ought to be enough to keep him up to the mark. More recently he'd come to the conclusion that this wasn't the kind of deal that a loving and forgiving God was likely to get Himself involved with. Consequently, he rendered all previous deals null and void and remade them with Sinatra. Thank Sinatra. However, even with the threat of these irritations hanging over him, Brian occasionally slipped. He wrote two subsidiary by-laws to the deal he'd made with Sinatra.

1) If the subject (Brian) should fail to complete any of the aforementioned exercises on any given day, provided they are completed the following day, in addition to the scheduled exercises for that day, then no penalty will be incurred.

2) As a penalty and a gesture of goodwill, any exercise completed late, i.e. after the twenty-four-hour period, would be subject to a ten per cent increase.

The New Deal – as he thought of it – worked very well. Brian thought it was only fair that he receive this punishment for his failure to complete the daily agreed tasks. However, in July, after a particularly bad period at work, Brian missed several days and built up a considerable backlog. To get back on course, the following day he would need to do 385 ankle and neck rotations – this included the daily ten per cent penalty – similarly 440 squats and press-ups and 715 sit-ups. The next morning, Brian phoned in sick and spent the entire day doing blocks of exercises, and at 8:45 that evening finally completed them to wipe the debt out. He also wiped himself out. He was aching and sore from head to toe. He'd strained several muscles, was physically sick three times during the night, and had to take the following two days off work as well. Brian enjoyed the irony but took little solace in the fact that he only started his exercise regime to get himself fit.

Having completed the two easy sets this morning, the neck rotations and the ankle rotations, Brian stood up and walked over to his bedroom window and looked out. It was a warm sunny day. A rare pleasure in September that made you appreciate warm sunny days more than those in June or July. He looked up and down the road, noticing how fluid and well-oiled his neck felt. The road was quiet, there was a light breeze, everything felt good, it was going to be a good day. A car crunched around the corner and slowly made its way down the road. It was a police car. It stopped a few doors away, possibly outside number 30.

Brian reached down for the binoculars he kept on the floor by the window. They were World War Two 1944 Carl Zeiss 10x50 binoculars. Exactly the same as the ones Clint Eastwood and Richard Burton had used in *Where Eagles Dare*. These were another of Brian's eBay acquisitions. He bought them two years ago after a three-year search for this exact model. It was very important to Brian to get the exact model. He could only fully relive the scene as Clint Eastwood in a snow camouflage suit if he had the right binoculars. There were always plenty of 30x8s but it took him the three years to find a decent pair of 10x50s. He was Clint Eastwood now scanning the snowy mountain with Richard Burton being Welsh by his side. DCI

Webster filled his view.

Brian had been thinking about DCI Webster a lot and he had a pretty good idea she had been thinking about him. In some ways this was quite accurate – she had indeed been thinking about him. Ever since the day she'd impressed Brian by remembering Peter Falk and the Columbo details, he knew there was a connection there. She had obviously made an effort to recall everything he had said. It was her way of telling him that she was interested in him. Interested in what he said, she was certainly interested in what he did, she never stopped asking him questions, and from those strange looks she gave him there was no doubt that she was interested in what he looked like.

Similarly, Brian was fascinated by DCI Webster. He dearly wished he had something less formal to call her.

'How lovely to see you again DCI Webster – or may I call you "D"?'

She had been on his mind a great deal since that day and Brian had imagined her in a variety of scenarios and outfits. Most nights he'd gone to bed fantasising about situations that would make him irresistible and her desperate for a man, a pharmacist if possible. Most of these fantasies involved a fair bit of adjustment, refinement and suspension of disbelief to be of any use. The latest one required that she be cured of her nymphomania through hypnotism and be prescribed anti-nympho drugs. After being hypnotized she would no longer be attracted to every man she met, but just the pharmacist who supplied the life-saving drugs. It would be Brian who performed the hypnotism and DCI Webster would need to be in a swimsuit – make that a bikini – for the hypnotism. He added a final refinement to the fantasy last night. DCI Webster would request that she be allowed to keep her police hat on during the hypnosis and to help the hypnosis work she would need a long massage beforehand. Yes, that one seemed to be sewn up now – he could start work on a new fantasy in bed tonight. He had a feeling handcuffs may be involved.

Brian knew how infatuated with him DCI Webster had become. He knew it was just a matter of time before she had to pay him another visit.

DCI Webster was sitting in the car thinking the same thing.

33

She was still sitting in the car but could come to knock on the door at any minute. Brian rushed into the bathroom and cleaned his teeth violently. He took a clean pair of trousers and shirt from the drying rack and put them on unironed. He felt the stubble on his chin and grabbed the BIC razor. There wasn't time to lather up so he just scraped the razor across his face dry, avoiding the dressing on his left cheek. He was particularly concerned about the undressed area around his mouth and under his nose, just in case he and Webster ended up kissing, which they often did in his fantasies. His shaving razor was cold – and it stings, he hurriedly thought in his Davy Jones voice, as he repeatedly scraped his face. The dry razor on unlathered skin was failing to cut the mustard, or the stubble under his nose for that matter. The repeated downward strokes were just snagging and painful. Going against the grain would probably result in a smoother finish, but may well be as painful, if not more so. It wasn't the sort of procedure to be done slowly, not that he had a lot of time to spare. He steeled himself, held his breath, and made a series of deft strokes, very, very quickly, upwards towards his nose. Scrape scrape scrape scrape scrape nick. In the blur of orange BIC razor, he just caught the tip of his nose, which briefly stung like a bar steward then welled red.

He tore a small square of toilet paper, stuck it to the cut, and finished his scraping.

She was bound to be knocking the door any second. He didn't normally use aftershave but this was different. The only aftershave he owned was an unopened boxed set that his nephews had given him two Christmases ago. He disturbed everything in the small bathroom cupboard looking for it. A bottle of cough mixture, a new toothbrush, and an unopened tube of Anusol clattered into the sink. He instinctively, but unsuccessfully, tried to catch them as they fell. Glancing at the tube he thought, *How the hell did they come up with the name "Anusol" for a tube of haemorrhoid ointment?* He was never quite sure how you were supposed to pronounce it. Was it 'Anus hole' or 'Anna-zol' or 'A-new-soll'? And another thing, why did all these specific treatments feel the need for a punned name? Earex, Blistereze. Might as well just call it Bum Cream or Arse Paste.

'Hi, I'm leading pharmacist Brian K Rayment. For all those rectal problems and indiscretions, I always use new Bum Cream – I can't be arsed to use anything else.' Bum Cream – don't be arsed to use anything else! Now available at Boots, Timothy Whites and all leading hardware stores.'

He found the aftershave. David Beckham's Eau de summat-or-other. He'd only just chucked twenty-eight bottles of it away on his neighbour's garage. He ripped open the expensive-looking packaging to get at the bottle. The top was screwed on tight and had a hermetically-sealed plastic covering. He scrabbled at it frenetically trying to slice through it with his fingernails and teeth. He looked like a desperate alcoholic who could stand the cold-turkey cure no longer. The plastic seal split and peeled off and he unscrewed the top as he simultaneously shook the bottle. He splashed himself randomly and was emptying a good palmful into his right hand when the wet bottle slipped. Again, an instinctive grab to catch it was this time successful. He caught the bottle firmly upside down and watched it empty onto the groin of his fawn trousers. There was a knock at the front door.

34

Brian dropped everything and got himself downstairs in his usual fast, shambling, trippy, stumbling way. As before, resulting in the Max Wall incident, he caught sight of himself in the hallway mirror. He saw and peeled off the square of bloodied tissue paper from his nose a bare second before he opened the front door.

'DCI Webster. How lovely to see you again,' said Brian as the first drop of blood reappeared on his nose like a ladybird. DCI Webster watched the ladybird grow, burst, and then dribble down Brian's upper lip before she could return the greeting.

'Good morning, Mr Rayment. You've met DS Wells.'

'Yes of course. I thought you may have come on your ...' he started, thought better of it and shut up. 'Do come in – you as well, Constable Wells.'

'DS Wells,' said DS Wells.

'You were saying?' Webster prompted when they were all sitting down. 'Thought I'd come on my ...?'

Hell's teeth. On her bike? On her day off? On her birthday? On her boss's recommendation? Yes that'll do.

'That last one,' he said.

'Beg pardon?'

'Sorry I just meant to think that, not say it,' explained Brian.

DCI Webster was getting used to Brian Rayment's MO when it came to conversation.

The blood from Brian's nicked nose was running freely again now and had found its natural course down his upper lip, along his top lip to the right, and into the dressing at of his mouth. It was quite a thing to witness. There was a clean white fresh dressing attached to his face apparently in anticipation of receiving the blood from another wound on his face. The once fresh white dressing was rapidly becoming a fresh red dressing.

Brian decided not to mention the nicked nose or the flow of blood. He hoped that it might go unnoticed or at least, as far as the police officers were concerned, taken in their stride. All police officers were surely used to seeing blood? Although perhaps a brief throwaway mention of it may be a good idea.

'Yes – I uh …' he started, tutting and raising his eyebrows at his stupidity. 'I just cut myself shaving. One of the many trials of being a male,' he said. Why did he say 'male' – why not 'man'? The police say male. *The suspect was a white male and getting whiter by the minute.*

'I'm sorry, Mr Rayment, we always seem to catch you at an awkward time.'

'Oh, Brian please – we know each other well enough by now,' said Brian. Webster ignored the offer.

'Would you like a moment to get sorted?' she asked, glancing, but pointedly, at the stained crotch of his trousers. Brian glanced there too.

'Oh that's just aftershave,' he said. 'I put it on for you DCI.' He tried the abbreviation.

Slightly alarmed, but her professionalism kicking in, she didn't show it.

'Why would you do that, Mr Rayment?'

He was embarrassed and struggling to start an answer.

'Well … I know it may sound silly … but I thought that if we should end up … you know … having a kiss an' that …'

'Christ on a motorbike!' said DS Dew whipping round to look at his boss's reaction. 'Are you an him…?'

'Shut it, Dew!'

'No, I just thought I should smell nice for you – like David Beckham. He smells like this.'

'David Beckham soaks his trousers in aftershave? As a matter of interest, where do you get all this information from, Mr Rayment?' Of all the questions DCI Lucy Webster wanted to ask that was the one that sprang to her lips.

'It's a special one he's had specially made that smells of him. It's called Eau de … Eau de …' Eau de what? What the hell was it called?

'Eau de Beckham's kecks,' suggested DS Dew.

'Both of you! Stop this nonsense! NOW! If you're happy to continue, Mr Rayment, we have a few more questions about your visit to A&E yesterday.'

'Yes I'm happy.'

'Good. Could you tell us, as clearly and as accurately as possible, how you came to sustain the injury to your lower cheek?'

'Yes – I – could – easily,' replied Brian, enunciating every word slowly, already starting on keeping things clear and accurate.

'Please – tell – us,' replied DCI Webster in the same tone.

'Well – it – all – started – when – I – was – making – my – way …'

'Mr Rayment – Mr Rayment, sir – your pronunciation is perfectly clear to us. When I said "could you tell us clearly" I was referring more to the content of what you say rather than how you pronounce the words when you say it.'

'Roger that!' said Brian, saluting. 'Well, it all started when I was making my way to A&E for my appointment to change the dressing on my arm.'

35

The next sentence he spoke would be a very important one. Brian had already thought extensively about this inevitable conversation. His dilemma was simple. Should he claim that (a) his Humphrey Rutherford creation had attacked him, (b) it was the suspect who stole his car, or (c) it was a completely new attacker? Which would help him the most? If he claimed it was Margaret Bogart it would surely appear outrageously coincidental that he was still the only person ever to see her and now for a second time. He feared that far from distancing himself from any crime it would heap more suspicion on him. To say it was the car thief who attacked him was highly risky, as he may well have been in police custody at the time and possibly still there this very minute. It had to be a new attacker.

Brian had made a decision as to his method of answering this. He had another random system of answering. Firstly he had to get them to ask questions, hopefully leading ones. The temptation, he knew from bitter experience, was just to ramble on himself. Rambling, though, could very quickly get out of hand. He would allow his answers to be police led. If the question ended in a vowel it was a 'NO' if it ended in a consonant it was a 'YES'. If it needed a more detailed response he'd be guided by the question. He hadn't entirely resolved this issue, but was, as always, happy to improvise.

'I was about a mile away from A&E when someone attacked me.'

'Carry on,' said Webster. Brian didn't want to carry on, he wanted a question so he could adopt his random answering system.

'Just attacked,' he said again, stalling and trying to provoke a question.

'Carry on,' said Webster again – *stop saying 'carry on'*.

'Just attacked,' he said again. Brian felt certain he could 'carry on' longer than they could.

'Did you see your attacker?' There it was – the question!

'Yes.'

'Could you describe him?'

'Yes.'

'Describe him please!'

'He was a man and he had a big … a big …'

'A big?'

'Mouth.'

'Do you mean he was mouthy, he spoke a lot, or that he physically had a big mouth?'

'Yes.'

'Which one?'

'No.'

'No?'

'No.'

'No, he didn't have a big mouth?'

'Yes.'

'I'm confused, Mr Rayment.'

'Yes.' His random answering system wasn't working, mainly because they were messing it up. They wouldn't ask proper questions. If they approached it like twenty questions – just yes/no answers – then perhaps we could get somewhere. He decided to abandon it and be creative. 'He had a big, mouthy mouth and small, tiny, titchy teeth.' It occurred to Brian that he never seemed to see or describe any normal-looking people. Maybe he should throw in a few normal attributes for the sake of realism. 'He had an ordinary nose and some ordinary hair.'

'What about his eyes? Did you get a look at his eyes?'

'Yes, they were ordinary, even more ordinary than his nose and hair.'

'Ears?'

'Ordinary.'

'Eyebrows?'

'Very ordinary.'

'Was he short or tall – what sort of height was he?'

'Sort of …'

'Ordinary?' suggested Webster.

'Yes, that's right – ordinary. Do you know who it is then?'

'No, not yet, sir. Build?'

'Ordinary.'

'Age?'

'Ordinary.'

'No such thing, sir. You can't have an ordinary age. Was he young, old, middle-aged, teenager …?'

'Yes, that last one. A middle-aged teenager.' Webster gave a sigh

'Could you maybe give a rough estimate of his age?'

Brian's mind tried to calculate how old a middle-aged

teenager would be. Teens, that was thirteen to nineteen. Middle-aged would be in the middle of that. What's the average? Thirteen plus nineteen is twenty-two. Twenty-two divided by two is -

'Eleven,' he said. Even as the word came out of his mouth he knew it didn't sound right. A quick double-check. Thirteen plus nineteen … Oh Bernard Ollocks it's thirty-two, not twenty-two!

'No – sixteen. He was sixteen.'

'He was sixteen?'

'Yes, sixteen. Thirty-two divided by two is sixteen, therefore he was sixteen.'

Brian noticed that DCI Webster and DS Dew were doing that slightly puzzled frowny look that most police people seemed to adopt these days. Maybe they were taught to do it.

'How did he attack you?' asked Dew

'Like this,' Brian leapt at DS Dew and made a stabbing action at his face. Dew's police training kicked in and in one impressive quick movement, he had Brian's face pressed into the floor, his knee in Brian's back with his arm bent behind him. Brian was screaming. DS Dew had grabbed and twisted Brian's bandaged arm and had pressed his shaved nose and bandaged cheek into the floor.

'OK! Let him go – let him go,' said DCI Webster, saving Brian's life.

Brian was quick to show his appreciation for having his life saved. He made his way towards Webster with outstretched arms and pursed lips, seizing the perfectly legitimate excuse to kiss DCI Webster.

Webster visibly recoiled. He was trailing bloodied and

seeping bandages, and a stream of smeared blood over the lower part of his face. He was stiff and sore from the recent counter-attack from DS Dew, so was lurching rather than walking towards Webster. Had Brian been in a position to witness his own progress, he would have recognised the resemblance to a 1950s sci-fi monster – *The Mummy* or *The Creature from the Black Lagoon* or maybe a combination of all those men-in-a-suit movie monsters.

'I'd like to kiss you to show my appreciation for saving me from PC DewDrop.'

'That's probably not a good idea is it, Brian? You're in a bit of a state at the moment.' Brian was quick to pick up on the fact that she'd called him Brian. The first time she used his first name. She also said 'at the moment'. Not a good idea to kiss 'her at the moment'. A clear implication that there would be a time when it would be a good idea. Emboldened by these two clear come-on signs from DCI Webster, Brian bashed on.

'No I quite understand,' he said backing off. 'Maybe, though, I could take you out to dinner tonight,' he continued, as another large drop of blood dripped into the still-damp aftershave stain in the groin of his trousers.

DCI Webster just stared at him for long seconds. She seemed to be weighing up just how to respond to the absurd suggestion. She then surprised all three of them by saying, 'Thank you, Brian – I'd love to.'

36

'I'll call you tonight when I've finished work,' said Webster to Brian. 'Thank you for your help. I think you need to go and get yourself cleaned up and sorted out now don't you, Mr Rayment? See you later. Goodbye.' The two officers got up to leave and Brian ushered them out, leaving a fresh drip of blood on his hallway carpet every three or four feet.

When they were in the car, DS Dew said to Webster, 'Do you think that's wise, guv? Meeting him for a meal? After all, he is the key witness in the case we're investigating.'

'I'm well aware of that, Kevin,' said Webster, who was getting more comfortable using first names, 'but we're getting nowhere, aren't we? The man's a complete idiot. I'm going to run this past the super and tell him exactly what I have planned. If he has any misgivings I'll phone up Mr Rayment and pull the plug on it. I just have a feeling though, if I can get him to relax a bit, he might open up and reveal something useful. Don't worry – I won't do anything without the full backing of the boss.'

'You should be careful though, guv. The two of you alone – you don't know what he's capable of.'

'At the moment he's not capable of very much at all. He's got a burnt arm and a mashed-up face and you softened him up a fair bit earlier on.'

Dew smiled at the memory. It was the first time he'd ever had the chance to put his 'restraint with necessary force' training into practice. He'd impressed himself with his agility and strength, though to be fair, he thought, Rayment was a pretty soft target.

When they got to the station DCI Webster knocked on the door of Superintendent Andrew Richardson.

DS Dew watched her go in. She came out twenty-three minutes later, gave the slight suggestion of a smirk and raised her eyebrows at him. She was under several strict instructions. She was not to wear a wire of any sort. Doing so without authority would get her struck off and any recorded information would be inadmissible anyway. She was not to question Rayment on any aspect of the case. She was not even to discuss any aspect of the case with him. She was not allowed to take notes. She was not to drink alcohol. She was not to arrive at the restaurant, or wherever it was they were going, with Rayment. He must already be situated there and she was to arrive after him so that it could still be taken, or seen, as a chance meeting. Superintendent Richardson and DCI Webster were the only two people who knew of the arrangement. They both also knew that they were sailing very close to the wind. The hope, and the only reason for the meeting, was that Rayment, in a more relaxed setting, would talk and reveal something useful that could then be followed up and hopefully push the investigation forward.

She phoned up Brian, who sounded excited and excitable. He immediately launched into one of his free-wheeling stream-of-consciousness approaches to a conversation. It was quickly in danger of convincing her it was a bad idea to be doing this.

Taking control of the situation, she suggested, reasonably forcefully, that they meet in the Marlborough Tavern – a gastropub that was local, informal and with several easy escape routes. She got the clear impression that Brian had been hoping for, and imagining, a much grander, romantic evening. However, frequent use of the name Brian quickly softened him into easy acceptance of her suggestions.

'You find us a table, Brian, round about eight. I'll be there as soon as I can. Don't worry if I'm a bit late – I sometimes get held up at the station. See you later, Brian. Yes thank you very much, Brian. Yes that's very kind of you, Brian. See you later.'

37

Brian was on the sofa in his living room still holding the phone. It was a regular traditional landline telephone that Brian had had for twenty-two years. He didn't much hold with mobile phones. Ten years ago he made an enormous mental leap and bought a basic mobile phone. It was a Doro 1370, a phone specially made with large numbers and loud volume for the old and infirm. Two years ago, much to his horror, Sandie had bought him a smartphone for Christmas. The worst aspect of this for Brian was showing the right reaction. It unquestionably was a very generous present but one that he did not want. In this kind of situation, he found it difficult to convey convincingly the appropriate sense of appreciation. Sandie on the other hand found it very easy to convey convincingly her sense of disappointment in his reaction. The whole concept of smartphones both appalled and terrified him. The screens of brightly coloured rows of 'apps' caused Brian to glaze over. Occasionally, feeling adventurous, Brian tapped one of the apps, opening up a whole new level of stress and irritation in the form of adverts, instructions and juvenile jingles. His default reaction to this was to switch the phone off and leave it for an hour or two to calm down. And another thing – what was all that swipe – swipe – swipe – swiping with your finger across the screen? Did these phone people just do it to annoy real people or did it have a function? Was it to warm the phone up or kickstart an app? And 'app'! Brian imagined all the heads of all the phone companies having a meeting in the penthouse suite of the most expensive offices in New York to discuss and decide on the most annoying name for a phone application. Brian frequently pictured himself hurling a smartphone straight down into the pavement. One day.

His mind was all of a fluster. The cocktail of mixed emotions all fighting for dominance had left him shaken. In Brian's mind, Sean Connery amended this to 'shaken but not shtirred'. Brian was sprawled in an unusual mid-leap position. The coiled cable of the phone had been stretched taut between the main body of the phone lying sideways on the floor and the handset. Ever since midday he'd been unsettled, wandering about, not able to concentrate on anything. He never moved more than a few yards from the phone. He'd been trying to estimate when DCI Webster was likely to call. He wasn't sure when her shift ended – this was the problem. From his extensive knowledge of police activity, learnt and filed away from shows like *Call of Duty* and *Prime Suspect*, Brian knew that police shifts were 2.00 till 10.00 – 10.00 till 6.00 – 6.00 till 2.00. If a shift ended at 2.00, she could be calling quite soon; if she ended at 6.00 he'd have the whole afternoon to get through. But wait, no it couldn't be 6:00. The 6.00 was the end of the graveyard shift, 10:00 the previous night till 6.00 in the morning, which means she must be ending at 2:00. She'd seen him and had been working in the morning so she must be on the 6.00 to 2.00 shift. Brian reckoned that the closer to 2:00 DCI Webster called the more interested she was in him.

He was jittery and on edge and mentally playing through films of all the possible ways the evening could go. A lot of them we're turning nasty in the last reel. These days he was finding it noticeably more difficult to come up with happy endings.

At 2.35 the phone rang. Brian leapt at it, listened for a few seconds of silence, then

'Hello. My name's Kevin' said a voice with a strong Indian accent, 'How are you today Mrs Raymond? I'm calling about a fault you have with your internet connection.

'I'm sorry,' said Brian, angry and irritable, 'you've called at a very bad time ...I'm in!' He banged down the receiver.

At 6:15 the phone finally rang again. Brian launched himself at it, landing in his current mid-leap sprawl. It was DCI Webster. An inspector calls. It was the sort of thing Brian may well have planned all day to say when the call finally came, but it came to him on the spur of the moment.

'An inspector calls,' he said.

'JB Priestley,' said Webster. She was good – she was very good.

'Alastair Sim,' said Brian.

'Inspector Goole,' said Webster.

'I beg your pardon?' said Brian.

'Inspector Goole,' repeated Webster.

'How do you mean?'

'Inspector Goole is the name of the inspector in *An Inspector Calls* by JB Priestley,' explained DCI Webster.

'Christ on a motorbike,' he said. He'd been saying it a lot to himself all day ever since he heard DS Dew Drop use it. He just waiting for a chance to try it out. It occurred to him, almost immediately, that DCI Webster had probably cottoned on to him copying Dew Drop, as it was not the sort of expression you hear twice in a day under normal circumstances. The reason he'd used it was due to his amazement that Webster knew more about *An Inspector Calls* than he did. That was definitely 1-0 to her and they hadn't even arranged to meet yet. What was this? He hadn't been concentrating. Oh – she was suggesting somewhere to meet. He wanted to treat her to a slap-up feed at the Royal Crescent Restaurant, where a side order of chips would set you back £12 and a room for the night was £470.00. What was she saying? The Marlborough Tavern? He instantly found himself picturing a Hansel and Gretel type pub-in-a-forest made entirely of cigarettes. She was telling him it was a friendly, relaxing gastropub. He didn't like the expression gastropub. The only time he ever heard gastro was in gastroenteritis. Already he was strongly associating this pub with getting gastroenteritis. He was certain that, however the evening played out, he would end up with stomach pains and throwing up all night. But she was being so nice about it she was using his name. She was also asking him to arrange things to find a table for them. It was clear she was falling in love with him.

'I think you're wonderful,' he said. She loved that – he could tell. She had used his name yet again. She was hooked.

'I think I've just fallen in love with you,' he said. He could picture her smiling and blushing. She would be putty in his hands tonight. He didn't like the smell of putty, the linseed oil was too cricket-batty, but he was fairly certain he would like the smell of DCI Webster.

38

As well as getting himself presentable Brian had one or two other things to organise – one or two surprises. He had about an hour before he needed to set off for the Marlborough Tavern. He spent a lot of the hour trying on just about every item of clothing he owned. He started with a dinner suit and bow tie, both of which were his father's, and clearly from a different era. Vintage was all the rage but the smell of mothballs probably wasn't. He thought too, that the dinner suit was possibly over-egging the pudding for a place like the Marlborough. He tried the other extreme and thought about going casual. It was no big surprise to Brian, when he looked in the mirror, to see that he'd gone too far down the casual route. The grubby white worn-out Nike trainers went reasonably well with the oil-stained track bottoms but the black Stranglers T-shirt, now a size too small, made him look strange, a bit like a serial killer. Not good. Over the next half hour of experimentation with his wardrobe, he neutralised the extremes and came up with an approximate midpoint. He wore a casual shirt with a chunky belted cardigan over some tailored slacks and slip-on shoes. The whole ensemble worked well together in a range of pleasing autumn colours. He looked neat and smart and confident. He looked like Ted Bundy.

He arrived at the Marlborough Tavern three minutes early so hung around outside for the three minutes so he could enter the place at exactly 8.00. He went to the bar and told the barman he was meeting a very special lady and asked if could he recommend a classy drink. The barman told him a margarita usually went down well. Brian told him he didn't think she would fancy a pizza, especially before they ordered their main meal. He told him he would wait for his lady to arrive before he ordered their drinks. Having found out what Webster wanted to drink, he would order the same for himself, just to show how much in tune they were. Also, he must find out her name. He couldn't call her Webster or DCI or CID or any other combination of initials all evening. When she arrived, six minutes late, Brian thought she looked stunning. Although the place wasn't busy she made a point of walking towards the bar and then 'noticing' Brian and making a detour to his table. Having only ever seen her in the navy blue standard issue police uniform it was a surprise to see her in grey. She wore a pair of high-waisted mid-grey wool trousers with a lighter ash grey sloppy joe pullover. Over this, she'd picked a darker grey duffle coat worn undone. Her hair had a redder tinge than he'd realised. And she was small. He knew she was small from the first time he saw her at his door with untrustworthy Higgsy, but in mufti she looked tiny. He leant forward to kiss her, actually, it was more a lunge than a lean and she backed out of it, very cleverly making it appear that she just hadn't noticed. He pulled a chair out for her in a very gentlemanly way – she sat down, thanked him and then he spoilt the moment by forcing the chair with her in it right back under the table, scraping the floor with a prolonged grating screech. Now she was quite firmly wedged into the table he moved in again to try for the kiss.

'Not here, Brian, not here.'

'Not here.' That was OK – that was good even. 'Not here' was a clear suggestion that there would be a place and the time that was right for kissing. Maybe later, maybe back at her place or my place. No not my place, he thought. Right! What now? Oh yes – drinks.

'May I get you a drink? What's your poison? I mean what would you fancy? Beer, wine, brandy, a margarita, maybe a capricciosa, quatro stagioni?' Because of the earlier confusion, Brian had somehow taken as read that classic pizzas were interchangeable with cocktails.

The absurd request relaxed Lucy Webster. She was tempted to order a quattro stagioni just for the fun of seeing Brian attempt to order it. She refrained, reminding herself that she was not here to have fun.

'Just a tap water for me, please – but you have what you want of course.' Tap water? That's not a good start. Brian made his way to the bar – it was clear. The barman raised his eyebrows and smiled at Brian with a 'what can I get you, sir?' expression.

'Two pints of tap water please.'

'Two pints?' the barman asked incredulously, the expression changing.

'Yes please,' said Brian, 'no ice. How much is that please?'

'No charge for tap water, sir,' said the barman as pleasantly as he was able. Brian carefully carried back the two sleevers of water and joined Lucy. 'Cheers. Bottoms up,' he said and started downing the water. When he'd drunk about half, he rested the glass down, took a breather, looked around the room, and then finished it off. Lucy was fascinated. The whole pint had taken Brian under a minute.

'Well that was delicious,' said Brian wiping his mouth. 'I think I'm going to have another one. Can I line one up for you?'

'No I'm fine, thanks,' said Lucy who had yet to take a sip.

During the pint, Brian's mind was working furiously. He couldn't take any more of this tap water lark, yet he wanted to appear at ease and comfortable with DCI Webster's choices. He made his way to the bar, catching the barman's eye again.

'What alcoholic drinks have you got that look like water? I know all about gin,' he whispered, 'but are there any others?'

'Vodka's the other obvious one. It's a bit of a speciality of ours. We stock a good range of both vodkas and gins. Care to try one?'

Brian realised he had some catching up to do and said, 'What's the strongest vodka you've got?'

'We have everything from a basic Smirnoff or Absolut, through a mid-range of different imported vodkas. The strongest one we have is a Scandinavian vodka known as Balkan 176. It's one of the strongest drinks in the world. It's eighty-eight per cent ABV. Or we've got a Devil Springs Vodka which is almost as strong at eighty per cent ABV. You usually have that with ginger ale.' Initials again. Always initials. What did ABV mean? The 'V' was undoubtedly vodka. What was AB? Anti-bacterial? Almost bearable? It had to be related to the powerful strength. Atomic blast? A-bomb? He'd call it Atomic Blast Vodka. This, as it happened, was a fairly reasonable description of the drink.

'I'll have a double of that Balkan 176 Atomic Blast Vodka.'

The barman smiled professionally and said, 'I don't think a double's a good idea, sir. I'm not even sure we're allowed to sell doubles. It is an exceedingly strong drink. There are thirteen health warnings on the label, including one in Braille.'

'Is that in case you get blind drunk?' said Brian.

'Good one, sir, very good. Shall we start with a single shot?' Brian never liked to be seen to be backing down.

'No no, I'll stick with the double shot if you don't mind – if you're allowed to that is – in a pint glass, please.' Shaking his head but saying nothing, the barman turned away to fix Brian his double shot of Balkan 176 in a pint glass. He brought it back round to the bar. Brian stared unbelieving at the three-quarters of an inch of clear liquid in the bottom of the pint glass.

'Is that it?' said Brian.

'That's two shots, sir. The pint glass makes it look smaller.'

'How much is that then?'

'£13.60, sir.'

'Farley Uckaduck! Can you top it up with water please?'

'How much water, sir?'

'Fu … fill it right up to the top so it looks like a pint of tap water. Come on – sharpen up, man!' said Brian, still bristling at the price. 'I want it to appear as if I'm on tap water.'

'It appears you're on another planet,' said the barman to himself as he topped up Brian's drink. But it did indeed resemble a pint of tap water.

39

'You were quite a time. What was all that about?' said Lucy, trying to kickstart some sort of conversation.

'No – I was just having a chat with the barman. Very interesting knowledgeable chap. He was telling me all about different types of … water.' He changed 'vodka' to 'water' at the last minute.

'Different types of water?' asked Lucy.

'Yes – he was telling me that tap water varies from town to town, county to county, country to country. If you drink tap water here and now, like I've just done, and then have another one in San Francisco, in ten minutes time, they'll be totally different. I suppose it's because some taps are made of brass and some are chrome. Some are fed by plastic pipes and some by copper pipes.' Brian was in full flow now and starting to enjoy himself. 'Yes, it's like a completely different drink. You wouldn't believe the different flavours. Believe it or not, Paul McCartney has bottled tap water from the Mull of Kintyre flown in each week.'

'Fascinating, Brian. Why don't you sit down and join me?' Brian sat down and joined her. Forgetting for a moment that he wasn't holding a pint of tap water, he took a long mouthful of the dilute Balkan 176. He sucked in loudly and his lips fired back in a grimace. He was making the same face that his childhood pet miniature schnauzer, Jackson, made when he was shown half a cut lemon.

'What is it, Brian? What's the matter?'

'Oh, it's just this vawter.' Changing 'vodka' to 'water' at the very last minute as before, he almost, but not quite, avoided the 'V'. Trying to pass it off as a temporary speech impediment he continued, 'Its vonderful, vonderful – I don't know vhy anyvun vould vant to drink anything else.'

Lucy Webster, being the sharp detective she was, had detected what Brian was doing and for that matter what he was drinking. She decided to leave it. To further quiz him on it would only lead them down another fruitless path. If he was drinking vodka that may well loosen his tongue.

'I dunno your name,' said Brian. 'I mean I know you're a DCI Webster – but I don't know what to call you.'

'It's Lucy,' said Lucy. There didn't seem any real harm in passing this information on – after all, it could be fairly easily researched.

'Lucy,' Brian tried it out. 'Lovely Lucy. Juicy Lucy.' By now he was planning how to film this meet-cute sequence. The sharp Marlborough Tavern scene would dissolve into a soft-focus dream sequence as Brian pictured himself in a boat on a river. The soundtrack to the scene of course would be 'Lucy in the Sky with Diamonds'. While picturing tangerine trees and marmalade skies, Brian had taken several more hefty swigs of his enhanced water which in turn was already enhancing his imagination to echo the psychedelia of the song. He continued his magical progress with Lucy as the song played on in his mind. He imagined Lucy as a girl with the sun in her eyes and

– Brian opened his eyes – she's gone!

He had a brief moment of panic but then saw that Lucy's grey duffle coat was still there. Also, she had drunk about two inches of her water. His reverie must have taken him out of the game for longer than he'd realised. Presumably, she hadn't done a runner and was just visiting the 'ladies'. The ladies already? She had only drunk a couple of inches. Maybe police people suffered from small bladders. Maybe it was a drawback of the job.

Lucy did indeed need to use the ladies. But just to get away from Brian and gather her thoughts. She was having very strong second thoughts about this whole idea. It seemed you had to treat this Brian Rayment like a firework that had failed to go off. She had to hold her nerve – let him have free rein and see if anything useful came out of the torrent of seemingly random rubbish. She looked at her watch and decided to give him another thirty minutes, then she was out of here. As she made her way back to the table, she saw Brian sitting there calm, quiet, and watching her return. When she was seated he said

'I'm a bit nervous. I've got some things I need to tell you.'

This was hopeful, Lucy thought. 'Well feel free, Brian. What is it?'

He was nervous and on the verge of speaking, but struggling to get any words out. This in turn made Lucy nervous. She picked up her glass and started drinking, primarily to hide her face and to have something else on which to focus her attention.

'First of all,' Brian started, 'and this has nothing to do with the other stuff I have to tell you – but first of all – I'm in love with you.' To avoid having to make any form of answer Lucy continue to drink and tipped the glass up to hide as much of her face as possible. Neither of them said anything for several seconds then Brian opened up again.

'It's about the murders,' he said.

40

This was both exactly the thing Lucy had been hoping for and the last thing she'd expected. She didn't want to interrupt – stop the flow – break the spell. She continued to hide behind her glass and sip her water.

'Not all the murders, only the ones in the garage,' said Brian. He made it sound quite reasonable. Lucy managed an encouraging nod. 'It's just that there are a few things I'd like to get off my chest.' Lucy's heart was sprinting. She was willing him to continue, to give her something to bust this devilish case wide open. He continued.

'It started several months ago. My neighbours, Tony and Marlina, had been driving me mad with their silly ways and their anger and their miserable attitude to everything. It got to the point where I just couldn't stand it anymore. I felt I had to do something about it. Tony was the main problem. Everything he did wound me up – annoyed me. He was truculent, unfriendly, so in the end, I decided to kill him.' Brian made this bold statement very matter-of-factly, like it was the natural and only conclusion to a tricky problem. Brian continued slightly less clearly, 'So I planned it using six melons like the Jackal and Edward Fox and a waffle iron.'

'Edward Fox and a waffle iron?' asked Lucy who seemed miles away.

'Yes, a waffle iron, because it's heavy and flat and it wouldn't leave a giveaway dent in Tony's head. Then, after I'd whacked him in the garage, Marlina came in to tell Tony it's tea time, so I barged her onto the floor till she was dead.' Lucy said nothing. 'Then another bloke came in who parked his car outside my house all week, so I hit him with Tony's Anglepoise lamp and his hand caught fire. So,' he summarised, 'I killed these three in the garage and I made very good time. It was all done and dusted in about six minutes. Anyway – you'll like this next bit – I searched around Tony's garage and found a gun. It was probably the gun he used to kill Len and Rose down the road. I decided to disguise the murders by doing some surrealism in the garage. I shot them all up with Tony's gun and put hieroglyphics on the walls, then I got some potatoes and other vegetables and set fire to the Shadows on Tony's CD player.' Lucy remained quiet. 'Finally, I painted Marlina with red lead and gave her a paint-tin hat like Isambard Kingdom Brunel and filled Tony up with pennies. I booted the garage door in then locked them all in from the inside and flooded the place and Bob's me uncle.' Brian gave a smile. He looked pleased with himself. He continued. 'Now that's just the first bit. The second chapter, so to speak, was a week later. Your lot didn't have a clue what was going on. It was me who rolled the three cars together and joined them up with petrol sheets and set fire to them. Yes! Hard to believe innit? It was me. I am that arsonist. You silly arsonist. Don't be such a silly arse, you silly arsonist! You're an absolute shower!' Brian was turning into Terry Thomas, Lucy was remaining silent. 'I was dressed like Humphrey Bogart with a hat like Margaret Rutherford.' Some of this was getting quite hard to explain clearly. Brian needed another drink. He finished off the vodka water. 'As I wassaying before I was s'rudely int'rrupted,' slurred Bryan, 'sheew's dressed like Humphreeb ogart inananormous mac anna soft ladies felt hat. Thass the felt hat that w's soft not the lady.' His mouth felt on fire the vodka water was the worst drink he'd ever had in his life. It was how he imagined dilute battery acid would taste. The inside of his mouth had a vindaloo throb. He needed to wind this up. Talking was becoming difficult, making sense even more so. 'When Ice truck the match the coat caught fire so I tookitoff and pretended to be the suspect and drove to hospitlinna Margaret Rutherford hat. The end.'

Brian bowed – let out a deep breath and looked over to Lucy to see her reaction. Lucy was asleep.

41

Seeing Lucy asleep was a surprise. Brian had no idea that the Rohypnol would work so quickly. Back in November of last year, right in the depths of the Covid 19 pandemic, Brian had been working a solitary shift at the pharmacy. A local woman had come in fully masked up for her regular prescription. She'd taken the opportunity to bring with her a large bag of unwanted and out-of-date drugs for the pharmacy to dispose of. The local NHS improvement team would make arrangements for a waste contractor to collect the medicines from pharmacies at regular intervals. As required by the NHS and the waste contractor, Brian sorted them into solids (including ampoules and vials), liquids and aerosols. Some additional segregation was also required under the Hazardous Waste Regulations.

The woman had a history of sleep problems and insomnia. In 2018 she had taken a holiday travelling around South America. After three days without sleep, she saw a local doctor in Mexico and was prescribed flu nitrazepam Rohypnol. She certainly got some sleep but the side effects were so extreme and unpleasant that she never took the drug again.

As Brian sorted through the various mix of medicines the woman had brought in he spotted the Rohypnol. It fascinated him it was the first time he'd ever seen or heard of any Rohypnol being in this country. The cultural stigma of the drug excited Brian. Because of this he would have loved to have owned it. However, he had yet to become a thief, as he had yet to become a murderer, and it was beyond his comprehension to steal anything. However, he had a small private locker at the pharmacy. For two days he kept the Rohypnol in the locker. But it bothered him. If he were to get caught with it in his possession, particularly as it had been handed in for disposal, at the very least he would lose his job. The next time he was in the pharmacy on his own he decanted the Rohypnol into a clean Optrex allergy eye drops bottle, a product freely available over the counter. There it remained until two weeks ago. Having now become a murderer, and hence free to commit any lesser crimes, he had no compunction in taking the Rohypnol home. He slipped it in his pocket during his midnight visit to the pharmacy for the bottles of aftershave and cologne for Tony's garage. He was very keen to use it to try it out but had no set plans about how and when. He just felt that one day it could well come in handy. When the arrangement was made to meet DCI Lucy Webster that evening he knew he should take it with him. He still had no real plan to use it but instinctively felt it may get him out of trouble, if only temporarily. He was astute enough to realise that it could potentially land him in much bigger trouble than it was likely to get him out of. It was a characteristic of Brian's life that he often ended up in these good-news bad-news knife-edge situations: salvation on one side – damnation on the other.

When Brian arrived he was nervous. There was the potential for many varied and hazardous outcomes to the evening. As the Stingray theme tune played in his head, he pictured the fixed gormless grin of Troy Tempest failing to register any reaction to the voice-over warning 'anything can happen in the next half hour'.

This was really what it boiled down to. Brian reckoned he had half an hour to make the right impact on DCI Webster. If things weren't going well after thirty minutes he would have probably blown it. If he was going to use the Rohypnol tonight he guessed this would be the point where it would happen. As far as Brian was concerned, the evening had got off to a horrendous start, when DCI Webster refused an alcoholic drink. His plans and schemes had all revolved around getting her reasonably drunk. At that moment, as he was discussing vodkas and tap water with the barman, his mind was wandering and setting up the shot. There would be a pan around the whole tavern, slowly making a complete 360-degree and then homing in on him, zooming in until his eyes filled the screen. His eyes would convey the change taking place in this poor man, from happy anticipation to a stunned realisation. The camera would zoom in until his eyes filled the screen.

Having realised his main plan was shot, he'd tried to average out the alcoholic intake between the two of them by adding an absurdly large amount of an absurdly strong vodka to his own water. It did indeed average out the alcoholic intake but in the same way as the man who has his head in the oven and his feet in the fridge is of average temperature. In reality, DCI Webster was stone-cold sober and Brian could hardly function. While still in the early stages of his malfunction Brian was aware enough to notice that DCI Webster had gone missing. It only took him slightly longer than it usually would to realise she had just gone to the ladies. He took this moment to remove the Optrex bottle from his cardigan pocket and squeeze several drops of the Rohypnol into Lucy's water. Despite his training, he wasn't particularly careful or scientific about this but just squeezed out a generous helping of drops.

Despite the onset of drunkenness, he felt very good doing this. It was another item on his to-do list that he could tick off. Another of life's little ambitions realised. 'Who, at some time,' he reasoned, 'hasn't wished to spike a young lady's drink with a drug causing memory loss?' All he was doing was making this particular wish come true. That had to be a good thing, didn't it? Who could criticise a man for making his wishes come true? Brian liked to live his life on that knife edge. He felt he should put his money where his mouth was. Though given that he made his living as a chemist and would almost certainly lose his job and therefore his income if the incident was found out, it was more a case of putting his mouth where his money was. He felt a need to test the amnesic qualities of the Rohypnol. He was going to put his faith in its ability to wipe out a person's memory and confess everything to DCI Webster. The murders, the arson, the lies, the whole lot, everything.

Having completed that part of the experiment he found himself faced with a new problem.

42

The two barely-legal shots of vodka had left Brian drunk and befuddled – the more than generous dose of Rohypnol had left Lucy unconscious.

They had arrived at the tavern at about 8.00. It was now 9.14. The place had filled up considerably, many of the clientele were eating. Waiters and bar staff were bringing out deserts and taking away plates. The place was alive with the clinking of cutlery and the chinking of crockery and glasses mingled with chat and laughter. Busy with happy life. Brian and Lucy were causing occasional little bursts of interest within the room. Every so often a small group would spot them and snigger or shake their heads at this mismatched couple who by mid-evening appeared to have drunk themselves into oblivion. Even in his advanced state of inebriation, Brian was still only too aware that a big problem lay ahead for them or more accurately for him. They couldn't stay here much longer in this state. They'd be asked to leave, or worse thrown out, or worse still, and ironically, the police could be called. Brian was not in a fit state to drive and he had yet to see whether he was able to walk. Lucy was not able to do anything. His first idea was to call a taxi but that would still entail getting Lucy out of the bar and into the taxi and then out again at the other end. And where indeed was the other end – where were they heading? He didn't have a car but Lucy presumably had driven here. That was the first thing to check. He stood up and tried walking the two feet to the other side of the table. He had mistakenly thought he'd be able to do this without drawing attention to himself. Holding onto the table with both hands as he walked around was probably the biggest giveaway. Oblivious to the looks and tuts and shaking heads he dipped into Lucy's duffle coat pocket. He brought out a large bunch of keys with a leather Fiat key fob. She was here with her car. Her car was probably more here than she was at the moment but a car was good. His new plan – Plan B – was to get the two of them into Lucy's car. That would give him a bit of thinking time or even time to have a nap. Brian very much liked situations where he had a Plan B. Having a Plan B made him feel very organised and on top of things. His mind went back to the large bunch of keys. Presumably, there would be her house keys on there. Possibly there could be keys to the police station or even the prison. That would be good. He would quite like to make a copy of the prison key. Somewhere at home, Brian had a tobacco tin already filled with plasticine waiting for just such an occasion. But then if she was still asleep in the morning he might be able to nip out and get every key copied properly. There was a heel bar and shoe repair shop quite nearby. Heel bars and shoe repair shops annoyed Brian – always had done. What was it about cobblers that made them think they could cut keys? If I want keys cut I want to go to a proper key-cutter. Just who the hell do they think they are, these cobblers? They come round here and set up cobbling shops, then start cutting keys all over the place. He halted this train of thought for a moment, which was, retrospectively, getting him worked up into a lather, to go back to the 'if she was still asleep in the morning' bit. He realised this was the biggest decision to make in his Plan B. It was bigger even than 'how would he get an unconscious DCI Lucy Webster from the table to her car?' Having made it to the car, having had a nap and having sobered up sufficiently to attempt driving, where would he be attempting to drive to? The options appeared to be three. One – back to the police station where he could drop Lucy and her car off and then walk home. He didn't like the sound of that very much, particularly the walking home bit. Two – if he could find her address in a wallet or purse he could take Lucy home to her house, he could get her indoors, maybe he could even stay the night. This sounded far more agreeable to Brian. Three – he could drive them home to his house and they could both stay there. This was certainly the easiest option, though he did like the idea of being able to have a bit of a nose around Webster's house. Whatever his final choice, the first part was to get the two of them out of this place and into Lucy's car. He needed to be thinking more clearly, he needed to sober up. Holding onto tables, he made his way to the bar. Never one to under-do things, he ordered a triple espresso and then as an afterthought a double espresso for Lucy.

'I'll bring them over to your table, sir,' said the barman, keen to avoid the mopping up job he could see on the horizon. Brian was grateful for the help. Lucy wasn't going to be drinking anything for quite a while so over the next fifteen minutes Brian drank all five espressos. During the espressos, he worked out a sequence of events. Firstly, and increasing in importance by the second, was a trip to the gents. Relieved, he went straight out of the back door and into the street to look for Lucy Webster's Fiat. It was dark and he was struggling to see any detail on the cars parked nearby. He hoped she'd parked nearby. He fanned the remote car key up and down the street, pressing the unlock button as he did so. After a second or two, the sixth car up chirped and the lights flashed. He was quickly inside the car and checking the action and position of the gear stick. As soon as he felt familiarised, he manoeuvred the car around as near as he could to the rear entrance of the pub, leaving the engine running. Feeling a bit more together now he walked back into the bar, picked up Lucy's duffle coat and brought it back out to the car, putting it on the back seat. From the passenger side using the seat adjuster he slid the passenger seat backwards as far as it would go then adjusted the rake so it almost flattened out to a bed. Now came the final and trickiest stage of the sequence. He had to physically get Lucy into the car. Leaving the passenger door wide open, he took several deep breaths, in a psyching-himself-up sort of way, and walked quickly back into the bar. This last bit had to be done slickly and quickly.

Brian pulled Lucy's chair out, slipped his arms under her and picked her up. She was lighter than he'd expected. He turned and headed directly to the back door, looking straight ahead, not catching anyone's eye, walking as quickly as he could. At the door, he had to turn slightly to accommodate Lucy in his arms. Without breaking step he swung her round and smacked her head into the door jamb, causing those who'd been watching to suck and wince. If Lucy hadn't already been unconscious she would have been rendered so now. The ultimate double-whammy. A kind of belt and braces approach to unconsciousness. Brian wondered if this worked concurrently or consecutively. When she came out of the Rohypnol unconsciousness, would she slip immediately into the knocked out unconsciousness? Or, would she experience a kind of double-strength unconsciousness now?

He was at the car and lowering her into the front passenger seat. Two or three people had come to the back door holding drinks to continue watching the entertainment. One of them was filming the procedure on his phone.

Once they were both in the car, Brian drove it back up the road and out of sight into the entrance of Victoria Park and switched off the engine and the lights. He sat there enjoying the sudden silence and darkness and stillness. Lucy lay beside him looking calm as if she were asleep. Brian leant over to look closely at her – she was beautiful. The intoxicating effect of the vodkas was wearing off. He no longer felt drunk but he also didn't feel sober. What was it he felt? What was the feeling the sensation? Sick. That was it! Sick! He felt sick! He threw up over Lucy, but she didn't seem to mind. The sick had very much the appearance and smell you might imagine from mixing two pints of water, two shots of vodka and five espressos. *Better out than in,* thought Brian, *marginally.* He was glad he hadn't yet covered her up with the duffle coat, which had been his plan. A duffle coat would take a lot more cleaning than the clothes she had on.

'Time to get you cleaned up and home to bed, my girl,' said Brian.

43

Having been sick Brian felt much better and was confident that he would be able to make the three-mile drive back to his house. It was 10.00 and there was still some traffic around. However, most people were already at the place they were spending the evening, so most cars on the road were just the early birds on their way home. Brian made one of his rare good decisions. He took a back route home, which was three-quarters of a mile longer, but much quieter. He saw just two other cars and a bicycle the whole way. Sitting in Lucy's car outside his house he realised he now had to go through the whole pub exit procedure in reverse to get Lucy indoors.

He was starting to get quite proficient at these sequentially driven recovery jobs. Lucy remained peacefully asleep and reclined on the tilted passenger seat, so he left her there. He went indoors straight to the kitchen, filled up every saucepan he had and got them on the four rings of the hob. He filled his two kettles with water and switched them both on, then unlocked the back door and went out into the yard. In the far corner was a large galvanised tin bath. It was partially hidden by some potted plants, a flower pot and a stack of earthenware saggers, and was full of dirty wet leaves. He moved the pots and saggers and was able to lift the tin bath clear, to empty out the leaves as best he could. He slid the bath directly under the brass garden tap which he turned on to full. While he left the tin bath to fill up, he went back indoors and upstairs to the spare bedroom. The spare room didn't get much use and had a vaguely musty, unused smell, but it also had a made-up ready-to-use double bed – Lucy's bed. He pulled the sheets back ready for her. What was next? What was next? Check on the pans, check on the tin bath, check on Lucy. The pans of water were starting to get warmer, the tin bath was overflowing and cleaning out nicely, Lucy was exactly as he'd left her.

He returned to the backyard, switched the tap off and emptied the tin bath. One by one, he brought the saucepans of now-hot water out into the yard and emptied them into the bath. He carried the heavy hot-water-filled bath back into the kitchen and onto the hob over all four rings on maximum. Lucy. Time to get Lucy in.

Leaving his front door wide open, Brian went out to the car and opened the passenger door. He had a clearer idea now of what to expect when lifting Lucy. She was light and manageable but he now had a longer trip and there was the flight of stairs to negotiate. Again he went into his deep breathing psyching-up routine that was becoming a default response to any tricky situation.

He reached in and picked Lucy up. He had a strange thought that she was too light to be a police person. He stood up, cradling her, and hipped the passenger door shut. 'Do it in one,' he advised himself. He strode into his house and up the stairs at the same pace, exhaling with loud blowing breaths on every step. When he was in the spare room he lowered Lucy carefully and lovingly onto the spare bed.

He looked at her and started another of his many mental tussles. She looked beautiful – almost perfect apart from the coffee-coloured sick over her clothes. He had to clean the clothes, which of course meant removing them. This is what was bothering Brian. It wasn't the done thing to remove a lady's clothes. He wondered if the clothes removal was an absolute, independent of circumstance. Was it more or less of a done thing to remove the clothes from a lady policeman whom he had rendered unconscious with a date-rape drug and then a backup whack around the head with a door jamb before being sick over? He decided on reflection that clothing removal was clothing removal regardless of the situation or status of the removee. The next item on the agenda was the relative severity of the three questionable actions taken on Lucy. Which was worse, slipping her a roofie, vomiting over her, or removing her clothes?

Using his own brand of logic, Brian thought the order of severity – most to least – was vomit, roofie, clothing removal. He reasoned that being sick over someone was about as bad as it got. There wasn't a pleasant way to do that. In the attractive-qualities-in-a-person stakes, it was pretty low down. Giving someone knockout drops wasn't too bad, as they wouldn't know an awful lot about it, so no real harm done there. Finally, the clothes removal. Surely that was a good thing – that was a nice thing to do, remove somebody's clothes – surely to goodness? There was also a sub-section to the vomit category. Was it worse to throw up over light-coloured clothing or dark-coloured clothing? Brian struggled with this one as he found it very hard to get away from the artistic considerations. Having someone throw up on your clothes is going to leave a bad taste in your mouth irrespective of whether they are light clothes or dark clothes. So that's equal points for both light clothing and dark clothing. The problem with dark clothing is that it's likely to absorb just about anything thrown up, on or at it. Unless it was a whipped cream or custard-based vomit, you're not going to get much showing up on a dark-brown pullover. However, a light grey T-shirt for example should give an excellent representation of most offerings. Lighter clothing is a clear winner on artistic merit.

44

It was time to get Lucy's clothes cleaned. Even though he realised it wasn't a bad thing to remove someone's clothes, he felt a bit bad about removing DCI Lucy Webster's. He decided that to do it blindfolded may be a good compromise. He didn't have a blindfold but he went to the cupboard under the stairs and sorted out an old balaclava that he wore in the winter. While he was downstairs he checked on the tin bath of water and found it was getting hot, but still not boiling. When he was back in the spare room, he put the balaclava on backwards. Perfect! He couldn't see a thing. Strangely he had looked in the mirror to put the balaclava on backwards. When it was on, he made his way back to the bed with arms outstretched. After three paces his legs made contact with the bed. With his arms and hands still outstretched he reached down carefully, not wanting to make sudden contact with a sicky area of her clothes. Working his way in from the edge of the bed his first contact with Lucy was her left hand. It felt warm and small as he held it in his own hand, and using it as a reference point, he quickly located the edges of her pullover, the hem, the cuffs, the neckline. Using just these extremities he started easing the pullover up and over her head. At one point he had to lift her head off the pillow, but it all went surprisingly smoothly up to this point. Because of the way she was lying the most difficult part was easing the sleeves down her arms. When it was finally off he turned it inside out and threw it behind him on the floor. He turned and felt for the waistband of her trousers. Having undone the two buttons on her waistband, he pulled the zip down, his knuckles brushing against the top of her pants. In the darkness, his imagination kicked in, this time running through all the possible variations of pants that Lucy may be wearing. He mentally tried out simple white cotton ones. They were good. Then he went through black and a selection of other colours. Continuing through lacy frilly and silky he reassessed the whole mental collection and voted plain black cotton the best, closely followed by plain white cotton. He took a moment to visualise Lucy in each of these just to make sure he had made the right selection. The doubt crept into his mind that these sort of pants would hardly be man enough for the job of a policeman, albeit a lady policeman. They probably had police issue pants made of reinforced fabric. Given that most DCIs were men, except for Helen Mirren and Lucy Webster, they were probably all issued with a good strong pair of fire-proof, bullet-proof Y-fronts with a pocket in the back for a notebook or something. He pictured both Helen and Lucy in a pair of such Y-fronts. The mental image of this was enough to shake him out of his reverie and back to reality. Still working in total darkness, thanks to the balaclava, he started to ease the trousers down over Lucy's hips. This quickly proved surprisingly difficult so he changed his approach. Making his way to the end of the bed he felt around until he'd located Lucy's feet. He pulled her shoes off, throwing them on the floor and then took a firm grip on the bottom of each of her trouser legs. He tried a test tug to see if it would be a good approach. There was quite a bit of resistance, but he felt sure that with a good solid continuous pull it would do the job. He envisaged a stage magician whipping out a tablecloth from under a fully laid table without disturbing any of the place settings, drinks or bottles. Standing where he was, right at the end of the bed wouldn't quite work for this trick. He could only manage a pull of twelve to fifteen inches from this position. To pull the trousers off cleanly, he would need to move away from the bed as he pulled. He moved away from the bed, skating his feet around, checking for any stray objects or clothing that may trip him up. It was all clear. He moved back to the bed and re-established the firm grip on Lucy's trousers. Once again the psyching-up deep breaths and slow blowing out exhalations. With the balaclava over his head back to front these exhalations created a cushion of hot air over his whole head and face. He counted down out loud – three, two, one. Holding on tight and pulling hard he moved backwards quickly. It seemed to take a long time but the trousers finally came off Lucy just as Lucy finally came off the bed. With only the trousers in his hands, Brian became aware of Lucy's predicament when he heard the sound of her head hitting the carpeted floor. Even in the darkness, the notion came to Brian that this was probably the third time he'd knocked Lucy out this evening. Was it possible to be knocked out if you were already knocked out? he wondered, and before long he was back on his 'consecutive' or 'concurrent' dilemma once again. He decided to deal with the clothing first. Lucy wasn't going anywhere – she was unconscious – possibly three times unconscious. He sang to himself as Lionel Richie:

'You're once, twice, three times unconscious – and I lo-a-uh-ve you'.

Still holding the trousers he felt around on the floor for

Lucy's top and taking the two items out of the room he pulled the balaclava off and went downstairs. The tin bath of water was bubbling and steaming now. He went out into the yard and threw the two items of clothing under the garden tap. With the tap running full he squeezed and rubbed the clothes, cleaning them as best he could. He came back into the kitchen, dropped both items into the bath of boiling water and added a generous amount of washing powder. Sorted! That was the clothing underway. Now he needed to sort Lucy. Brian ran upstairs, then stood on the landing outside the spare room. The balaclava was there on the floor. This was going to be a tough job, if not impossible, to get Lucy comfortable and settled for the night if he was wearing a balaclava back to front. He knew it was wrong to see Lucy in her underwear. Dilemmas – always dilemmas. Which would he rather? He wrestled with his conscience. It was a tough fight, but eventually he won. He walked in and saw Lucy looking angelic lying on the floor in her grey bra and grey pants. Grey, of course. Grey. He hadn't been sure if black pants or white pants were better, but grey was of course the perfect compromise – the perfect solution. Lucy knew this, of course, and that's why she wore them for him. He remade the bed, which was in quite a state after the trouser-removing trick. Once it was properly remade, he folded the sheets back again, ready to receive Lucy. He went round to the detective chief inspector lying on the floor in her grey underwear and lifted her up much as he'd done earlier, to and from the car. The only difference was this felt so much nicer, so much softer and warmer. Once she was on the bed, he rearranged her arms and legs until she looked comfortable. There was a nasty swelling with a cut on the side of her head. It didn't detract from her beauty, but it was still a nasty swelling. He gazed at her lying there and struggled to believe it was really happening – that he was really here – that she was really here. He'd had many dreams similar to this and he knew he would have many more that started exactly like this. He would remember this scene and relive it over and over again for the rest of his life. He hoped his powers of recall would be up to the task. He fleetingly thought of taking a photograph of her but then put his hands over his ears and shook his head to shake away the wicked thought. But it came straight back. Again he shook his head, this time chanting 'Wa wa wa wa wa' to divert his mind and extinguish the thought. It still came straight back. OK! He needed a different approach. He needed to confront this thought, analyse it, look at it logically. What were the pros and cons? It was quite a thing to experience Brian's logic at work. Many people had been on the receiving end of, or maybe more accurately, fallen victim to, Brian's logic. Few had understood it. He deemed it perfectly acceptable to drug Lucy with Rohypnol. This was because it fell into several acceptable categories. Research, hobbies and life hacks.

'Having trouble with that new girlfriend? Not sure how the evening will turn out? Simply slip her a roofie and your evening is sure to go with a bang.' However, taking a photograph of the unconscious Lucy he saw as inherently wrong. He was not the sort of person to take advantage of an incapacitated woman. It simply wasn't cricket. As soon as he had the 'not-being-cricket' thought, his mind was off again looking for cricket links to help the analogy along. Working through 'bowling a maiden over', 'fine legs', 'dolly', 'bodyline', 'appeal', 'bouncers' and 'leg glance', he ended with 'full toss'.

But now he asked himself what his reasons were for wanting to take the photograph. It was purely to help him maintain as accurate a mental image as possible. An aide-memoire. Another life hack to make life easier. After all, this situation may well be a one-off. For all he knew, Lucy may kick up a stink about the whole event. Women were funny like that. She may complain to her superiors about being drugged. She may even instigate some trumped-up charge against him. And what if? … Oh no! … He didn't even want to think about this! What if the amnesiac qualities of the Rohypnol hadn't worked? What if she remembered every single thing he told her? It would be no use pleading or trying to lie his way out of that one. That would be it. He'd be sunk. That would be the end of him. What options would he have? He could kidnap her again, he could threaten her, he could blackmail her, but he had nothing to blackmail her w … And there it was!

45

An idea that a short while ago seemed unthinkable now seemed essential. He needed photographic evidence that he could use to save his skin, if push came to shove. It was purely self-preservation. It was probably the most basic and deep-rooted of all man's instincts. The self-preservation angle gave complete justification in Brian's eyes to photographing the unconscious Lucy. His phone was in the pocket of his Ted Bundy cardigan. He went downstairs to fetch the phone but first checked on the tin bath of boiling clothes. The clothes were on a full rolling boil rather than a simmer. They would be as clean as they were ever going to be now. Having no traditional wooden laundry tongs, he took a pair of small chrome pickled onion tongs from the kitchen drawer. Picking up the two scalding items with some difficulty, he dripped them across the kitchen to the far corner where the washing machine was and threw them in. He set the machine on rinse and spin and went to get his phone. He was starting to get used to seeing the semi-naked Lucy lying there. His fears and concerns about photographing her in this state had vanished so he set about the task. He started with a video shot. A nearly complete circuit of the bed with the phone camera held high above his head and pointing down. Keeping the camera recording, he followed this up with the same circuit but with the camera held at chest height. The final circuit was a low angle tracking shot. He filmed this last one by making his way around the bed on his knees. He was already planning the edit. He would take the film back to black and white and cut repeatedly between the three angles. He would add a lot of contrast and 'noise' to the image. This would be his long-awaited response and follow up and homage to Warhol's 1965 Chelsea Girls.

He felt that Lucy was fairly well documented on video and just a few more stills should be sufficient. He took 312 shots of her from every possible angle: 215 full-body pictures and the rest a good selection of close-ups. Now the photos were in the can, so to speak – Brian liked to use proper movie terminology – he needed to set down some regulations regarding his viewing of them. He firstly decided that he would only view them in case of an emergency blackmail situation, which would require a choice of the best images to use. He considered this for a while then realised that the whole collection could be at risk if they were just shut away until needed. It would be perfectly valid to check them every so often, he reasoned. He would be allowed to check them once a year – no, make that twice a year – just to reassure himself that they were safe and hadn't been tampered with. Six months was a long time to leave it. A lot could happen in six months. He revised it to once a month and then ten minutes later to once a week. Trying to be as fair as he could, he ruled that any viewings should last no longer than five minutes. After a bit more fine-tuning and safety precautions he had his final regulations set out clearly. He would be allowed no more than two viewings daily, with a maximum viewing time of fifteen minutes. To aid with security he would have a backup set of the pictures and video with him at all times.

Having sorted out the question of the photographic dossier on Lucy, he finally, but somewhat reluctantly, covered her up with the sheets and blankets. He thought how comfortable and relaxed she looked and what a lucky girl she was. He kissed her goodnight and told her to sleep tight and advised her not to let the bedbugs bite. Given that the bed hadn't been used for over a year he guessed that this was probably fairly sound advice, though he wasn't sure how an unconscious person could go about preventing bed bugs from biting. For the third time, he heard the washing machine give the three long beeps, signalling that the rinse and spin cycle had finished. He went down the stairs two or three at a time and took the two spun items out of the washing machine and pushed them into the tumble dryer. With a practised familiar action, he flipped the dials to maximum heat for about two hours. It was an old machine that he'd had now for eighteen years. It was very noisy and made a constant hypnotic trundling sound. During the two hour cycle, it would probably chug away on the kitchen floor and move about an inch and a half.

Things were getting sorted. Lucy was tucked up in bed and her clothes were clean and drying. The hunger hit him suddenly as soon as he let down his guard and relaxed. Brian hadn't eaten since breakfast time. His whole day had been one long expenditure of nervous energy. When it came to eating he liked to think of the visual element of his food. Whenever possible he would have a colour theme to his meals. When he had chosen a theme he would stick quite rigidly to this. This resulted in some very unusual meals and also some interesting culinary discoveries. He recently had a red lunch of strawberries, tomatoes, peppers, radishes and chillies – his spicy fruit salad. The yellow breakfast he had two days ago was very successful. Smoked haddock and sweetcorn with butter, cheddar cheese and English mustard, all garnished with a couple of slices of lemon. As far as Brian was concerned, it was the perfect breakfast. Nutritional, tasty, and above all artistically pleasing. This, however, wasn't the time for artistic priority, Brian needed to get some food on board. Experience had taught him the best colour scheme for a bulk-priority meal was white or cream. It was 11.15 in the evening when Brian started preparing his second meal of the day to the background thrum of the tumble dryer. At 11.45 he sat down to a lovely looking cream-coloured meal. Four thick slices of lightly browned and buttered toast each topped with a generous heaped mound of mashed potato, basmati rice with a horseradish dressing and a side order of pasta with a bread and onion sauce dip. The whole lot was topped off with shavings of Roquefort cheese. The occasional blue vein of the Penicillium mould was the only colour in the meal but it offset the bland off-white colour beautifully. Brian enjoyed it immensely and finished every last mouthful. At 12:20 a.m. he was sick again.

46

Wednesday 29 September 2021

After he'd mopped up the kitchen floor Brian had a shower and changed his cheek dressing, arm dressing and clothes. He checked on Lucy. She was still soundo and didn't appear to have moved. As he was checking on her, the background rumble of the old tumble dryer downstairs suddenly squawked and stopped like a stylus removed clumsily from a record. He went downstairs and opened up the dryer and was enveloped in a cloud of very hot air. He could hardly touch the two items inside, but he managed to get them out and tossing them from hand to hand quickly cooled them down. When they were a cosy, comfortable warmth he buried his face in them. They smelled fresh and clean and they were Lucy's. This would be a nice surprise for her. He would leave them washed, clean and folded ready for her on the chair beside her bed. He took them upstairs and into her bedroom. He threw them both down on the chair but picked up the trousers again, shaking them out to fold them. He held them out in front of him. They were shorter than he'd remembered. He knew Lucy was small but he hadn't realised just how short she was. They were barely three feet long from top to bottom. He threw them back on the chair and picked up, and shook out, the pullover. It looked like something you might buy at a school shop. He wasn't entirely sure but Brian was starting to get a fairly strong feeling that the clothes had shrunk. If they had shrunk then it was Brian who'd shrunk them. This revelation led to a classic instance of Brian's particular brand of logic. When Lucy woke up she would quickly see that her clothes were smaller than they had been. This could mean one of just two possibilities. Either the clothes had shrunk or Lucy had grown. If the clothes had shrunk it was only reasonable to assume it was Brian's fault. If Lucy had grown that was her own fault. Therefore, to shift the blame and suspicion away from himself, he had to convince Lucy that she had grown. He sat down in his front room in the dark and quiet, just thinking about the problem. After about fifteen minutes Brian had worked out the solution. He stood up and set about putting it into action. He would need Lucy's full address for this, so went to her grey duffle coat and searched the pockets. Apart from her car keys the only other items were a wallet and a Samsung Galaxy mobile phone which appeared to be out of juice. He would have a closer look at the phone later on. For the time being, he needed the address. There were several bank cards, security cards and police-related documents in the wallet. One of these appeared to be a letter from her boss, which was headed with her full name and address. He flattened this out on the chair and with his phone took a photograph of it. He needed to get to the pharmacy now. He put on his coat and checked he had the pharmacy keys. He had a quick look at Lucy, who appeared not to have moved. Maybe a more rigorous test was needed to see if she was ok. He poked his finger into her cheek then her forehead. No reaction. He tapped his fingers on her forehead. Still no reaction. Finally, he wrapped the top of her head quite sharply with his knuckles shouting 'Lucy – Lucy – Lucy' in her ear. No reaction. He remembered that to check if someone was still alive, you held a mirror to their mouth to see if it misted with their breath. Brian could think of no small mirror in the house. The bigger mirrors were all part of wardrobe doors. Then he remembered that the hallway mirror was just hooked onto the wall. He went downstairs and unhooked the five-foot by two-foot mirror and struggled with it upstairs. He struggled with it much more, holding it over Lucy's mouth. He hoped to hell that she didn't choose this moment to wake up. Having taken a brief moment out to picture what it would be like to wake up from a drug-induced sleep and be staring into your own face two inches away, he checked the mirror for misting. Thankfully the mirror showed a small circle of fogging in front of Lucy's mouth – she was still alive. He took the large hall mirror back downstairs and replaced it on the wall. With a final check that he had the keys, he left the house and made his way to the pharmacy.

47

Once he was inside the pharmacy Brian switched on the computer and printer. While it was booting up he went into the back storage room to search for a specific drug – Macimorelin acetate.

He opened up the most commonly used program on the pharmacy's only computer. Its primary use was for filling in and printing out prescription labels. He typed in Lucy's full name and address. Under that, in the medication details, he typed 'Macimorelin acetate – one tablet to be taken twice a day with meals – 56 tablets'.

The tablets contained a man-made growth hormone that is prescribed for adults with growth hormone deficiency. Brian knew that it couldn't possibly be responsible for the massive overnight difference in dimensions between Lucy and her clothing. He also knew that Lucy would know that too. However, it could throw in that all-important red herring, that water-muddying element that would shift the attention away from him.

At the bottom of the label template, he added the words 'GROWTH HORMONE – WITH CARE' in capital letters just in case Lucy didn't quite pick up on the idea. He also took care to delete the name of the pharmacy and to change the font from 'Arial' to 'Lucida sans'. When he hit 'print' the printer whirred out a sheet with two labels. One for the bottle, one for the box. He stuck the labels on a generic bottle and its accompanying box. In the bottle, he had already placed just eight of the Macimorelin acetate tablets. He was hoping to plant the suggestion in Lucy's mind that she'd already taken forty-eight of these tablets – three-and-a-half weeks' worth. The final stage of the set-up was to age the box and bottle to look as if they'd had some use. He opened and closed the box and unscrewed and screwed up the bottle many times. He handled them roughly allowing the box to pick up a few bends and the labels to become slightly grubby. After a few minutes of playing with them, they looked convincingly as if they'd had a few weeks use. Brian switched everything off and locked everything up and was soon on his way home.

As he drove home he remembered a story he had heard about Flanagan and Allen, a British comedy musical act from the 30s and 40s. Bud Flanagan was a well-known practical joker. During one short season in Blackpool, he sought out the services of a local seamstress. One morning he took Chesney Allen's stage suit to the seamstress and asked her to take up the trousers and the jacket sleeves a quarter of an inch. He collected the suit an hour later and returned it to their dressing room. That evening in the dressing room, as they prepared to go on stage, Bud Flanagan remarked that Chesney seemed to be growing. Chesney laughed it off and thought no more about it. The next day Flanagan once again took the suit to the seamstress and asked her to take the trousers and sleeves up another quarter of an inch. That evening in the dressing room he repeated his observation that Chesney appeared to be growing. Chesney looked at his sleeves and agreed they looked a bit short. Flanagan repeated his trip to the seamstress every day that week and each evening acted more adamant that Chesney was growing. Finally, Chesney Allen showed some real concern and Bud got his payoff. The memory of this anecdote was almost certainly what gave Brian the idea of the growth hormone tablets.

Once indoors, he placed the tablets on the cabinet by the side of Lucy's bed with the box lying down beside them. He checked that Lucy's keys, wallet and phone were all back in the deep pockets of her duffle coat. It had been a very long day so Brian went to bed.

48

Brian fell into a deep sleep very quickly. The nervous and physical energy expended throughout the day had exhausted him. He soon found himself in the midst of a dream, a re-edit of the black and white film *Gaslight*. He knew the 1944 film well. All the actors were in it – Charles Boyer, Ingrid Bergman, Joseph Cotten – and playing their parts well, following the script, but Brian and Lucy were in it too. He had seamlessly created integral roles for the two of them, which over the course of the dream became the two leading roles and finally the only roles. Throughout the dream, Brian was 'gaslighting' Lucy.

The phrase 'to gaslight' someone was derived from the film, where the protagonist, Charles Boyer, deliberately tried to drive the victim, Ingrid Bergman, insane by psychologically manipulating her environment and tricking her into believing that she was insane. In his dream, Brian continued to trick Lucy and force her to fall in love with him. In the final reel, she stripped naked and pleaded with him to marry her, which he agreed to do for half a million pounds and a Mercedes-Benz 300SL Gullwing and a made-to-measure bright yellow chequered suit. It was no surprise when Brian was nominated for, and then went on to win, an Oscar for best actor – his twelfth to date.

At 9.20 in the morning, he opened his eyes and tried to sort out the reality in his life from the fantasy. The one bit he struggled with was the strong feeling that DCI Lucy Webster was asleep in her grey underwear upstairs. This just couldn't be true – could it? It seemed far more like one of his dreams than anything that could have possibly happened. He was picturing tablets and shrinking trousers and other absurdities, none of which helped to clarify things. He got out of bed and went straight upstairs to check. She wasn't there. Of course she wasn't there, it was another one of his vivid nocturnal flights of fantasy, though the spare bed did have a sort of slept-in look about it that he didn't recall. As he got on with his day – washing, shaving, breakfast, coffee – other unlikely happenings and memories interrupted his thoughts and seemed to take on an increasing and convincing reality. He now clearly remembered being at the pharmacy and typing something on the computer. At some point last evening he had driven someone else's car. And he had definitely boiled some clothes. He was fairly certain he won an Oscar, which was presented to him by Helen Mirren in grey underwear and a police hat. Things were gradually coming back to him, though some of them were still not filed in the correct real-life or fantasy categories. Things finally came back clearly all at once in a jolt when he opened his phone and saw first the photograph of the document from Lucy's wallet and then, as he scrolled through his pictures, about six feet of photographs of Lucy in her grey bra and pants. For the second time that morning, he rushed upstairs for a closer look at the situation. As well as Lucy being gone the tablets and her clothes were also gone. Now that he was awake and fully up to speed with yesterday's events, there were a lot of worrying questions.

The main one, and all subsequent questions, would hinge on this: had the Rohypnol worked? Did Lucy have any memory of the things he told her? If the drug had worked, how much did she not remember? Lesser questions, but still of concern to Brian, were: was she angry with him? Had she reported any of yesterday's events to her superiors? What did she make of the shrunken clothes? Did she wear the shrunken clothes home? Did she even go home? Where was she now? How long would he reasonably have to wait for the police to come and arrest him if the Rohypnol had not worked? If he got life imprisonment, how long would that actually mean? Would he get a cell to himself or would he have to share? If he did have to share, would they allow him a curtain around the toilet? Could he have his own pillows? Were there tea-making facilities in the cell? Are you allowed to have pets in prison? Would Lucy come and visit him? Are you allowed to have friends to stay in prison? Did he have any friends? Would the chatty postman who spoke to him every day count as a friend? How easy was it to escape from prison? Would it be easier to escape with other prisoners or just have a plan to escape on his own? For the rest of the day, Brian worked on his escape plan.

49

While Brian worked on his escape plan, which currently involved Lucy smuggling into prison a pair of bolt cutters, a large tin of treacle, some super glue and a sharp knife, Lucy had questions of her own.

Lucy woke up that morning groggy, with no idea where she was and no concept of how she'd ended up there. There was a strong scent of washing powder, not her own. She leant out of the bed and picked up her clothes lying on the chair. They had been washed, and dried – someone had laundered her clothes. What had happened last night? What had she done that necessitated her clothes being cleaned? Lucy still had no idea where she was or if anyone else was in the house, but instinctively felt that she should keep quiet. She needed to use the bathroom, so wrapping a blanket around her shoulders she went out of the room to explore. She immediately saw she was upstairs and there were three other doors, all shut, on the landing. She gripped the white ceramic doorknob of the first one and pressed her ear to the door. She heard nothing, so slowly turned the knob clockwise. It was a smooth action and turned quietly but finally opened with a click. With the door open a bare two inches she could see it was dark and she could also hear snoring. She turned the handle back the other way and held it there as she pulled the door closed and carefully released the knob. The floor wasn't creaky at all, and the carpet was thick. She was able to move silently along to the next door. She went through the same process of opening this door but immediately saw it was light and it was the bathroom. She went in shut the door and locked it with the slim brass sliding bolt. She was quite desperate now so went straight to the toilet and sat down. She physically jumped and gasped as she saw the woman facing her. A woman with a blanket around her shoulders and grey pants around her ankles sitting on another toilet facing her. The mirror was one of the biggest she'd ever seen and appeared to take up most of the opposite wall. It made the bathroom look twice its actual size. When she finished, she opened first the airing cupboard then the two doors in the vanity unit to try and pick up some clues as to the occupant. Neither was very forthcoming. The airing cupboard was crammed to capacity with nothing but sheets, blankets, bedspreads, pillowcases and other bed linen. The two small cupboards under the sink were home to spare toilet rolls and cleaning agents. Lucy made her way back to the bedroom to get dressed, wondering what sort of person would have such a mirror in such a position.

Back in the bedroom she shook out her grey trousers to put them on and saw immediately that they were small. Her first reaction was naturally that they weren't hers. That would explain the different smell she had noticed earlier. But they were exactly the style make and colour of the ones she owned. Why would somebody go to the trouble of exchanging them for an identical smaller pair? She noticed the frayed edge of the label she had cut out of her own pair because it had rubbed and irritated her when she was wearing them. These were her trousers. They'd shrunk. That at least tied in with them being washed, which was very marginally less freaky than thinking of them being exchanged for a smaller pair. With no other options she put them on, or more accurately she forced them on. They were comical and like something a leading lady playing Peter Pan might wear in a pantomime. As she picked up and shook out the grey top the thought went through her mind, just as the truth of that thought was confirmed, that the top had shrunk too. It had changed from the elegant grey swagger top to a bust flattening skin-tight crop top. Again, without a choice, she put it on. She saw her favourite grey duffle coat and her heart sank. Not that as well? But it was untouched and fit Lucy as well as it ever had done. Her keys, phone, wallet, everything seemed to be there. She tried switching her phone on but it was dead. Damn! She was about to make her exit when she noticed the tablets and box on the bedside table. She wondered what they were and if someone had made her take them. It was a shock, quite a big shock to see her name and address printed on the bottle and packet. These were her tablets, tablets that had been prescribed specifically for her. She read 'GROWTH HORMONE – WITH CARE'. For an instant, her mind played with growth tablets and shrunken clothes and she saw the absurd possibility that they could appear to be connected. For some reason, Brian Rayment entered her thoughts. She put the tablets in the box then in her pocket and quietly made her way out of the room and downstairs. As she walked down the stairs she saw and recognised the hallway from her previous visits to Brian Rayment. A lot of things jumped into place and now made sense – a Brian Rayment kind of sense.

50

Back at home, the first thing Lucy needed to do was to call in sick. She was still feeling groggy as well as thirsty and starving. However, the main reason to call in was to buy herself some time to put her thoughts and last night's events in order. She plugged her phone in to charge it, but then used the landline to phone the station and tell them she was unwell. She got through directly to DS Dew and told him she had been awake all night with severe food poisoning. She asked him to pass on the information to the superintendent, and told him she'd be back in as soon as she was able, but for the moment was in desperate need of sleep. She hoped the story would keep any questioning phone calls at bay for a while. After breakfast and coffee, she started to feel more normal and clearly remembered getting ready and setting off to meet Rayment. He had been waiting for her at the Marlborough Tavern and there was a strange episode with him ordering their drinks. He had either already been drinking or was adding shorts to his pint glass of water – quite probably both given the drunken state he was in. She remembered telling Brian that she only wanted tap water and the lunatic brought back a full pint glass of it. She wondered whether he had any social awareness or skills at all. After this things were getting difficult to recall, but she did remember going to the loo. That's right – it came back to her now. She left Brian on the pretext of needing the loo, but had used the time in there to set her phone on record, turn up the volume to maximum and put it in her pocket. She distinctly pictured herself going back to her seat and then that was it. That was it completely until she woke up.

She checked on her phone. It still only had an eleven per cent charge but that would be enough to start. She kept it plugged in and continuing to charge as she opened up her images file. The last one showed a black thumbnail with the white arrowhead indicating a movie clip. The small white figures told her it was 9 mins and 59 seconds long – the default setting. She tapped it and a muffled and tipsy sounding Brian Rayment was saying, '... all the murders, only the ones in the garage. It's just that there are a few things I'd like to get off my chest. It started several months ago. My neighbours, Tony...' Then there was scraping and rustling and the recording was inaudible for about twenty seconds and then cut back in, '... annoyed me. He was truculent, unfriendly, so in the end, I decided to kill him. So I ... it using ... lons like the Jackal ... dward Fox and a waffle iro ...'

'Edw ... ox and a waffle iron?' That was her. Lucy recognised her own voice, but she sounded tired – that was strange.

'Yes, a waffle iron – bec ... dent in Tony's head. Then aft ... I'd whacked him in the garage, Marlina came in to tell Tony it's ... so I ba ... till she was dead. Then another blo ... in ... killed these ... and I made very good time it was all done in about six min ...' There followed a long period of muffled interference with nothing useful or discernible. Then finally the last few words before the clip ended, '... surrealism ... I shot them all up'

Even though the quality was very poor the surviving words were dynamite.

Lucy listened to the recording several times, trying to decide if it amounted to a confession or not. It was quite fragmented. The problem was what could she do with it? Who could she show it to? She had been under strict orders that if she was going to meet Rayment she should under no circumstances make any recording. What she'd done was illegal, and far from convicting Bryan Rayment it could get her thrown out of the service or worse.

So, she summarised for herself, she had a recording of the suspect saying, amongst other things, 'I decided to kill him' and 'I shot them all up,' which would be inadmissible in court and to whom she could show no one.

How come she had slept through all this? Why couldn't she remember it? She was as certain as she could be that she had had no alcohol. If Brian Rayment had spiked her drink with alcohol she would have known about it. The thing that was bothering her most, which she had pushed to the back of her mind, which she'd refused to think about as yet, was how she ended up in Brian Rayment's bed and what had happened while she was there. There was also the matter of the shrinking clothes and the growth tablets to add to the equation. She was weighing up the trouble she would be making for herself against the help this would give to the investigation. If she was going to tell anyone about any of it she had to do it soon. If it came out later she'd be in far greater trouble. Withholding information, illegally obtained information at that. Instinctively she felt her best policy at the moment would be to keep quiet. She still had the information herself, which maybe could be put to good use.

The thing she must do above all else was see Brian Rayment again and quickly.

51

Before she could make final decisions on anything else, she needed to confront him and fill in the missing gaps from last night. She couldn't turn up at his house in police uniform, in an official capacity, and would have to make it an informal visit. She was only too aware of the big mistakes she had already made and that she was now in danger of compounding them. Everyone at the station knew she was supposed to be asleep at home recovering from food poisoning. If anyone decided to check up on her, or call round to see her, or worse still, spot her on her way to see Rayment, she might as well hand her badge in now. She sat there staring out of the window. Her eyes suddenly stung as they unexpectedly brimmed with tears. The first tears rolled down her cheek – she was crying. The truth of it was she hated her job. She'd like nothing more than to hand her badge in now. The atmosphere at the station was difficult, to say the least. She would never be one of the boys. She was in charge of a working team of twelve, all men. Most of them struggled with the idea of a female boss. She'd made the unforgivable mistake of being a successful woman in a man's world. The feeling of resentment, whether real or imagined, was nevertheless always there. On one occasion, after a successful investigation, which resulted in the arrest of three notorious and vicious gang members, Lucy had even tried to buy the team's friendship. She invited them out that evening to the local pub, all drinks on her, by way of celebratory thanks for their hard work and a good result. All but Kevin Drew had just one drink then left. The evening was over in less than ninety minutes. When she started as a rookie nine years ago, the job was unbelievably exciting. As a PC she had done exceptionally well and was quickly promoted to sergeant, then in two more years to inspector. Within the Bath and West Police Service, hers was a meteoric rise through the ranks. Eighteen months later she was chief inspector, the youngest chief inspector the force had ever known and the first-ever female chief inspector. The work was much harder and less enjoyable but the pay was good and she continued to do well. By the time she was thirty, she was promoted again to detective chief inspector to become the youngest DCI in the force and a classic example of the Peter principle, a concept whereby employees are promoted based on their success until they reach the level at which they are no longer competent or suitable. Lucy knew she wasn't suitable and she frequently doubted her competence. Paradoxically the work was stressful, difficult and yet boring. The graph of her job satisfaction had plunged over the years, finally flatlining with her appointment as DCI. She frequently thought about chucking it all in, just handing in her notice and taking off somewhere. She needed some excitement, something out of the ordinary to ignite the spark of life within her once more. Even some of the criminals and miscreants she came into contact with had far more exciting lives than she did. Take Rayment, for example. He was a highly unusual man bordering on lunacy at times, she thought, but his life seemed challenging. Different things happened to him – things out of the ordinary, things that would excite you. She wondered what it would be like to live just twenty-four hours in the life of Brian Rayment. This brought her right back to her earlier thoughts of trying to fill in about twelve of those twenty-four hours by meeting up with him again. If she'd been told just a few days ago that she would arrange to meet Brian Raymond socially, end up in his bed, and not remember much about the evening, she wouldn't have believed it. Now, not only was this true, but she was considering a follow-up meeting. Although it was easy to see the craziness of these considerations, to Lucy there was undeniably a frisson, an aesthetic chill of excitement or espionage about it. The whole element of subterfuge had a very James Bondy sort of feel. Lucy wondered if these were subconscious or deliberate actions on her part. A death wish. Maybe deep down she was trying to put herself in a situation where she would be fired, so the decision would be taken out of her hands. Was she in any state at all to be making any decisions of importance? Before she could overthink herself out of it, she phoned Brian.

'Hello this is www dot Brian Rayment and Sons Limited dot com hashtag. I am not an answering machine I am a real person. If you are a questioning machine or a foreigner with a pretend British name who doesn't know who I am, goodbye.'

'Hello, Brian. It's DCI Lucy Webster – Lucy. Can we meet, please? There are some very important things we need to discuss.' Brian was sitting by his phone, listening to his own message and Lucy's response. He was ecstatic. He knew she would come round to his way of thinking eventually but he didn't imagine in his wildest dreams that it would be this quick. The woman was infatuated with him! He knew he had made a big impact last night: the chat, the drink he'd got her, the careful drive home, carrying her over the threshold, cleaning her sicky clothes, the fairly fresh bed had all combined to sweep the girl off her feet. And now she had phoned him up to pop the question.

'No need for any discussion! The answer's, "Yes", said Brian.

'Good. When's convenient?' asked Lucy. 'The sooner the better would suit me.' Good grief! The woman was keen – he had no idea. He was impressed with his own powers of seduction.

'Well, I suppose a few days to a week just to arrange things?'

'No no no! I can't wait that long, Brian. I need to come round today, as soon as possible.'

'We'll need to book up a registry office or a hotel or something and … and … and we'll need a registrar. We'll need someone who can do it for us. I think you can get doctors or some professional person, a vicar, a teacher or a dentist or a policeman or a judge, but not a postman or a tattooist,' said Brian. 'I don't mean a postman or a tattooist are the only people you can't use, but they're very good examples of people you can't use. Whereas,' he continued, 'you'll be perfectly OK if you're a vicar or a policeman.' As he was talking he was Googling 'Quickest way to get married in the UK'.

'I am,' said Lucy, confused, as she often was after one of Brian's explanations.

'You are? Are what?' said Brian, equally confused.

'I am a vicar or a policeman,' said Lucy. 'I mean I am a policeman – a police officer.' Lucy briefly wondered whether Brian Rayment's conversation technique was catching.

'I know you are … but … well you can't do it to yourself can you?'

'Do it to myself?'

'Marry yourself. You can't marry yourself, can you? Even a vicar couldn't marry himself. I think you'll find you always have to have someone else to marry you.'

'Yes, I do believe you're right, Brian.' She said patronising him. 'It always takes two. Three is illegal, one's impossible – always got to be two of you.'

'Here it is! I've just found it!' said Brian. He read off the screen, 'Any UK registry office will require a minimum of twenty-eight days' notice from the proposed ceremony date. Seems like even if we phoned up today we still have to wait a month. The only other thing we could do,' he started tentatively, 'is to go to Las Vegas. You can get it done the same day there. I've looked into it. For $120 you can get married within ten minutes, have two red roses and a ten by eight photograph with Elvis Presley. Not the real Elvis Presley of course, but someone who looks a bit like him. For another $100 you can get Elvis to sing a couple of songs. I think he gets to choose, so it could be "Hound Dog" or "An American Trilogy". I don't know about that but it's certainly something to think about.'

Lucy was lost.

'Well maybe if I could come round soon we can have a chat about it. What do you think, Brian?'

'Yes. Sounds like an excellent idea. I'll need a bit of time to put some trousers on though.'

'Hopefully that shouldn't take too long. Shall we say half an hour?'

'I've got to put pants on too – and socks.'

'OK, should we say another thirty or forty seconds?' Lucy was very definitely getting the hang of this Brian Rayment

WHICH WOULD YOU RATHER?

mode of conversation.

'Perfect! See you soon, darling.'

52

'Come in, come in,' said Brian. 'Make yourself at home. How about a glass of champagne to celebrate?'

'No thank you, Brian. Very kind, but no thank you.'

'Well I'm going to have one,' said Brian. 'I might have a cup of tea as well. Thinking about it, I'll just have the tea. Fancy some tea? I am making some.'

'I'd just like to talk, Brian, but if you're making one, let's have some tea then, OK.' While Brian busied himself clattering around in the kitchen, making the tea, Lucy tried to collect her thoughts into some sort of cohesive order. The collecting of thoughts was interrupted by a crash in the kitchen followed by a 'Bugner! Joe Bugner! – Bugner! – Bugner! – Bugner!' from the kitchen. When Brian was a teenager he once heard his mother change the swear word at the very last minute into Bugner for Brian's benefit. He was always very impressed with this quick-thinking sidestep, and the fact that it had been done for him. He'd adopted the use of Joe Bugner's name ever since. Brian detested swearing and blasphemy. He felt it showed a lack of vocabulary – a lack of inventiveness. However, he often had the need of some expletive when other words just wouldn't do, so the 'Bugner' worked perfectly. He also used names as a camouflaged vehicle for swearwords. Last week he successfully called the local shopkeeper Barry Astard without being rumbled. Recently, when he heard Sergeant Dew use the expression 'Christ on a motorbike' Brian's first reaction was that he would never consider taking the Lord's name in vain like that – but what did 'taking the Lord's name in vain' really mean? Was the expression blasphemous? If so, how? Why? If he'd said 'Peter on a motorbike' or 'Bridget on a motorbike' there would be nothing offensive in that. Why did 'Christ on a motorbike' sound suspiciously offensive. Maybe it was the word 'Christ'. Brian had had it in his mind that there was a group of people who were nervous about using the word 'Christ' in the same way that some people never like to use the word 'black' in front of Black people. As if the very word is offensive. How about 'Jesus on a motorbike'? Now that's just an amusing thing to imagine – a strange juxtaposition because motorbikes weren't around when Jesus was around. The same as Abraham Lincoln throwing a frisbee or Adolf Hitler playing a Fender Telecaster. Jesus was a carpenter but it's still quite difficult to think of him using a rip saw, even more difficult to imagine him wearing a mask and goggles and using an electric sander. But this wouldn't be taking the Lord's name in vain. At best it could be classed conceivably as taking the Lord's name in an anachronism. There would have been chisels in those days though, and saws and drills and spokeshaves. Most of the tools of the time would have had very sharp blades. This was another thing that didn't sit comfortably with Brian's image of Jesus. When he thought of Jesus he didn't think of him holding a sharp bladed tool. Ray Winstone yes – Jesus no. And another thing, as a carpenter, what sort of woodworking was he involved with? Did Jesus make fruit bowls, or maybe bedside cabinets, fitted kitchens, bunkbeds for the children's room? Maybe it was more in the line of folding picnic tables. It's true he wouldn't be able to finish them off nicely with wipe-down Formica with that printed tablecloth check design. Also, when he was doing his carpentry, did Jesus wear that long white nightie thing that he used to wear or did he have a sensible pair of dungarees or a boiler suit? These things worried Brian. Having thought about it Brian was very clear in his mind that the phrase 'Christ on a motorbike' wasn't offending anybody and was used purely to create a funny image. He genuinely felt that God, Jesus and the Holy Ghost – all three of them – had a sense of humour and would find the image funny. This started him on another line of enquiry. If Father, Son and Holy Ghost were all the same, three-in-one like the easing oil, how did it work with the Holy Ghost being a carpenter? And what would the Holy Ghost have worn?

'Special offer this Christmas! New Levi 3-in-1s, a hard-wearing denim dungaree as worn by the Holy Ghost. One size fits all three.'

The tea was ready and Brian had it laid out neatly on his best tray with his two best cups and saucers. He was about to carry it in when he remembered the chocolate digestives. He opened the end kitchen cabinet and took out a plate and reached to the top shelf for the recently opened packet of chocolate digestives. The cellophane wrapper had already started to split, and reaching for the biscuits set it well underway. The entire pack of biscuits, bar two, fell bouncing, breaking and crumbling onto the tray of tea. One 'Holy Ghost on a motorbike', several more 'Bugners' and another five minutes, and Brian was carrying the repaired tray of tea and biscuits into Lucy. There were originally sixteen biscuits in the packet of dark chocolate digestives. Brian had brought thirteen of them in to go with the tea.

'There you go,' he said handing Lucy a cup of tea. 'I've already been mother.'

'Thank you very much, Brian.'

'Would you like a chocolate digestive?' he asked. 'There are six and a half each.'

'No thank you. I'd just like to have that chat if we could.'

'I won't be offended if you only have four or five,' he said.

'No thank you – I'm fine.' Lucy took the first sip of tea, which was hotter than she'd expected, given the long-winded kerfuffle in the kitchen. As she took a second sip, half a chocolate digestive floated to the surface and bumped her lip.

'I wondered where that had gone,' said Brian, smiling – pleased to have solved the problem.

Time to take charge! thought Lucy.

'Brian I need you to tell me exactly what happened last night – don't leave anything out. I remember everything up to the point where you bought our drinks, two pints of water. I'm well aware that you had something else in yours. Now tell me what happened from there.'

Brian took a slow deep breath as his eyes glanced down and to the right repeatedly. Lucy recognised the movements as a sure sign of somebody about to lie.

'Well I started talking telling you things, but you got bored so you decided to fall asleep.'

'Yes, carry on,' said Lucy.

'Well, then I took you home and cleaned the sick off your clothes. They're very tiny clothes aren't they?' he added quickly. An impromptu attempt to exonerate himself from any shrinkage that may have been noticed.

'So how did you go about cleaning my clothes then, Brian? Did you remove them?'

'Well yes, I had to. I couldn't clean the sick off while you were wearing them.'

'Brian, do you realise you are telling me that you removed the clothes of an unconscious female police officer?'

'Well I wouldn't quite put it like that,' said Brian.

'How would you put it exactly?' asked Lucy.

'I'd say it was more a case of cleaning the sick off my fiancé's tiny clothes.'

'Brian! Will you give it a rest with the tiny clothes bit? I know whatever you did, you shrunk my clothes. I'm not a complete idiot.'

'I only shrunk them a little bit. I did a sum. I estimated it was fourteen or fifteen per cent shrinkage, but hardly anything.'

'You've rendered them useless, Brian. I might as well just give them to a children's charity.'

'Oh, I know a really good charity shop that sells a lot of children's clothing. It's in the middle of town, "Save the something or other", you could take them there or I'll take them for you.'

'Brian, can we back up a bit. What did you mean by fiancé?'

'Well now that we're getting married, you are my fiancé. I know I haven't given you a ring or anything, but we're arranging the date and the registry office, all that sort of stuff.' Hearing all this, a lot of the previous conversation and the earlier phone call made a lot of awful sense to Lucy.

'Brian, what on earth made you think I was your fiancé?'

'Nothing made me think it, I volunteered to think it.' Lucy filed it away as something else to discuss later.

'Can we get back to last night, Brian? Tell me exactly what happened after you cleaned and shrunk my clothes.'

'After I cleaned and shrunk your clothes you looked a bit tired or dead. You hadn't moved for two hours, so I put you to bed and tucked you up. Then I held the big hallway mirror over your face to make sure you were dead.'

'And was I dead?' said Lucy, momentarily entering into the spirit of things.

'No, you weren't dead. You were alive and well, but sound asleep or possibly unconscious.'

'Let me get this completely clear, Brian. Are you telling me that you undressed me when I was unconscious in order to clean my clothes?'

'Yes but I didn't see anything and I didn't look at you because I was wearing a balaclava.' As much as she wanted to, Lucy found all these openers impossible to ignore.

'How would a balaclava stop you looking or seeing?' Lucy asked.

'Well obviously I had it on back to front didn't I?' said Brian with an air of slight exasperation. 'I just undressed you by feel.'

'YOU DID WHAT?'

'I just accidentally felt you when I was fumbling about with your clothes.' *Fumbling was not a good word to use. I shouldn't have said that,* thought Brian. 'My fingers accidentally brushed your grey pants.'

'How do you know they were grey?' asked Lucy.

'I thought they felt a bit grey. Anyway, I whipped your trousers off like a magician without spilling a drop or knocking anything over much,' said Brian. 'Except I also accidentally whipped you off the bed and banged your head again,' he added. Each sentence the man spoke threw up three or four new things that needed an explanation.

'Have you any idea at all,' started Lucy, 'how I received this nasty wound to the side of my head? I didn't have it last night when I met you but I woke up with it.'

'As I recall,' started Brian slowly, obviously thinking marginally ahead of talking, 'you banged your head going out of the pub door on your way to the car.'

'I have no memory of that at all,' said Lucy. Brian was quick to seize this golden opportunity.

'No that's exactly what I thought. It was quite a hefty whack you gave yourself,' he said, squarely placing the blame with Lucy. 'When you hit your head it made you go all unconscious and you lost your memory. That's why you can't remember anything else that I did – I mean that happened.'

'I was indeed unconscious, Brian, and I don't remember anything, so it's just as well I had this in my pocket.' She left Brian wondering and brought out her phone. It was paused at the recording. She pressed play and let Brian hear it. What followed was the longest uninterrupted section of Brian's confession. When it had finished, she stopped the phone and just waited for Brian's reaction.

'How did you get that? You shouldn't have recorded me! You weren't even on duty! That's illegal!'

'Yes, Brian, I rather think you're right. I'll have to see what the superintendent says about it.' Brian was silent but took his own phone out. He was trying to find something.

'Maybe you could ask your superintendent what he thinks

of this as well,' said Brian, holding the phone to face her and showing her one of the photographs he'd taken. The tables having been turned, it was now Lucy's turn to go silent.

'I theenk, Meester Bond, this is, how-you-English-say, "stalemate".'

'How many photos do you have of me?' said Lucy, trying to keep her cool.

'Meester Bond, I theenk ziss depends on how much of my talking you have.' 'Do you know it's an extremely serious crime to take photographs of somebody you've rendered unconscious and stripped?'

'Indeed, Meester Bond. Entrapment! Eet eez also an extremely serious crime – No? especially while you are pretending to be in love wizz zee entrapee.'

'I'm not pretending to be in love with you!'

'Ah, eenteresting Meester Bond, so you admit zee entrapment?'

'I don't admit anything. I want to see all those photographs!'

'And I want to hear all of that recording,' said Brian finally dropping the Blofeld voice. It was not in Lucy's best interest to let Brian hear the whole recording. It was so broken up that the poor quality would probably reassure him. Much better that he think she had a complete uninterrupted recording. Brian was coming to much the same conclusion about the photographs. He too would be in a far stronger position if he let Lucy imagine what he might have.

53

Lucy had spent many hours mentally having this conversation with Brian and considering the possible outcomes. One such outcome had been that, in her role as a police officer, she would arrest Brian on suspicion of murder, search the place, and remove any incriminating evidence. Each time this idea had entered her head, she had fairly quickly abandoned it as she realised it was possibly too extreme a response and, in the long run, could be more detrimental to her than to Brian. However, having just learnt that Brian had an unknown quantity of photographs of her, at least just in her underwear and possibly worse, it was looking more like an option to be considered. There was still a strong element of risk and she'd have to play it very carefully and act quickly. She reasoned that arresting Brian would give her the ideal chance to officially confiscate his phone. If she then acted quickly she could remove all the photographs, wipe the phone clean of any images and data, release Brian and hand him back his phone. It would be a big gamble, but she felt it was one worth taking. Brian would be very unlikely to report it. In her coat pocket, she had brought her badge, ID and even a pair of handcuffs. It was an instinctive decision on her part. She had a momentary welling of pride and thankfulness for her foresight in taking this action. Considering it further she decided that a smart move would be to get Brian to open his phone and show her another picture. If she could then contrive to get him handcuffed to somewhere in the room and then get the phone off him already unlocked, it would make the deletion that much easier. She could leave the room, delete the photographs, return to Brian, make out it was all just a bit of a warning, release him and hand his phone back. It was conceivable that within a quarter of an hour they could be back where they were now but with the dodgy photos erased.

As it happened, Lucy and Brian had begun to think and scheme in a very similar way. Brian would say this was irrefutable proof that they were perfectly matched. Lucy would say it was evidence of Brian's lunacy rubbing off on her. While Lucy had been plotting her arrest of Brian, he in turn had been planning a citizen's arrest of Lucy. Brian had no real idea of what was involved in a citizen's arrest but he felt sure he could give a convincing performance. Over the years Brian had watched countless courtroom dramas and crime series. It was just a matter of what role did he want to play in this forthcoming live drama? He was fairly sure he didn't need handcuffs or any specific wording but just to take charge of the situation and to make sure the suspect knew they were under arrest. Some situations demanded impeccable timing and weeks of research and planning, but this wasn't one of those times. This was an improv show. Brian would be in his element. He knew improvisation was his strength, and he thrived on it and excelled at it. He took a deep breath and launched into his citizen's arrest of Lucy. He stood up, faced Lucy and, clicking his heels, gave a very smart formal salute. It just seemed the right way to start something like this.

He opened up, 'I put it to you my learn-ed lud that you did wilfully and with malice aforethought seek to profit by attempting to incriminate a murder suspect, to wit, me. Furthermore, by unlawfully impersonating the fiancé of that suspect, to wit me again, you showed a clear intent to deceive.' This was going very well, thought Brian. He continued, 'Without any regard to human life you did use an illegal electronic recording device concealed about your person for the sole intention of entrapment. I, therefore, have no option but to impose on you ...' *No no – careful! This was sounding too much like a crusty old judge about to pass sentence, rather than a citizen's arrest – but it was sounding rather good. Should I change tack?* he thought. *No! Bash on with it!* He continued, 'I, therefore, have no option but to impose on you the maximum possible sentence, for better or for worse, for richer for poorer, ashes to ashes, dust to dust, in sickness and in health, as long as you both shall live. If any man knows any just cause or impediment why we two should not be joined together, let him speak now or forever hold his peace. And now may you live together in holy matrimony and taken from this place forward to a place of execution and may God have mercy on your soul. DCI Lucy Webster, I am arresting you on suspicion of impersonating my fiancé, to wit you.'

'Oh shut up, Brian. Don't be so damned silly.'

Brian was very rarely rendered speechless, so he didn't quite know how to handle it. He tried to say something but physically couldn't say anything. How could a person you were placing under arrest just tell you to 'shut up' and 'stop being silly'? It was completely the wrong reaction. It just wasn't true to life. You'd never get that happening in *Prime Suspect*. And from Lucy of all people. You'd think being a lady policeman, or police person or whatever it is they call themselves these days, she would have seen every episode of *Prime Suspect*, and would therefore know how to behave in a situation like this. But no. There she is, bold as brass, telling him to shut up and not to be so silly. It beggars belief.

Well, that worked well. Brian had gone completely quiet. This was the perfect chance to capitalise on the situation. Speaking very sharply, as she had done when she'd told him to shut up, she said, 'Show me one of the photographs you took of me, Brian. Straight away! Now!' As if in a trance, he took his phone out, found a photograph and handed the phone to Lucy. She could hardly believe it, he just handed the phone to her. She placed it on the table behind her and out of Brian's immediate reach. While he was still in the trance-like state she barked, 'Give me your hand!' Brian responded and stuck out his right hand. Lucy snapped one of the handcuffs over his right wrist and gave him a sharp painful downward tug so she could snap the other cuff around the radiator feed pipe. As she did so she said to him, 'I'm Detective Chief Inspector Lucy Webster. Mr Brian Rayment, I am arresting you on suspicion of murder. You do not have to say anything, but it may harm your defence if, when questioned, you do not say something you later rely on in court. Anything you do say will be taken down and may be used in evidence. Do you understand?'

'No of course I don't understand!' said Brian from his very uncomfortable position on the floor crammed up and joined at the wrist to the radiator. The whole reason for the arrest was for Lucy to get her hands on Brian's phone and hence the photographs. She was only too aware that the phone would eventually time out and lock, so she needed to get on with the task at hand.

'Well, you just have a think about it for a bit, Brian. I'll be back shortly and explain it to you if you can't work it out.' Lucy picked up the phone and went out of the room. In the hallway, she looked on Brian's phone for 'gallery' and opened up the 'images' folder. She was alarmed to see row upon row of photographs of herself. Thankfully they appeared to be subtle variations of the picture she had already seen. Choosing 'select all' she highlighted the pictures and went into 'share' where she sent them to her own email address. She wanted to study these in detail later to find out exactly what Brian had been up to. This took longer than she'd expected. The horizontal blue bar showed three per cent complete. She knew Brian was safe and secure, but he was making quite a racket, clanging and banging on the radiator, and shouting that he didn't understand. While the pictures were being sent, she decided to help herself to a cup of tea in Brian's kitchen. She shut herself in the kitchen while she made the tea. Consequently, Brian's hollering was significantly subdued.

The shouting gradually subsided and was replaced with a rhythmic metallic banging, presumably of the radiator. While she made and drank the tea she sat at the kitchen table reading Brian's newspaper and even answered and filled in a couple of crossword clues. She periodically checked the progress of sending the photographs. It had reached ninety-one per cent complete. Lucy watched the completion of the last nine per cent to a backing of Brian's radiator bangings, which were still going strong.

Finally, when the pictures had all been sent, she selected

them all again and pressed 'delete'. This time it was almost instantaneous. The pictures went and were no longer on Brian's phone. She was just having a look at other folders on Brian's phone when the regular metallic knocking stopped and was replaced by uncontrolled manic screaming. Lucy raced back to the room where Brian was handcuffed. As soon as she opened the door she was sprayed with a wide fountain of warm water. Brian appeared to be in an impossible near-foetal position with one arm bent awkwardly under him and still attached to the radiator, which had fallen on top of him. His kicking, pulling and banging had finally yanked the radiator off the wall and fractured one of the pipes. Water sprayed into the air in a powerful arc as it had been doing for over a minute now. Brian was completely soaked, as was the floor and most of the furniture.

'Do you know where the stopcock is, Brian? The stopcock to turn off the water?' shouted Lucy.

'Yes – it's in the kitchen – under the sink,' gurgled Brian. Lucy went straight over to him and unlocked the handcuffs.

'Go and switch it off, Brian! You're not under arrest any more!'

'Does that mean I didn't do it?' he asked

'Brian, go and turn the water off as quickly as you can! You're free! You're released.'

'I'm free! I'm free! I'm innocent! I didn't do it!' sang Brian.

'TURN OFF THE WATER, BRIAN! NOW!'

'Yes, m'lud, your honour.' Brian went into the kitchen rummaged around under the cupboard and a few seconds later the water stopped and everything went quiet. He went dripping back into the room and sat down looking at the broken radiator, the soaked carpet, the damaged furniture and the soaked Lucy. He thought the soaking Lucy looked the best. He told her so. 'The wet suits you,' he said to her. 'It makes you look like you've just come in from the rain, or just had a shower, except that you've got all your clothes on of course, which spoils the effect a little bit.'

'I wasn't going for any particular effect, Brian. Are you alright by the way? Did the radiator hurt you? How is your wrist?' Lucy asked.

'Well my wrist is a little bit sore and I whacked my shin, but the worst thing is I got a bit of a pain up the bollocks because I accidentally sat on my heel and squashed them when you handcuffed me to the radiator. But I'm sure it's nothing a small operation wouldn't put right,' he added.

'Do you know the rain suits you as well, Brian. It makes you look more sophisticated, more intelligent?' Brian looked at Lucy with a puzzled expression. She was smirking. They looked at the devastation all around them, then at each other, then they both laughed.

54

Lucy was keen to get back to the station as soon as possible. She didn't want things to look any more suspicious than they already could do. It was clear to her that she had to slot back into regular duties as smoothly and quickly as possible. The best approach would be to make light of her meeting with Brian – laugh it off and tell the super just how unproductive it was, and how it was a complete waste of time. That would of course mean lying. As it happened she was thinking constantly about Brian Rayment. Not all good things, not all bad, just the whole hard-to-fathom package. When she left him earlier she was nervous. She had committed goodness knew how many misdemeanours and indiscretions. An unofficial 'arrest' while she wasn't in uniform. An arrest that had lasted forty-two minutes. Unlawfully handcuffing him to a radiator, using far more than necessary force. As a consequence of these highly questionable actions, a great deal of his property had been damaged and would undoubtedly be very expensive to repair or replace. She had deleted everything from his phone, which she had then dropped, albeit accidentally, into two inches of water, probably ruining it. Finally, she had caused him to have 'a pain up the bollocks' when he squashed his testicles against his heel. Even though it was something she would never experience, nevertheless it made her wince. Despite all these things she'd inflicted on him, Brian was in good spirits and appeared to hold nothing against her. When she asked him about the fractured radiator and the leak he simply and very reasonably replied, 'These things happen – don't worry about it.' No threats of reporting her or suing her, he seemed to hold no ill will against her at all. This was such a marked difference from the way her so-called colleagues treated her. Not just her; there was an overall tension at the station. Everyone seemed ready and keen to criticise or blame. This stemmed from the many pressures of the working environment of a police force. The dreadful shift work. Sometimes eight-hour shifts, but more usually ten or twelve-hour shifts. Although it didn't divide into a twenty-four hour day, the ten-hour shift was the most common. It necessitated overlap, which enabled communication between officers passing work from one shift to the next. However, these ten-hour shifts were often extended with emergency overtime for whoever happened to be on duty. These long days frequently led to increased health issues, problems with home and social life and extra mental stress. The pressures of poor pay, long hours, potentially dangerous or threatening confrontations and the ever-present risk of reprimand and ridicule after a cock-up.

It was three in the afternoon and Lucy was back home getting changed into her uniform. At 3.40 she walked into the station, went straight to her office and started work. After ten minutes she left her office and made her way to Superintendent Andrew Richardson's office. She knocked on the door. 'Come in,' called Richardson's distinctive voice.

'Afternoon, sir. Sorry about missing this morning.'

'That's alright, Lucy. Feeling better now I trust?'

'Yes thank you, sir. Finally got some sleep.'

'So how did things go with our Mr Rayment last night?'

This was it, thought Lucy, the big lie. In her whole police career, she had never lied to any of her bosses, to any of her colleagues for that matter. Now she was at the very point of telling a whopper. If it ever came out, she would lose her job immediately. Momentarily poised on a cliff edge and ready to abandon this decision, she took a deep breath, preparing to tell everything.

'Well, sir, it was quite unbelievable actually,' she started and then, 'a total washout. He said nothing, gave nothing helpful at all. A real waste of time.'

'Oh well, nothing ventured nothing gained. There's a meeting in half an hour at four-thirty or in the main incident room. See you then.'

'Ok, sir. Thank you.' Lucy made her way back to her own office already regretting the big lie she'd just told. This would undoubtedly play on her mind. She knew what she was like, but there was no going back now. Even if she ran straight back in now and apologised, it was there. She lied. She'd been prepared to do it. She sat at her desk considering. If she did want to undo it, to back out of it, to apologise, minutes were precious. She needed to go in straight away and explain she'd made an error of judgement. She may be able to put it down to the food poisoning or the lack of sleep or even just bad judgement. Trying to play out the possible conversation with the superintendent in her mind it wasn't going well. Other useful, possibly usable, phrases came to her. 'Sickness and sleep deprivation.' 'I wanted to write it up fully and completely before

I told you, sir.' 'He threatened to kill me if I said anything.' That was probably the best one, but a little unfair on Brian. How about, 'He threatened to kill you, sir, if I said anything.' No this was getting ridiculous. This was starting to sound like Brian Rayment himself. OK. Last run through. She'd go back to his room and say, 'Please, sir, I'm so sorry – I lied. I was worried. I didn't know what to do. Brian Rayment threatened to kill me if I said anything, but he confessed last night and he attacked me, and I think he drugged me.' She stood up to go to the superintendent's office, and saw him walk past the window towards the main incident room. She looked at her watch. It was nearly 4.30 and she'd blown it. The lie would have to stand. And then a strange thing happened. As soon as she had it in her mind that this was now a fait accompli, she relaxed and she could almost feel a physical weight lifting from her shoulders. She felt pleased with the lie.

It was a short afternoon until the end of the shift at 6.00. Naturally, she was keen to look at the photographs she had sent to herself from Brian's phone. She headed home to her modern apartment. It was one level of a converted Georgian terraced house in Camden Road and had limited but extensive views across the hilly Somerset landscape. At this time of year, it was cold and dark, but the lights across the city were beautiful, and she usually took time out to look and appreciate them. Not tonight. Tonight she headed straight for her computer. The idea of a laptop had never appealed, and she still used the old desktop PC that she'd had for five years. It was very slow and often seemed to spend most of its time buffering. She switched it on, booted it up, then went to get changed and put the kettle on as it slowly came to life. Opening her emails she saw at the top of the incoming list the one she'd sent from Brian's phone. The rows and rows of attached photographs lined up as solid opaque grey squares. She selected them all and clicked open. Nothing happened other than the computer seized up. She saw the familiar 'page unresponsive' at the top of the screen. It was impossible to open any other page or file. The whole computer screen was covered with a milky see-through barrier preventing access of any sort. It was either switch the computer off at the mains and start all over again or sit it out. She sat it out. After a quick shower, the seven o' clock news and a cup of tea, she went back to the screen. Two pictures had now fully opened in their thumbnail form. Another twelve had partially opened – all from top to bottom in decreasing levels of revelation. As far as she could tell from these first few, they were all just subtle viewpoint variations of the one picture he'd shown her. The complete set of pictures finally opened at 3.42 in the morning. Lucy had fully intended to keep checking the PC throughout the night, but had fallen asleep almost immediately. She awoke at around 7.30 and started to doze again, then was wide awake when she remembered the photos. She went through the open-plan flat to the PC. It was an unusual experience seeing so many similar but different pictures of her unconscious self. She went through them one by one. It was fairly obvious that Brian had made several circuits of the bed from different heights, taking photographs all the way. Now they were safely in her hands and out of Brian's, she was able to look at them objectively. They were good pictures, she liked them and the subtle shifting repetition made them reminiscent of a strip of a movie film.

55

Thursday 30 September 2021

Lucy shut down the computer, went through her usual morning repertoire and made her way into work. Approaching the station the nervousness returned, as she worried and wondered all over again if she had got away with the lie. When she arrived at the station, it was alive with the bustle of a changing shift and new cases to be assessed, reviewed and have officers assigned. Updates on existing cases were given to the new incoming shift. She sat in on the updates, such as they were, of the Garage Murders case. Because she had missed so much of yesterday, the briefing was chaired by DS Dew. He wasn't particularly good at holding the floor and presenting the information. He was hesitant, repetitive and nervous, making everyone else in the room nervous on his behalf. The bottom line was that there was nothing new to add. The case had gone decidedly cold. There had been three phone calls from members of the public claiming to have seen the huge Humphrey Bogart woman. Two of the calls claimed to have seen her at Bath Bus Station at around 11 p.m. last night. One of these came in quite soon after the sighting, just before midnight last night. The second call came early this morning, but both calls related many specific similarities. The general public made notoriously bad witnesses and commonly overestimated people's height, but both these callers put the woman at about six foot four and wearing a 'greatcoat' from one – a 'large winter overcoat' from the other. They also said that she was being very loud and was swearing a great deal and, finally, they had both claimed to have seen her throwing something at a bus. One said a rock, one said a bottle. The main task today regarding this case was to question people, at and around the bus station, for more information. Two other officers were to try and track down local CCTV camera footage to see if it could reveal anything further.

When the briefing was over, the remaining officers from the previous shift went home and the new shift started to get on with their tasks for the day. Lucy went to her office. There was plenty of catching up to do from the lost day yesterday. Throughout the day, however, Lucy had the uneasy feeling that people were deliberately avoiding her or ignoring her. They were never really a chatty or jokey bunch at the best of times, not with her anyway, but today she almost had a feeling of being ostracized. She put it down to a guilty conscience and did her best to get involved with the catch-up work. The uneasiness had almost left her when at 2.30 she saw Detective Higgs go into Superintendent Richardson's office. Although she could hear nothing she could see straight into Richardson's office. The blinds weren't drawn so she had a clear view of the two of them talking. She noticed that at one point they both glanced around and looked directly at her, briefly, then continued their conversation. Just that quick moment's glance unnerved her and sent her right back to the guilty feelings of unease. The two of them seemed to be in there talking for a long time. They were standing up and were not very animated.

When their meeting was over, DC Higgs left the office and walked past her window. He shot her another quick unsmiling glance without stopping. In another couple of minutes, Superintendent Richardson also left the office. He too walked past her window so she gave a brief smile and nodded to him. He glared at her and carried on. It was a glare – he definitely glared at her! For the rest of the afternoon, Lucy felt dreadful. She couldn't concentrate on anything. They knew. They knew she had lied. It was a long afternoon and she didn't get very much work done. Several times she considered asking to see the super and telling him she detected an 'atmosphere' and asking him if there was some sort of problem. She decided it wasn't a good idea and could be construed as the action of a guilty person.

At 5.45 a decision was made for her when Superintendent Andrew Richardson stuck his head through the doorway of Lucy's office and said, 'Can you come into my office please, Lucy – soon as you can!'

56

Brian had spent the rest of the day dealing with the flooding and the leaking radiator. He was, of course without water, so it was fairly high on his priority list. The carpet still had puddles in it where it was completely submerged. He found that by bouncing lightly up and down on one spot he could make waves appear on his carpet. It occurred to him that this would be the perfect time to wash the carpet given that it was already soaking wet. He went to the cabinet under the kitchen sink to look, with more hope than expectation, for some carpet shampoo. There were two bottles of strong bleach, a limescale remover spray, three-quarters of a box of washing powder, a never-used bubble bath and an abrasive cream cleaner. By a process of elimination, he narrowed it down to the washing powder and the bubble bath. As well as two plastic bowls and a bucket, there were also a variety of scrubbing brushes and sponges in the cupboard under the sink. He carried a bowl, the brushes, sponges and cleaners back into the sopping carpet. Before he got started on the possibly long task of cleaning the carpet, he went to see if his phone was working yet. He'd found it submerged under a carpet puddle when DCI Webster left. It was no surprise to find that it wasn't working. Earlier on he spent half an hour with a hairdryer and paper towels trying to dry it out. It briefly came to life but very soon went to black screen again. In his mind, Brian had already written the phone off and was running through possibilities for an upgrade replacement. Under the heading of 'nothing-to-lose', he heated the oven, switched it off, and placed his phone in the hot oven with the door shut to dry it out as the oven slowly cooled. It was a fairly big and pleasant surprise to find that the phone worked when he took it out of the oven. He had a quick check through the various files and apps on the phone and found that everything was in working order except that all his camera images had disappeared. The strange thing was that the images he had on other files, screensaver shots, pictures people had sent him on WhatsApp, were still there. Only the pictures he'd taken with the camera we're missing. He checked the video folder. All his video clips were there. He was devastated that all those lovely shots of Lucy were gone and that all that remained was the video clip, which he looked at again. The loss of the 123 still images rendered the solitary video clip even more valuable and precious to him.

He closed down the video file and opened up the phone to his saved contact list. He selected the number he was looking for, and finally got to check that the phone itself was working as he dialled the number for Bryan Ferry. After three rings, Bryan Ferry's recorded answer phone message kicked in. When he heard the beep, Brian left his own message.

'Hi there, Bryan, it's Brian Rayment from Brownlow Buildings, number 26. I'm afraid it's a bit of an emergency here. One of the radiators is leaking badly, so I'm totally without water – well – water I can use that is. Plenty of unwanted water and the place is getting cold. I'd appreciate it if you could get back to me as soon as possible, with a view to fixing it. Many thanks, speak to you soon, yours sincerely, Brian Rayment.' He had to stop saying 'yours sincerely' on phone messages. Someone had told him recently that it wasn't the done thing, but it was a habit he was finding hard to break.

Bryan Ferry was a local plumber, whose number Brian had got from the Bath Local Look magazine. Mr Ferry had more 5-star reviews than any other local plumber. It was perhaps predictable that most of the reviewers felt obliged to incorporate some sort of Roxy Music/Bryan Ferry pun in their feedback.

'I danced away all night after Mr Ferry expertly fixed my heating.'

'My washing machine gave up in the midnight hour but as always, Bryan Ferry was soon round to help.'

'Bryan Ferry is a very reasonable price and whatever problem I have he's able to fix it. You can't ask "More Than This".' All of the reviewers no doubt thought they were being very clever and original. Bryan Ferry suffered from having the same name as the famous star. However, he suffered with good grace and was usually able to produce a smile each time he heard one of the frequent puns. He found it a little hard to swallow though, when people asked him if he knew he had the same name as a famous pop star. Did they think he had reached the age of fifty-one without discovering that? Sometimes he would just wind them up, or have some fun with them. 'No, I didn't know that. Who is he, one of the Rolling Stones?' Or, 'Yes I heard that. Big fat blond-haired chap isn't he? Plays the trombone I believe?' Generally, he tried to be affable and go along with people's clever jokes. He was astute enough to realise that a good ten per cent of his work came from people who were happy to use him, so that they could tell their friends that Bryan Ferry had come round to repair their immersion heater or fix a leaking tap. Having left his message, Brian returned to the job of cleaning the carpet. He started by giving a good squirt of bubble bath onto a small area of the carpet. He scrubbed it for a while with a little nail brush. It started to lather up a bit, but the sheer amount of water absorbed the bubble bath with not a lot to show for it. In the airing cupboard upstairs, Brian had a pile of dust sheets that he kept for decorating purposes. He brought them all downstairs and spread them about the floor, stamping on them, jumping on them, walking over them to try and absorb as much of the water as possible. When all five sheets were soaked, he threw them over the washing line in the back yard to drip dry. The carpet was still damp, but he was sure it would be much more receptive to the bubble bath and washing powder. Meaning business now, he emptied a good handful of washing powder, as well as another generous squeeze of bubble bath, onto the carpet. The phone rang.

'Hello, Mr Rayment, it's Bryan Ferry here.'

'Hello, Bryan Ferry' said Brian, not missing an opportunity to use Bryan Ferry's full name. 'Thanks very much for getting back so quickly.'

'That's alright. I was only ten minutes at the last job. I thought it was going to take a couple of hours. The lady told me her washing machine was leaking. Turns out she had a split in the bowl she was carrying her wet washing in. I could be with you in about forty minutes and hopefully get you sorted.'

'Fantastic,' said Brian, 'see you shortly then. Yours since—' he started to say 'yours sincerely' again, but stopped just in time.

He changed it, very cleverly he thought, to disguise what he was going to say. 'Your sense of urgency is very commendable, Mr Ferry,' he said.

'Is it? Yes. Well, thank you. I'll see you in about forty minutes then,' said a slightly surprised Mr Ferry. Forty minutes. That should be ample time to clean this carpet, thought Brian. He picked up one of the scrubbing brushes and started going vigorously at the pile of washing powder and bubble bath. The words washing powder and bubble bath had mistakenly led Brian into thinking warm, comfortable, swirling and restful thoughts. He imagined the carpet cleaning would be a gentle and relaxing way to spend half an hour. He could already see it was going to be hard work. He spent another vigorous five minutes with the scrubbing brush and worked up quite a solid lather but this was doing him in. He needed some strong elastic bands. No, they wouldn't be strong enough. Something more sturdy was needed. Bungees. They would do the job. He went into the backyard and opened the small shed door. At the back of the shed, there was a stack of plastic storage boxes. He'd been meaning to label these. Each time he needed something, he had to look through the whole lot and, if he was lucky enough, he came across what he was looking for. He lifted the first box down and opened it up. It was full of small off-cut sized wooden blocks and three dirty gardening gloves, one with a split finger and hole in the thumb. The other two were a mismatched pair. This was just rubbish. Why did he keep these things? He put the whole box outside in the yard to be ditched, and lifted the second box down. On opening this, he discovered his electric sander with rolls and sheets of various grades of sandpaper. He mislaid this over a year ago, and had convinced himself that

Tony had borrowed it and kept it. The third box was extremely heavy and full of used nails, screws and unclassifiable clips, springs, washers and bits of metal, all oily or rusty and all useless. This too went into the yard to be discarded. Brian had often heard the term hitting 'pay dirt' in American movies. He was never entirely sure what it meant, though its meaning was fairly clearly implied. Whatever it meant, he felt he'd hit it now with the fourth box. When he opened it up he could see straight away it was full of rope, bungees, coils of wire and straps. He took the entire box indoors and then from his carpet cleaning collection, sorted out the best two scrubbing brushes. Over the next ten minutes, using a combination of bungees, rope and straps he went about lashing the brushes to his feet. He had to pull the various ties up tight between rows of bristles to fix the brushes in position securely enough. The bungees and straps he wrapped around his feet and scrubbing brushes and then up around his ankles, where he secured them. They looked like what was once called 'invalid shoes' but probably had a safe allowable name these days. Footwear for the hard of moving. *Good name*, he thought, discovering that this new footwear did indeed make moving hard. Tottering over to the carpet he tentatively tried out his new Acme Carpet Cleaning Shoes. He started with a single-footed scuff backwards and forwards. Then he changed weight and did the same thing with the other foot. He soon got into a bit of a rhythm with it: four on the right foot, four on the left foot. The scuffing of the brushes made a singularly pleasing sound reminiscent of a soft shoe shuffle routine. The kind of thing you'd see from a speciality act in one of those 1930s Hollywood musicals. To create a more pleasing and regular rhythm he swung his foot forwards, backwards, forwards, then down on the right foot then forwards, backwards, forwards, down on the left foot. This gave Brian a good solid backbeat to work with. After a set of right swings – a set of left swings, a set of right swings and a set of left swings – he broke into

'I'm scrubbing up my rug,

Just scuffing up the rug.'

After a few script changes and rehearsals, he said to himself out loud, 'Right! This is it! This is the performance! Whatever happens now, this is the live performance that everyone's going to see.' He gave his now much improved soft shoe shuffle intro and at full volume broke into:

'I'm scu---ffing up the rug

Just scu--ffing up the rug

What a glooorious feeling

It (scuff scuff) makes me feel smug

I'm laughing at suds

All over my floor

I've wiped out some neighbours

But (scuff scuff) who's keeping score.'

There was thunderous applause to this and Brian took a bow, promising to work on further verses later on with an assurance of a late-night performance of the complete routine.

57

Once Lucy was in Superintendent Richardson's office, he asked her to take a seat but made it sound very much like an order. When she was seated he turned his back on her and looked out of the window. Finally, after a long heavy silence, he said to her, 'Is there anything you'd like to tell me, Lucy? Think very carefully.' She'd been thinking very carefully all afternoon but none of her careful thoughts had led to her changing her mind. If she wasn't going to change her mind she had to continue thinking very carefully and act as if everything she had told Superintendent Richardson was accurate and truthful.

'Tell you about what?' she asked with puzzled innocence.

'Lucy! I'm just giving you a final chance to tell me anything you may think I need to be told.'

'Sir, I've absolutely no idea what you are talking about. Can you give me a clue what it's in connection with?' Richardson breathed in deeply and exhaled loudly. He seemed exasperated.

'Detective Sergeant Higgs claims that you weren't at home sleeping off food poisoning, but you were meeting with Mr Brian Rayment at his house. How do you respond to that?' He may as well have said 'how do you plead?' There was no possible chance of turning back now. Whatever information he threw at her she had to respond to it from the stance of a reliable police officer who had recently reported truthfully and accurately to her superintendent.

'I always thought Higgs was untrustworthy and shifty, and this just confirms my low opinion of him. Why on earth, when I'm feeling sick and lacking sleep, would I go to see that man? It's a ridiculous claim. What has Higgs said exactly?' This was a big gamble. Lucy had no idea what was coming next. In some corner of her mind, she was already working out what she might do with her life, having been thrown out of the police service. She clenched her teeth and set her jaw, determined not to change her expression whatever Superintendent Richardson said next.

'Higgs says he knows you were at Rayment's house and that he has proof.'

'Impossible! What proof?' Lucy almost shouted.

'He says he has the proof at home but needs to go through some files to collect it.'

'Go through some files to create it more like,' said Lucy.

'Look Lucy, I think it would be best if you took some time off for a day or two – paid sick leave or holiday, I don't mind. Just until we've looked unto this.'

Lucy acted incensed.

'What is this guv? Are you trying to say I'm guilty of lying to you?' she said in a raised voice.

'No I'm trying NOT to say you're guilty of lying to me,' Richardson said with finality. 'The alternative is to suspend you. I have no choice. If an allegation such as this is made it has to be investigated. If you take the time off now I can avoid the suspension for a day or two. If nothing comes of it you'll be straight back and Higgs will be the one under investigation.

Don't question me, Lucy, I'm on your side I'm trying to help. Take the time off now – straight away – and nothing will show on your record. And in case it should cross your mind, whatever did or didn't happen yesterday, under no circumstances make contact with Mr Brian Rayment. Do I make myself clear?'

'Sir.'

'Just so you know, DS Higgs is finishing his shift today at ten. We've told him to gather any evidence he claims to have and present it when he starts his shift tomorrow at two tomorrow afternoon. I imagine we'll be in touch fairly soon after that '

'Thank you, sir.' She returned to her desk, collected her things together and left the station. As she drove home, Lucy contemplated what the future had in store for her. It really wouldn't bother her if she left the job. The truth was, she would welcome it, but it would have to be on her terms. She wanted to be able to walk in and tell them 'I'm leaving'. She wanted to hand in her notice officially, work out the four weeks' notice, have a leaving party, maybe get presented with a watch, move on to a better life and receive a half-reasonable pension. Being fired for misconduct would destroy these wishes.

Despite what Superintendent Richardson had said, she had to find some way to make contact with Brian Rayment. Lucy had a feeling that he would know something about how Higgs had been aware of their meeting. She was still wrestling with the problem of making contact with him, when she stepped inside her apartment. After less than a minute in the flat, her phone rang. It was Brian. He started to tell her some absurd story about Bryan Ferry mending the radiator and how it was another of these foolish things that reminded him of her. She leapt in and hijacked the phone call.

'Brian I need to ask you something very important.'

'The answer is still yes,' said Brian. 'Anytime you want. We never decided on an exact date did we?' Sometimes it was easier to ignore Brian Rayment than to get sidetracked trying to understand just what he was talking about.

'Brian, I need to ask you, has DS Higgs tried to make contact with you? Has he called round or phoned you up?'

'DS Higgs? DS Higgs?' Brian tried to remember DS Higgs.

'You know. The one you said was shifty. The one you didn't trust. Looks like Lars Mikkelsen,' prompted Lucy. When she had first mentioned Higgs looking like Mikkelsen, Lucy had been very surprised that Brian knew who she was talking about. Although Mikkelsen was well-known in Denmark, he was hardly a household name in the UK. About three years ago, one of the officers had been watching the Nordic Noir series, *The Killing*, and was the first to notice the striking resemblance between Higgs and Mikkelsen. He came in the following morning, full of it, telling anyone who would listen, how Higgs was the spitting image of the Copenhagen mayoral election candidate Troels Hartmann. Nobody had heard of the drama, the character, or the actor – so the lookalike jibe didn't gain an awful lot of traction. He was briefly known as the Copenhagen Copper for about a week and then that was dropped, being far too long and not derisory enough for a usable nickname in a police station.

'Oh yes! I remember him. Nasty bit of goods,' said Brian.

'Has he been in touch, Brian? Has he called you, or turned up at the door, or asked you questions?'

'No, he hasn't. I'd have remembered him. Shifty bit of work … What car does he drive?'

'Car? I don't know. Why?'

'Try and think when you've seen him drive home or arrive at work.'

'Why do you want to know?' asked Lucy.

'Oh just answer the question! Do you know what car he drives?'

'I think it's one of those new Minis that are quite big. It's cream coloured, or stone they'd probably call it'

'He was here!' said Brian.

'What? Where? … When?'

'When you came round earlier. There was a cream-coloured Mini outside Tony and Marlina's ex-house.' That sounded wrong. It sounded as if he was blaming the house for Tony and Marlina no longer living there. Like the house had just upped and scarpered. 'There was a cream-coloured Mini with a dark-coloured man inside. He spent the whole time looking out at my house,' he said.

'Did you say a dark-coloured man? DS Higgs isn't dark coloured,' said Lucy.

'No, I know he's not. He's Light poached salmon - No. 286. I meant his clothing was dark-coloured, ergo he appeared as a dark-coloured man in a cream-coloured Mini.' Brian had a mental flash of Morgan Freeman wearing a short pleated tennis skirt.

'Did you say "ergo"?' Lucy asked. Brian wondered if Lucy was going to go through everything he'd said and ask him if he'd said them.

'Yes I said "ergo" … but I don't think I said Morgan Freeman … or tennis skirt … but I may have done. I lose track of what I've said out loud sometimes, but I'm pretty sure I said "ergo".'

But it seems like it was your Higgs – spying on us.'

'He's going to try and get me sacked. I shouldn't have come round to see you earlier. I lied to my boss about it, I compounded the lie when he questioned me and now it turns out Higgs has got evidence – proof of me being with you when I said I was ill at home. He's bringing it all in to show the boss at two.' Whatever codes of behaviour she had already breached, she had now certainly breached a handful more. It was such an unlikely situation that she should be discussing her possible sacking offences involving a murder suspect with that self-same murder suspect. But even harder to believe was that she found this unusual and eccentric man easier to talk to than any of her friends or work colleagues. She found him gentle, understanding and, in a strange way indeed, enjoyable to be around.

'Don't worry, I'll sort it,' he said. Of all the things that he could have said, this was the very one thing above all else that Lucy needed to hear.

58

Brian's soft shoe shuffle routine with the scrubbing brush shoes had started to create an impressive lather on the carpet. Unfortunately, Brian's attention had been focused more on the song and dance routine than the cleaning. consequently, there were two parallel channels of heavily scuffed carpet with parallel walls of dense white suds. He kicked the suds around and added more bubble bath and washing powder. Trying various approaches, which included skating, running on the spot and twisting, he bashed on with the carpet cleaning. The twisting was by far the best method and also lent itself to another song and dance routine. 'Twisting The Night Away' soon evolved into 'Twisting The Rug Away', which, as he was later to discover, was all too good a title. Brian had worked his way all over the visible area of carpet and had created a floor of thick white foam when the front doorbell rang. He ran, if the impeded movement could be called running, to the front door. As he got his fingers on the lock, the scrubbing brush strapped to his right foot got securely enmeshed with the deep coir welcome mat. His foot stayed where it was as he angled himself slightly to open the door.

'Hello, Bryan Ferry,' he said as he fell on the floor screaming, in considerable pain from his freshly turned ankle.

'Are you alright? What's the matter with your feet?' asked Bryan Ferry. He was concerned at Brian's screaming and had just noticed the bungees, rope and scrubbing brushes. It looked like he was wearing some type of built-up special-needs shoes.

'It's these cleaning shoes, they're difficult and a bit painful to walk in and because of them I've just done my ankle in, I expect I might have screamed a bit.'

'Yeah – I imagine they … Yeah I can see – yeah.'

'Come on in and I'll show you the radiator. There it is,' Brian said, limping into the room and making no mention of the white foamed carpet. It looked like it had snowed in the room yesterday and kids had left bare patches where they'd been scooping up handfuls for snowballs.

'What's happened here?' asked Bryan Ferry, concerned that he was facing a modern plumbing problem that he'd never encountered before. 'Did the radiator cause all this?'

'No, I tipped a bubble bath on the carpet to make use of the hot water,' explained Brian.

'A bit shallow I imagine?' Brian gave a blank look by way of response.

'So what can you do about the leak?' he said, returning them both to the reason for Bryan Ferry being there.

'Well I can see the cold feed pipe is fractured, so that will need replacing, but the radiator's old and it's half off the wall. I think it's a bit distorted – looks like someone's given it a good kicking. It would be just as easy to replace the whole radiator.'

'Right. How much would that cost?'

'Well I'll have to check, but I think I've got a new one of these in the van. I can do you a good deal if you have that.' Ever since he first met Bryan Ferry seven years ago Brian had waited for an opening such as this. It was too good to miss.

'Make me a deal,' he said, 'and make it straight.' Looking directly at Ferry he continued. 'All signed and sealed, I'll take it.' He might have got away with it had he left it there but Brian couldn't resist the temptation to carry on.

'To Robert E Lee I'll shoooow it,' he warbled.

'Yeah alright, alright, I geddit,' said Bryan Ferry, which slightly spoilt it for Brian, but Ferry, give him his due, entered into the spirit of things.

'We've been around a long time,' he continued. 'So I'll do for cost price, say a hundred quid all in, supplied and fitted – for cash, OK?'

The radiator was removed, the new one fitted and the whole system bled and up and running in a remarkably short time. As always Bryan Ferry was very neat and did a highly professional job – very much like his namesake. For the entire duration of his visit, no further mention was made of the dense white suds covering the carpet or Brian's scrubbing brush shoes.

When the plumber had left, Brian was keen to get in touch with Lucy to tell her that the whole thing had been sorted. She had appeared concerned at the broken radiator and leak and he was sure she would be as impressed as he was at how quickly and well the problem had been resolved. He rang Lucy's number and she answered quite quickly. He just managed to tell her that Bryan Ferry had fixed his radiator when it became clear that she was quite agitated.

59

Poor Lucy was in a state. She sounded stressed and worried. It appeared that the slimy Copenhagen Copper DS Higgs was trying to drop her in it. She seemed convinced that Brian was somehow involved. When Lucy had been around earlier, just at the time she was building up to proposing to him, he had noticed a cream car parked outside. It was one of those new huge Minis. These days, whenever he saw one, he had the repeating thought that the old and new versions of the Mini were very similar to the old and new versions of the Daleks. Comparing the new big pumped-up Minis to the original genuinely tiny little Minis was very similar to a comparison of the more recent all-new bigger, brighter, bulkier Daleks and the original 1964 Daleks fought off by William Hartnell.

The cream car that he'd seen outside was a big Maxi type Mini belonging to DS Higgs. DS Higgs – Distinctly Shifty Higgs. Dirty Scumbag Higgs. Dodgy Suspicious Higgs. *Right well, I'm going to turn you into Decidedly Scuppered Higgs you Diarrhoea Stinking Higgs*, thought Brian.

On the night when Lucy slept over – for that was how he saw it – Brian had discovered the notebook in Lucy's purse. The back half of the notebook was a telephone address book. Working on the premise that information was power, Brian had copied down all the names, addresses, phone numbers and email addresses for the people recorded there. He had no reason to do this other than they may one day come in handy. Today was possibly that day. Lucy had the contact details for most of the people she worked with. It only appeared to be members of the police service whose details she'd saved. The front of the book had notes regarding cases and enquiries. Other names and numbers had been jotted down. There were several dates and times with arrows linking them to names. There were a few crossings out. Brian's name was there twice. Once as 'Brian Rayment – 10.30' – once as 'Rayment / hat?'. All of this was too much to copy down, so while Lucy had been sound asleep in bed, as Brian remembered it, he photographed each page. Unfortunately, these had all been lost along with the complete photo-shoot of Lucy. He was now very glad he'd gone 'old school' and written down the names and addresses with pen and paper. The action of physically writing made the recall of what had been written that much easier. He could now mentally run through most of the names on that list and he knew that DS Higgs was amongst them. He went to the list now and found his address. Using the postcode he soon brought up an online map of the house location. He shifted to Google Earth to get a close-up roadside view of the house. There it was and – Well! – Look at that! – There was the car! The final proof that it had been DS Higgs who had been spying on them. Dirty Spy Higgs. Brian zoomed in and had a good look all over the face of the house to get to know it. He zoomed into the general area of the front door and the letterbox in particular. It appeared to be a regular-sized letterbox. As he was getting to know the look of the place he was also working on the rudimentary outline of a plan, which at the moment involved putting something through the letterbox. The idea came to him to try Higgs's number – still looking at the screen and the image of Higgs house he dialled the number. It rang for five times and was then answered by a spritely sounding woman.

'Hello, Marjorie Higgs.' Brian was very tempted to answer this with, 'Oh hard luck love!' but didn't. He started to improvise.

'This is Superintendent Andrew Richardson. I've got a package of files for DS Higgs. Do you know when he's likely to be back?'

'Hello, Andrew I didn't recognise you. Your voice sounds a bit rough. Are you keeping alright?'

'Tail end of a cold, Margaret-jorie,' said Brian, improvising quickly and impressively, despite stumbling over Marjorie's name. 'Fancy you noticing that. You'd make a good detective.' They both laughed at that. 'So do you have any idea when he's likely to be back?' asked Brian breathing through his mouth and trying to roughen up his voice a bit.

'Yes, Ken's shift finishes at ten, so he'll probably be back indoors by ten-thirty. Can I leave him a message?' Ken! That was it – Ken. Why didn't he remember that?

'No that's alright. You can just tell him when he gets in M-Marjorie' said Brian, adding even more of a full-of-a-cold element to his voice.

'Well, I won't see him till the morning. I go out every Thursday evening to meet my sister and her husband, and I won't be back till long after Ken's asleep. You do sound rough don't you, Andrew? You should be back home in bed. You're not still at that station working are you?' Brian reigned in the flu symptoms a bit and ignored her concern for his well-being.

'It's just that I've got this important package for him. Is there somewhere I could leave it where it would be safe?'

'Yes, you could leave it in the porch. It's always open and it's perfectly dry.'

'Do you think that will be safe? From prying eyes, I mean' said Brian using his normal voice again. 'It's very sensitive material.'

'I'll tell you what,' said Marjorie Higgs in a conspiratorial tone, 'seeing as it's you. There's a pair of my gardening gloves in a small basket in the porch, on the floor on the right-hand side as you come in. We always leave a front door key in one of the gloves. If you open the front door you could leave your package just inside in the hallway. As long as you lock the door again and put the key back in the glove.'

'Much appreciated, Marjorie. I'm very grateful,' said Brian – and he was. 'Have a nice evening, Marjorie.'

'I will. And you take care of yourself, Andrew. You sound terrible, I hardly recognised you.'

It was rare that Brian's improv sessions turned out to be so successful or fruitful. In a few minutes, he had arranged easy access right into Higgsy's Housey. He had already abandoned the initial 'letterbox plot' or 'letter-bomb plot', as he changed it to at the point of abandonment. Even though nothing had taken place and it was all at the initial ideas stage, it gave Brian a greater sense of achievement to be abandoning a letter-bomb plot, than to be abandoning a letterbox plot. There was a lot to organise and set in motion before Higgsy arrived Homey.

He scoured the house for a variety of everyday items that he needed. He was hoping to avoid the need to go shopping and so was very pleased when he was able to make such a good start. After an intense half hour, he had gathered together a biscuit tin, some candles, a length of yellow-sleeved electrical wire, some duct tape, two nine-volt batteries a nearly solid lump of grey plasticine, that hasn't been used for twenty years, and the Margaret Rutherford hat he last wore three weeks ago. The one thing he just couldn't put his hands on was an alarm clock. This was a shame because it was a key part of the whole plan. He'd have to leave that for the moment and pick up the search later. He left all the items he had found, together on the sofa, and went to his computer. He Googled 'Humphrey Bogart' images and the screen filled with superb studio portraits of the iconic actor. Brian selected a picture that had one of the worse likenesses but was square on to the camera. He enlarged it to fill an A4 sheet and printed a copy. It wouldn't be so wise to use a well-known picture of Bogie. When the portrait had printed he held it up by the side of his face and looked in the mirror. It was a good size, slightly big if anything but that was fine. He cut around the face to create what was in effect a Humphrey Bogart mask. Using a short strip of the duct tape folded double, he stuck the mask to his forehead and helped keep it there by donning the Rutherford hat and jamming it down to his eyes. Looking downwards behind the mask he was able to see his phone that he'd just taken from his pocket. It was difficult to navigate clearly but he soon set it to front camera. Shooting blind, he fired off several what he hoped would be selfies. He changed the angle of the camera and took several more. Then another half dozen while shaking the phone to create some blur, then a final burst, angling his head differently with each shot. He looked down behind the mask again to check that the photographs had come out and that he was actually in shot. He could see that he had a good selection of pictures. On a roll now and starting to speed up he removed the mask and hat, took the phone to the computer and plugged it in, bringing the twenty or thirty shots up on the screen. Half of them he could delete immediately. They were either too blatantly a mask, or had clipped off part of his face. He also deleted the last two shots he had taken, as the flash had accidentally been tapped on, and the pictures were burnt out almost white. This left him with six shots to choose from. Repeatedly running through the six shots, he quickly narrowed it down to two that were emerging as the best two shots. Making the final decision between these last two took longer than all the other deletions, but he finally picked the winner. Of all the images, this was the most convincing as a real person. There were no creases in the paper showing, the hat and the face sat well together and there was a slight element of blur, which was perfect – just what he wanted. Having a tendency towards obsession over such things, he still felt it needed tweaking. He copied it into Photoshop and then darkened it considerably, lessened the contrast and added even more blur. The final procedure was to come in tight on the face and crop it closely, removing any edge or slight suggestion of it not being a real person. He printed a copy and held it out at arm's length. Studying it with his eyes half-closed, he once again admired his own skill.

60

He was staring at an image of someone who bore more than a passing resemblance to Humphrey Bogart, with some sort of hat pulled down over the eyes. The image was indistinct, staring out of the shadows, and had quite a threatening look. It was perfect. That was stage one complete and ready to go.

Now he had to make the bomb. First thing's first. He couldn't decide whether to take the role himself or hand it over to Mark Strong. Ideally, he would have liked Mark Strong to audition for the part, but being honest to himself, Brian knew the real reason for this was to watch Mark and get a one-to-one masterclass on how to tackle the role. Maybe it would be better if Mark took the role, and he could direct the scene. It was a well-established pattern, that the most successful actors of any generation, in time, move on to become directors themselves. Brian was quite excited by the idea of directing this particular scene. He already had some camera shots and lighting worked out, but there was a snag in that there was a bit of a paradox for Brian. He was happy to direct Mark Strong in the role, but of course, Mark Strong wasn't here. This meant he would have to play the part of Mark Strong, an actor taking on the role of the assassin bomb-maker. This was quite a nice solution for it meant that Brian could legitimately be billed as actor-director.

'Assassin' was now bothering him though.

Should it be assassin or murderer? This was a thing he needed to get right. After all, he had killed three people – he needed to know what his title should be. Assassin sounded so much cooler than murderer. 'Assassin' had a bit of class to it. Bryan Ferry, for example, the real one, could have been an assassin, but he would never have been a murderer. However, Bryan Ferry the plumber, thought Brian, continuing this line of enquiry, Bryan Ferry the plumber – he could have been a murderer. Brian knew he wouldn't be able to rest and continue with the bomb-making until he's sorted at the question of assassin vs murderer. He went back to his PC and Googled 'assassin vs murderer what is the difference?' After reading several short concise definitions he came away knowing for certain that he was a murderer. It was disappointing, but at least it was sorted. Brian was the director and surely it was the director's prerogative to make any changes he felt necessary to enhance a film. Brian summarised to himself. So in real life I'm a murderer, but in the film I shall be playing an actor, who is playing an assassin. That seemed to cover everything and now he needed to crack on. He started with the five white six-inch candles. With the sharp knife he squared off the wick ends then taped the candles together tightly. With more of the strong duct tape, he securely fixed the bundle of candles into the corner of the biscuit tin. The two batteries he taped together in a similar way, and then fixed them securely in the opposite corner of the tin. Next was the plasticine, but this needed quite a lot of work to get it softened up into a usable malleable state. When it had warmed up and was easy to shape, he pressed the whole block of plasticine into the edge of the tin directly under the candles.

The whole scene would start in the other room with a long slow tracking shot along the floor. The camera would move slowly at ground level through the irregularly foamed carpet; the lighting would be very dark with knocked back colour, almost black and white. The soundtrack comes from a background radio playing '5 Minutes' by the Stranglers. It would sound very distant to start with but would increase in volume as the tracking shot progressed and the colour and brightness of it increased. Finally, the camera would find a pool of light and someone working under a strong lamp. The screen would be filled with two feet wearing expensive shoes, and the legs of the chair in which the shoe-wearer is sitting working. The camera stops there momentarily and we hear small noises of the bomb-maker at work. The stripple of a length of duct tape being unrolled, clicks and rubbings, a brief sawing from a knife, then the film pans upwards over the bomb-maker's hunched body and around until we see the partially constructed bomb in his hands. The lighting now is strong and contrasty under the closeness of the lamp, the colour is bright and the Stranglers are at full volume as the track ends with the ticking clock.

61

The ticking clock! Packed away in a suitcase from when he went on holiday two or three years ago. He ran upstairs, opened the loft hatch and lowered the ladder. In the attic, Brian had kept all the old suitcases he'd ever owned, many of which had broken handles or wheels and were worn too much to use. They were useful for storage, and all were crammed much fuller now than they ever had been in their working lives as suitcases. He was looking specifically for a dark red faux leather 'Revelation' case. The attached straps with buckles had become loose due to unravelled stitching – this was why the case had been relegated to the attic storage system. It was easy to see under three other very heavy-looking cases. Brian briefly considered trying to haul it out from under the three, but quickly went for the ultimately quicker option of lifting the other suitcases off, one by one. Protected by the other suitcases, the top of the Revelation had remained shiny and dust-free. The heavy brass zip that ran right around the soft top had a lovely smooth uninterrupted action that immediately became familiar again. So many zips, whether on clothing or suitcases, were a struggle. There was the common irritation of them pinching the edge of the pleat designed to conceal the zip. Once the pleat or fabric had been pinched you could usually say goodbye to the next five of ten minutes.

The suitcase was one of those that had rigid sides and base, but a soft flexible top. Brian lifted the top and flipped it backwards, revealing a treasure trove of forgotten items and memories. There were several books he'd been meaning to read, a very nice chunky pullover that he had assumed he had left in Croatia, there was a bundle of two sets of knives, forks, spoons and teaspoons. These were all held together with a thick elastic band which snapped as soon as he picked the bundle up, sending the cutlery onto the attic floor. Why had he even saved these things? What are they doing in the suitcase? It came back to him. He and his sister Sandie had taken them for possible use on picnics or when they went camping. It hadn't been worth the effort, given the palaver they had caused at customs. The cutlery had been confiscated at customs and Brian was told he could pick it up on his return journey. The customs officer had told him that they needed to confiscate the knives and the forks but he could hang on to the spoons and teaspoons because they weren't regarded as offensive weaponry. Brian put forward a reasonably forceful argument for the spoons being offensive weapons so that they could be kept all together with the knives and forks. This put Brian into the slightly dodgy situation of claiming that he was indeed intentionally and knowingly carrying offensive weapons to the airport. Brian kept the four spoons with him, unused for the duration of the holiday, and under pressure from Sandie, retrieved the knives and forks on their return. They had remained in the case since that day. Brian found going through the case very exciting, in a child-on-Christmas-morning sort of way. A great deal of the stuff in the case had been added after the cutlery holiday. Two new shirts, still in their packaging, he was thrilled to find. He had bought them, put them away safely and forgotten about them. Now he'd found them again he was certain they would move into first and second place in his 'favourite shirts' list. Brian had favourite lists for shirts, trousers, shoes, films and CDs. They weren't actual physical lists. He didn't need physical lists, as he kept a good mental record of all of them. There was a set of child's toy handcuffs, again, still in their packaging. They were good quality ones – metal and with two keys. He had bought them for his niece when she was five years old and into cops and robbers. He'd put them away safely, as with the shirts, until her birthday but again, as with the shirts, he'd forgotten them. He'd discovered them once before, years later, and still considered giving them to his niece. However, the idea of an uncle giving his 17-year old niece a set of handcuffs was creepy, to say the least, and so they went back in the case. A small package of bubble wrap was found to contain two Corgi 497 'Man From Uncle' cars. Oldsmobile Thrush-busters. They were both fairly extensively chipped. One of them was missing the gun clicker on the roof, although both Illya Kuryakin and Napoleon Solo were still present and correct. The other was missing Napoleon Solo but the clickers still worked. The bubble wrap was an indication of the value Brian placed on the two toy cars. It was a restoration project that now was unlikely to get off the ground. He smiled to himself as he realised quite a big coincidence. He hadn't given a thought to Napoleon Solo, or to be more precise, Robert Vaughn, for probably a decade, and yet today he'd thought of him on two separate occasions. Just now, seeing the two Corgi cars, and lying in bed this morning. He had experienced a very enjoyable dream involving him being invited on various TV quiz shows. He'd won *Who Wants*

To Be A Millionaire? without phoning a friend or asking the audience, got the highest score ever reached on *Celebrity Squares* and he was currently on *Celebrity Mastermind*. His specialist subject was the life and times of Steve McQueen. His final question, the one that would win him the series and the trophy was, 'Brian K Rayment, can you name' – wheeeep – wheeeep – wheeeep – 'I've started so I'll finish, and of course, this will now be your last chance to take the Mastermind title, trophy and the twenty million pound prize money donated by Sir Mick Jagger. Can you name the other six actors to appear with Steve McQueen in *The Magnificent Seven*?'

He woke up at this point and started to put in some sensible time on the answer. He could remember five of them, he even remembered Horst Buchholz, but it was one of the obvious ones he kept forgetting. Lying in bed and marking them off on his fingers, he could now remember six of the seven. Then it hit him! Steve McQueen of course! He was given Steve McQueen. The much bigger problem was how should he present his answer? He could start with something along the lines of, 'Well, there's Horst Buchholz of course and Brad Dexter.' Then he could slowly pretend to remember Steve Mc Queen, Bronson, Robert Vaughn and Coburn, spinning it out to the last few seconds when he would finally get the obvious Yul Brynner. Or the other way he could do it is the rattle off the first six and then say 'No, it's no good I just can't remember the seventh one.' He could allow himself to be pressured, 'Go on Brian! Have a guess! Might as well have a guess – nothing to lose.'

He could finish with, 'No I've no idea! … OK … Total shot in the dark … Horst Buchholz.' Brian decided he was going to do it that way.

He came across his mpharm degree certificate, a letter from Sir Harold Wilson's secretary, who had replied to Brian's complaint about the flagpole in Harold's garden in the Scilly Isles and … the alarm clock!

62

Brian took the alarm clock back to the partially completed bomb. The clock was exactly as he'd remembered it. A traditional alarm clock with two bells on top. He recalled that it had a very loud tick. He turned the key in the back of the clock a good dozen times, and it started ticking. It didn't matter if the clock kept good time or not, but the ticking was an important element. On the back of a clock there was another small, milled dial to set the alarm, and next to that, a short lever to prime it. As Brian recalled, you could lift the lever to get the alarm to ring at any time, provided the clock had been wound up. He lifted the lever now and the little cream clock leapt into life, vibrating with the ringing bells being struck with the small oscillating hammer. Before he went any further he needed to do a quick test. Taking one of the short lengths of wire he'd already cut, he wound one end of it around the alarm lever. He gave a couple more turns of the wind-up key ensuring there was enough clockwork power to give the bells a good test. Brian then yanked the wire upwards, triggering the alarm once again. Lovely. Fixing the alarm clock securely inside the biscuit tin was no easy task. It was heavy and awkward. The clock face needed to be visible and the alarm bells must remain free to operate. He found the best approach was to use several strips of duct tape to hold the base of the alarm clock securely to the base of the tin. This also gave him completely free access to wind up the alarm clock and do some further tests. He had now reached the final stage that would bring the whole thing together. Using the wire strippers he exposed each end of the ten different lengths of yellow-sleeved wire he'd snipped off. The three longest lengths he coiled carefully and tightly around a pencil, then slid the pencil out leaving a very impressive looking coiled wire. Very bomb-like Brian thought.

The soldering iron had been plugged in for twenty minutes now. He knew he wouldn't feel completely like a bomb maker until he started using the soldering iron. He soldered three of the lengths of wire, two straight and one coiled, to the back of the alarm clock. He then soldered two more lengths, one of each, to the batteries. Finally, to complete the soldering, he attached the other end of a straight wire from the clock to the battery. Using the four remaining free ends of wire and one new piece of coiled wire, he linked the remaining elements of the bomb together. The bared wire ends pushed easily into the wax candles and even more easily into the plasticine. The bomb itself was complete. Of course, it wasn't a bomb, just a collection of household objects and rubbish, but the effect was astonishing. It was the archetypal movie bomb and yet Brian still felt something was missing. It looked too clean. It didn't look worked on or assembled. A real bomb would have a grubbiness, an oiliness to it. He went to the small storage cupboard under the stairs and fetched the remainder of the box of latex gloves and his can of three-in-one oil – his Father, Son and Holy Ghost oil.

'Ease your worries. Ease your guilt. Ease your body, with

the new Three-in-One Father, Son and Holy Ghost easing oil.'

Brian stretched and snapped on a pair of the latex gloves and squeezed out a small drop of oil into his left hand. He worked his oily fingers all over the plasticine and candles to start with until they took on a grimy, greasy, sweating look. He was going to move on to the batteries and the alarm clock, but found it wasn't necessary. In his massage of the plasticine and candle, they had picked up enough of a smeary patina to do the job nicely.

There was one more thing he wanted to do with the bomb. He wasn't at all convinced it would work, but it was certainly worth a try. It took him six attempts, but with minor adjustments each time he got a working trip switch to set the alarm bells ringing. It was a refinement of his earlier first test with the wire loop. Eventually, he found he had to solder the wire to the alarm lever and the other end to the metal biscuit tin lid. When the lid was lifted it pulled the alarm lever and set the bells ringing. The one problem now was getting the lid to fit on snugly. Even though it was a very deep biscuit tin, it was slightly too shallow to close the lid properly, because of the clock being taped in an upright position. Brian tried tipping it backwards, which annoyingly but not surprisingly made it even taller. He solved the problem by simply unscrewing and removing the base of the alarm clock, which lowered it enough, when it was re-taped into position, to get the lid of the tin on firmly.

He gave the clock a final wind up and took his time setting the tripwire up. The whole tin was ticking more loudly now. A lucky side effect of the enclosed tin was that it acted as a sound box for the ticking clock. As he carried it to the far side of the room he envisaged a camera following him closely, keeping focused on his hands for the whole shot up until the moment he placed the ticking bomb on the table. He walked back to the far side of the room and looked at the tin from a distance. After a moment he strode purposefully towards it and lifted the lid. The stark ring of the alarm split the silence of the room. Zoom in to close-up of Brian slowly, almost imperceptibly, breaking into a smile.

63

Brian peeled off the old oily latex gloves and binned them. Then, having put on a fresh pair and a spare pair in his back pocket, he slid the print of the Humphrey Bogart photograph inside a large travel atlas to prevent it from creasing. He carefully picked up his movie-prop bomb, as if it were a real one, and made his way to the car. It was 8:15, which gave Brian a generous two hours. He knew exactly where Ken Higgs lived and had already worked out the route to take. It was only three miles away, but he knew it would take him at least twenty minutes, even at this time of night. This was due, as always, to the ever-present roadworks, traffic lights and consequent traffic snarl-ups. He wasn't too worried about the hold up as Higgsy would have the same problem later. Brian had brought with him the Margaret Rutherford hat, which was now getting far more use than he originally imagined, and the largest coat he possessed. A thick navy reefer jacket. At just before 8:40 Brian pulled up outside number 146 Shakespeare Avenue – the house that he had earlier spent some time looking at on Google Earth. You need to think straight now, Brian. He'd already realised his first mistake – he should have worn the reefer jacket. It was now quite a reach and a struggle to get the large coat from the back seat and put it on while sitting in the driver's seat of his relatively small car. When he'd finally got the coat on and buttoned, he pulled up the collar high and put on the hat, pulling it down over his eyes. He didn't want to be seen or recognised or give any neighbours a chance to provide a good description of him. Wearing the hat and the coat, he hoped that any description given would be sufficiently close to their Rutherford/Bogart suspect. He walked up to the front door with the bomb and the atlas and rang the front doorbell. This was just a precaution, he didn't expect anyone to be in and no one was, so he let himself into the porch. Marjorie's detailed description of where the key was hidden was faultless, and he went straight to it. He supposed an enhanced power of description was one of the resulting benefits of being married to a policeman. Well done, Marjorie. Having checked around through the windows of the porch, to see there were no overly interested neighbours or passers-by, he opened the front door and slipped inside, shutting the door after him. The place was in darkness, but with outstretched arms he made his way down the hallway to the back of the house. He kept his eyes shut as walked from the front door, straight through to the open-plan kitchen area in the rear. Whenever he was in a completely dark place, Brian shut his eyes. To be walking around with your eyes open and not be able to see is an unnerving thing. If you walk around with your eyes shut, you expect not to see. By the simple measure of shutting your eyes, you can turn an abnormal, even scary situation, into a normal one. When he was obviously at the back of the house, he felt around the walls for a light switch and flicked on the first one he found on a wall to his right.

It appeared to be the main living room area. The whole of the floor was open plan and the living room was an extension of the kitchen area. The only sound was the ticking from the biscuit tin. Looking back from the living room area towards the front of the house, Brian assumed he was looking into some kind of study. Although there was no light on in that section the light he'd switched on was illuminating it enough to see. A small red LED light glowed brightly in the dim room. It came from an ancient-looking computer monitor in standby mode. Brian went over to the computer, took hold of the mouse and jiggled it on the mouse mat. He hoped it might awaken the dormant computer and yet it was still surprising to see the screen flash on into life when it did. Looking at the desktop he was overcome with a mix of pride and smugness and a dash of scorn when he saw that Decidedly Sloppy Ken Higgsy Higgs was still only using Windows 7. Surely everyone had moved on to Windows 10 by now. Brian gave an audible 'Huh!' to register his derision. He was extremely tuned into the shortcoming of the Windows 7 system and the benefits of Windows 10 having spent a good six-months deliberating and researching and preparing himself to bite the bullet and make the upgrade. He finally bit the bullet and forked out for Windows 10 and its subsequent, unwanted but inevitable, upheaval of getting to grips with a new computer system. This was only a few weeks ago, just before his little murder spree in the garage, when Tony and Marlina bit their bullets. Thinking back to that interesting night in the garage, which seemed an age ago now, he was annoyed at the line the press coverage had taken. In nearly all reportage of the murders and the ensuing search for the suspect, they had referred to 'the five-times killer' or 'suspected of killing five'. Brian had always detested the idea of anyone taking credit for something they hadn't done. He had only killed three.

'Oh you only killed three did you?' asked Brian, being both advocate and defendant now. 'Well that was jolly decent of you!'

'What I'm saying is, everyone seems to be claiming that I killed five people, whereas, in fact, I only killed three people – just sixty per cent of the killage claimed.'

Brian frequently got himself involved with these internal courtroom dramas, which were played out to his rules and rulings, very much on an 'anything goes' basis. He always came out the winner, but there again he always played all the roles. He judged himself to be very knowledgeable on most aspects of the law and based his courtroom knowledge and performances on his extensive viewing experience of British police and legal procedural dramas. Occasionally he would borrow from the American and Hollywood style of prosecution, wandering around the courtroom and gripping the wooden rail of the jury's stall to deliver his impassioned closing speech to a riveted and tearful jury. On the most memorable of these cases, Brian was prosecuting himself for being rude to a librarian. His closing speech, delivered as Kevin Costner with an educated deep southern accent, reduced every single member of the jury to tears and he was of course found guilty. He was sentenced to death, but a compassionate and heartfelt plea for leniency from Costner got the sentence reduced to life imprisonment.

'I put it to you, Mr Rayment, that murdering three people in cold blood, rather than five, doesn't make you any the less of a murderer – maybe a less proficient one.'

'Well I put it straight back to you, my learned advocate, that sixty per cent is regarded as a fail in most exams, therefore I am a failure as a murderer. Consequently, if I failed as a murderer, by definition that means I am not a murderer, it means I haven't succeeded as a murderer, I didn't pass the murder exam. If you had only achieved sixty per cent in the advocacy exam you would not be a solicitor – you would not now be acting as a legal advocate. Am I making myself clear?'

'I don't know whether you're trying to be funny or facetious or whether you are just a lunatic, Mr Rayment.'

'Yes! There's rather a lot you don't know isn't there, my learned prosecutor? Let me help you out! I am indeed a lunatic but I was also trying to be funny. So, as you can see, you had two out of three – sixty-six point six per cent this time. However, being under the required seventy per cent, you would still fail even a mere accountancy exam with that success rate. I must say I am beginning to question your qualifications. I put it to you, to use your own hackneyed legal jargonise, that you are a combination of overconfidence and cluelessness. An ill-informed popinjay. A pompous under-educated nitwit. This being the case there is no charge to answer and I should walk from this court of law a free man.'

'Sir! You are a bounder and a cad and you are an insult to honest murderers and other members of the legal profession. I challenge you to a duel at five a.m. in the morning somewhere misty and cold. Pistols at dawn at thirty paces.' Brian took the spare pair of latex gloves from his back pocket and slapped himself around the face with them, thus securing the fixture for the duel with himself. 'Pistols at dawn is a bit archaic don't you think? But I would expect no more from a milksop fop like you. Why don't we bring this up to date and say Thompson submachine guns at ten feet?' Brian was beginning to work himself up into a bit of a state, to the point where he had forgotten who he was arguing with, what he was arguing about and how exactly he had ended up scheduled to fight a duel with himself, with machine guns no less. One of him wasn't going to survive!

64

While Brian was otherwise occupied in playing out the court scene between himselves, the monitor had timed out and gone to black screen again. He jiggled the mouse once more and the PC lit up again. He took a good look around the desktop to see for which programmes Higgsy had saved shortcuts. The pictures file was huge and full of holiday shots of Higgsy and presumably Marjorie. The folders of photographs were arranged chronologically with the most recent at the top of the page. The newest file was dated two days ago and was titled 'BR + DCIW'. Brian clicked on the file opening it up to reveal twenty-four photographs. There were shots of Brian's house, shots of Brian leaving the house and of Brian returning home. More of Lucy arriving at the house and going into the house. Several obviously zoomed-in blurred shots through the window of the two of them and finally a few shots of Lucy leaving and Lucy driving off.

Brian's immediate knee-jerk response was to delete them all as quickly as possible. Last year though, he recalled his computer chap saying to him that even when you deleted items they were always retrievable somehow – if you knew what you were doing. 'If you knew what you were doing! Cheeky devil.' At the time this wasn't what Brian wanted to hear. He had wanted to delete some things get rid of them permanently, destroy them so that no one could ever find them again, but also remembered the computer chap saying that there was a much better way to get rid of unwanted items. Change them in some way and save them in their new form. Right Mr DS Dirty Smutty Higgs, I'll happily change these for you. Being very familiar with Windows 7, Brian soon found Windows Explorer and Googled – 'naked man's bottom'. He was hunched in close to the screen, squinting to improve his focus, but the rows of images that suddenly appeared made him back off with a start. He winced as he selected the most objectionable fat arse in front of him and clicked 'copy'. Opening each picture from Higgsy's recent file, in turn, he clicked 'paste' followed by 'save'. Within moments the BR +DCIW file comprised two dozen identical shots of the awful fat arse. 'Show that to your boss then, Higgsy.'

While he was in photo-manipulation mode, he had a quick nose around Ken and Marjorie's holiday picture files.

Brian thought Marjorie looked like a schoolboy. It was a strange phenomenon he'd noticed before and had tried to explain to a number of people, none of whom had been convinced or interested. He had frequently noticed that mumsy-type women aged between, say, twenty-eight and forty, could often look very much like thirteen to fifteen-year-old schoolboys. Once you had the idea in mind, it could be humorous or unnerving depending on the situation of observation. He once saw his bank manager at a wine and cheese party, arm in arm with what looked like a thirteen-year-old boy called Michael Mullis with whom he'd gone to school. The fact that Mullis was wearing a dowdy tweed skirt did nothing to improve the impression. It happened when these mumsy wives had a rounded, scrubbed, homely face and a head of shortish thick wavy hair. You could always find some second or third-year grammar school boys, usually the shy types not into sport, who had the same exact look. Looking at these photographs now, Brian was keen to superimpose Marjorie's head onto a schoolboy's body. This would be quite a simple task to do in Photoshop and Brian found himself looking on the desktop to see if Higgsy had the Photoshop programme. Yes! There it is! He opened it up and while it was loading, went back to the holiday photographs. He scrolled through them all again until he came across the one where Marjorie looked at her most teenage boyish. He clicked on and copied the photograph, then went into the now-open Photoshop. Once he'd opened a new document he clicked 'paste' and the image of Marjorie appeared on screen. Now he just needed the schoolboy. Having just used it, he went straight back to open up Internet Explorer again and entered a search this time for 'Schoolboys in short trousers'. Unfortunately, most of the thousands of shots seemed to be school photographs of rows of seated boys or 'back to school' photographs from retailers selling school uniforms. He put in another search for 'Teenage boys in shorts on their own'. This was better but still not quite right. After a few more searches, including 'Young teenage boys in a natural setting', 'Teenage schoolboys in a field', 'Teenage schoolboys in vests and pants' and 'Young teenage schoolboys at home', Brian finally found the right picture, which he copied and pasted next to the picture of Marjorie. First, he had to balance the size of the pictures, which meant reducing the picture of Marjorie and Ken so that Marjorie's head was the same size as the schoolboy's head.

Now he had to tweak the colour and tone. Marjorie was a bit washed out, whereas the schoolboy was bright and contrasty. With some minor adjustments to each picture, they were soon well-balanced and had a similar tone, colour, intensity, and overall look about them. The picture of Ken and Marjorie showed them posing on a brightly lit pavement in front of an empty road. The overall effect was of a uniform pale grey background behind them. This was why he had chosen this particular picture of the schoolboy, as he too had an almost identical pale grey background. The similar background made the final cloning procedure very easy. Brian selected the soft cloning tool and transposed the schoolboy's body into Ken and Marjorie's photograph. Within a minute or two, Ken was posing on the sunny pavement with a fourteen-year old schoolboy who happened to look a bit like Marjorie. Both of them were smiling a lot, which put an extra little spin on the image. Brian was very pleased with the result and, as usual, extremely impressed with his own skills. It seemed a shame to delete all this talent and craftsmanship so he saved the picture of Ken and the schoolboy Marjorie, and copied it back into their holiday photo file for them to appreciate another day.

65

Bernard Ollocks! The time was going on. It was almost 9.30. He was supposed to be the Notorious Bath Bomber and here he was, honing his photo-manipulation skills. But this was more time well spent, this was what life was all about, this was what computers were all about. What better or more useful way to spend your time, than cloning the body of a schoolboy onto a middle-aged woman's head convincingly? Brian always fancied his chances as a forger. He felt sure he could have made a real go of it, had he not been a successful pharmacist. He had the eye, you see, and a capacity for taking pains and giving attention to detail, which he regarded as the minimum requirements for being a forger. He guessed it would also be useful, even necessary, to spend a little time inside – not a long stretch, just six months or maybe a year, to pick up some useful tips and contacts. He would need to learn about access to vintage papers, inks, paints etc. He would need to work with a good 'dip' – someone who could steal passports, driving licences and other documents to order. He would also need to know and trust several fences. One specifically for forged notes and currency, another for paintings and artwork and probably a third specialist fence for driving licenses, passports and other person-specific sensitive documents. During his brief part-time teaching spell at Somerset College of Arts and Technology – SCAT – (he was sure that was deliberate) he became quite friendly with Steve, the head of the design department. Steve had a healthy side-line forging vehicle tax discs for both students and other staff members alike for sixty quid a pop. This was at a time when the only checks made were from traffic wardens or bobbies on the beat looking in vehicle windscreens for out-of-date discs. Steve was averaging about three of these a week. On one occasion a student told him he only had £40 available so he produced an eight-month disc for him, knowing full well he would need a replacement in eight months. Brian had been as impressed with this piece of business acumen, as he was with seeing Steve make good financial use of his artistic skills.

In the past, Brian had spent many an hour weighing up which would be the best items to forge. Banknotes were not a good idea. They would take a lot of work for very little return. He quite liked the idea of forging high denomination foreign currency, as the scarcity of everyday use would render them almost free from criticism or scrutiny. He had even considered creating non-existent currency, for example a $200 bill. There would be nothing to compare it with. If he could convince people that such a thing existed, he was home and dry – it wouldn't matter what the design was, provided it looked sufficiently like a banknote. However, the effort was still likely to outweigh any return. Brian had already dabbled in some very low-level forgery, that both fulfilled his creative desire and bought him a few drinks along the way. Following his pursuit of minimum work for maximum return, he decided that forging the autographs of famous celebrities was the best way to go.

This all happened at a time before he was a criminal – before he'd murdered three people, before he'd stolen two jerry cans of petrol. At that time, the idea of forging autographs for monetary gain concerned Brian greatly and offended his sense of morality. The big problem of course was selling them. He could hardly walk around the streets of Bath shouting, 'Get your autographs here. Authentic autographs! All your favourites! Fresh this morning!' or some such thing. At the time, he had planned to do a boot sale. Like most people these days, he had lots of rubbish and excess 'stuff' that he needed to get rid of. A loose idea was forming in his mind, that any autographs he created he could have on his boot sale table in amongst all his other items and see what response they got, if any. It wouldn't be a hard sell. He would give people the excitement of discovering them for themselves. Two days later it was no longer a loose idea but a fixed plan that was underway. He scoured the local charity shops, as he often did, specifically looking for a teenager's pop star picture book from the 60s. In the Bath Women's Aid shop, in amongst a stack of children's books, he found a very battered, 'Thank Your Lucky Stars' annual from 1966. He was looking for a picture of the Beatles from the mid-60s period, and there were plenty in this Lucky Stars book. He bought it for £1.50. Before he went off hunting for the book, he had already done some research on the Beatles' signatures, and had printed off several very good examples. His first thought was to have four good clear autographs on the picture, but thinking about it, that would be a very unlikely item to come across at a boot sale. He decided on two signatures – those of John Lennon and Ringo Starr. He had a whole backup story worked out about the other two being backstage when the autographs were obtained. After several A4 sheets of practice signatures, he added his version of John's and Ringo's to the picture. On the day of the boot sale next to Lansdown Racecourse, Brian brought along the picture, with his unwanted items, trinkets and rubbish. It was now placed behind glass in a small wooden picture frame which immediately made it appear treasured – special. It was the only thing on Brian's table in which anyone was interested. And everyone was interested in it. While Brian was still transferring his sale items from the car to his pasting table, someone asked, 'What do you want for your picture?'

'I hadn't really thought about that yet,' said Brian who hadn't really thought about that yet.

'Are they original?' Now Brian had thought about this. He guessed that some people may ask this, although he hadn't realised that everyone would ask their version of the question. He didn't want to lie. Lying was very bad and he prided himself on not telling lies and so used one of his prepared and carefully worded answers.

'Well, I didn't actually see John and Ringo sign it.' Perfectly true.

'How do you know they're authentic?'

'I've compared them to several originals and they look authentic to me. I've absolutely no reason to think the person who gave me the picture was lying.' Clever – still all true. There was a quiet spell while the punter examined the picture closely, changing the angle to get more light on it while avoiding reflection.

After a long studying look, 'Who gave it to you? When did you get it?' This double-barrelled attack was more difficult to answer and remain truthful. 'The lady in the Bath Women's Aid shop a week ago' wouldn't have helped the chances of a sale.

After a brief moment's thought, in which he acted the part of someone trying desperately hard to remember an important piece of information, Brian came up with, 'I got it from a lady I've known for a few years now … and … I'm … afraid I can't quite remember exactly when I bought it,' he said, still acting 'trying to remember'. This was still all technically correct but getting decidedly more difficult with each question.

'How much did you pay for it then?' Whoa. This one's tricky.

'Ha-ha,' Brian gave a short laugh, just to buy himself a small amount of time. 'Ha-ha, a lot more than I was hoping to pay!' he said with a conspiratorial raising of the eyebrows. He was pleased that he'd still managed to answer this with a degree of honesty, given that the book cost £1.50 and he had hoped to get it for a quid. All of these answers though were sailing quite close to the wind as Brian employed his own kind of honest dishonesty. There was certainly an element of 'Intent to Deceive' about it all.

'So what are you asking for it then?'

'Make me an offer.'

'Twenty quid.'

'Ha-ha. No I don't think so'

'Fifty?'

'No.'

'Fifty-five'

'No.'

'(Big sigh) Sixty.'

'No – I'll open the box, Michael.'

'Do what?'

'Michael Miles – your Quiz Inquisitor on *Take Your Pick*.'

'Sorry, you've lost me.'

This was another of those observations that Brian had meant to think rather than voice out loud. The exchange with the boot sale punter had reminded him of the New Zealand quiz presenter Michael Miles, who, on his weekly show, *Take Your Pick*, offered contestants the choice of increasing amounts of money or the opportunity to 'open the box' containing an unknown prize – hence the show's title.

With the deal on hold at £60, the interested punter moved on to check out the rest of the boot sale. Throughout the sunny morning, another twenty-six punters looked at the picture and asked the same questions. Brian delivered his answers more and more convincingly as time went on in much the same way as an actor will relax into a role more and more with each performance. He turned down offers of £70, £72 and even £80. As the boot sale was winding up and Brian was packing his unsold items back into his car, the original punter returned and bought the picture for £100. Brian had sold his first forgery without ever having to lie or even claim that the autographs were original.

66

It was five to ten now and Brian had a bomb to set. While on Ken Higgs' computer earlier, and during his transforming of Marjorie Higgs into Higgs-minor the second-former, Brian had stumbled on an improved idea for using the Bogart image. Brian noticed a second red LED standby light belonging to a Hewlett-Packard All-In-One printer – not identical to, but of the same series as the one Brian owned. Having lifted the lid he took the Bogart print from the atlas and placed it on the printer screen. This action opened the option/prompt box on the PC screen and Brian selected 'scan'. He adjusted the preview so that the image filled the scan page. He pressed 'scan' and within seconds the scanned image was on the screen. After another brief visit to Photoshop, Brian had the Bogart image filling the screen. To the side of the image in bold white type were the words:

TOMORROW YOU WILL DO THESE THREE THINGS.

1) TELL SUPERINTENDENT RICHARDSON YOU WERE WRONG AND HAVE NO EVIDENCE OF MISCONDUCT WHATSOEVER AGAINST LUCY WEBSTER. 2) APOLOGISE TO LUCY WEBSTER FOR CAUSING HER STRESS. 3) GIVE HER £50.

IF YOU FAIL TO DO ANY OF THESE THREE THINGS I WILL KNOW AND I WILL BLOW UP YOUR HOUSE WITH YOU IN IT. YOU WILL

BE VICTIM NUMBER FOUR. FORGET ABOUT RAYMENT AND WEBSTER. LET THEM GET ON WITH THEIR BORING LITTLE LIVES. I'M THE ONE YOU'RE AFTER. I KILLED THE THREE IN THE GARAGE AND I CAN KILL YOU ANYTIME I WANT – MR DS DEEP SHIT HIGGS. THE NEXT BOMB WILL BE REAL.

He left the image on screen and placed the bomb on the mouse mat, resting against the mouse. Hopefully, the slightest movement would take the screen out of sleep mode and display his warning. He wound up the clock one last time. The trickiest bit was priming the alarm, which was a delicate operation. It took only two attempts this time, and it was set. The whole tin, acting as the amplifying soundbox, was ticking loudly now in the silence of the empty house. When Higgsy lifted the lid, the screen should light up and the alarm would split that silence.

Brian removed his Bogart print from the scanner and made his way into the hallway. He was looking for keys. Most people kept their keys somewhere in their hallway. There were no obvious prominent hooks or holders. He checked the single hallway window sill, but nothing there either. There was an old fashioned telephone desk on the right-hand side with address books, phone directories and a mug full of pens and pencils. On the side of the mug was a cartoon policeman answering a telephone saying ''ello 'ello 'ello'. A red coloured phone was on charge there, and just tucked behind it on the polished wooden top was a small desk-tidy with eight untidy compartments. There were a few safety pins, a drawing pin, two pieces of chalk, a couple of BIC pen tops, a champagne cork and … three bunches of keys! Two of the bunches were clearly car keys for different cars, with some other unidentifiable but interesting looking keys. The third bunch appeared to be made up of duplicates of the interesting looking keys. The third bunch he left, the other two he took. Having pocketed the keys he turned out the light and left Higgsy's house, checking the front door was locked with his new keys.

It was fairly tight. Brian left Shakespeare Avenue and turned right to head home. After a couple of minutes and just a few hundred yards, he passed Higgsy, already indicating to turn into Shakespeare Avenue, who had made extremely good time by the looks of things, in his awful big cream-coloured Mini. Brian spent an enjoyable twenty-minute drive home imagining in real-time Higgsy's next twenty minutes.

The next ten minutes of Ken Higgs's life followed Brian's imagined version very closely. He entered his house as usual and flicked on the hall light. There was no Marjorie to meet him; he knew she had gone to her sister's. He went through to the kitchen, opened the fridge, took out a beer, flipped the lid off and drank half straight down from the bottle as he tried to locate the ticking sound he could hear. Things took a turn for the worse for Ken Higgs when he walked through into his studio and saw the biscuit tin and located the ticking. For any police officer, a ticking biscuit tin is a cause for concern, for Ken Higgs it was very nearly a cause for a bathroom visit. It was the association of ideas – ticking coming from an unrecognised closed container doesn't have the feeling of something that is going to end well. Higgs went through the kitchen to the back door and opened it. Keeping calm, as per his police training, he walked through and picked up the tin, held it at arms-length and walked outside, placing it on the ground and shutting himself back in the kitchen. After several minutes upstairs, Higgs returned to the kitchen door dressed entirely in cricket gear. A hard helmet with a visor, cricket box, pads and wicket keepers gloves. He was aware of the absurdity of how he must look but it was the most protective gear he had in the house. At the station, he could have put on the correct gear with a protective Kevlar vest. He went out through the kitchen door again and even with the hard helmet he could hear the tin was still ticking. He remembered a police training lecture, years ago, on explosives, when the lecturer had told them that a ticking bomb was unlikely to go off suddenly. The ticking indicated that there was a timer, which would be set to explode the device at one specific time. Keeping this at the forefront of his thoughts, Higgs reached for the tin at arm's length and, keeping the tin on the ground, slowly eased off the lid using the edge held away from him. He had it clear in his mind that as soon as the lid was free he would dive back indoors and shut the door. The biscuit tin lid was a snug smooth fit that overlapped the tin by about a centimetre. As he eased it up, a millimetre at a time, it occurred to him that if you absolutely had to choose, gun to your head, the worst possible thing to wear while trying to defuse a ticking bomb, you couldn't do much better than pick wicket keeper's gloves. They made the job extraordinarily difficult, but did give him a stronger reassurance than their actual protection warranted. He continued to ease the lid, then it popped. The noise and vibration of the piercing alarm jolted him like nothing else ever had. The initial assumption that it was the bomb going off followed by the instant realisation of it being an alarm bell was a difficult sequence to take in your stride. He threw himself backwards, turning towards the kitchen and clamped his arms over his head, waiting for the explosion. He remained in this position for some while, looking like an inconsolable wicketkeeper who had just lost England the Ashes, having missed the easiest of catches. When he finally got the feeling that no explosion was imminent, he scrambled up and went back indoors. As it happened, this was the precise moment that Brian, who had by now arrived home, was going back indoors.

67

Neither of the two police officers, Ken Higgs nor Lucy Webster, slept very well that night. Brian on the other hand slept soundly. As soon as he got back indoors, Brian went straight to his drinks cabinet to pour himself a brandy. He had begun to remove the top of a half-litre bottle of Sainsbury's basic line brandy. It was marked with five stars. Brian would have given it two but it usually served its purpose. In a what-the-hell moment, he screwed the lid back on, returned the bottle, and reached for an expensive-looking unopened box on the top shelf of the drinks cabinet. It had been a present for his forty-fifth birthday, and he was waiting for a reasonable excuse to open it. Brian didn't know a lot about alcohol but he knew what he liked. He liked getting drunk occasionally, for a start. In the normal daily routine of his life, Brian was quite rigid about his alcohol consumption. He would allow himself one unit per day, possibly half a lager, a small glass of wine or an occasional tot of brandy. But today was a day of celebration of a job well done. If he couldn't let his hair down today when would he? He opened the box very carefully so as not to damage it. He always had the idea with boxes that if they were in good condition, the item contained within could be returned for a refund, if ever there was a problem. Provided of course that the box was still intact. Even though he was now intending to drink some of the birthday brandy, he couldn't break the habit of many years with the box. He poured a good double measure of the Remy Martin XO cognac. When he had first been given the cognac, he checked the price of it and was appalled to find out how expensive it was. He worked out, even back then, that it was £6 a shot. Given inflation, the drink in his hand now was probably £15 worth. Years ago, as part payment for an illustration job, he was treated to a slap-up feed at what was described as 'the second-best Chinese restaurant in the country'. The client who was treating him bought him a brandy after the meal, which turned out to be a Louis XIV brandy and cost £40 a shot. Brian wondered now, as he did then, how do you enjoy a £40 brandy any more than a £6 brandy? How is it possible to show an extra £34 worth of enjoyment? Do you lick your lips more and go 'mmmmm'? Do you sip it and make it last all evening? Do you close your eyes and smile in delirious ecstasy? Do you keep talking about it? What do you do? How do you show that extra enjoyment to the person who's forked out for it? Brian took his £15 brandy – call it £14.50 – into the front room and sat relaxing and drinking it on the sofa. The heady warmth enveloped him as he relived his perfect execution of the planting of the bomb. He was halfway through the second replay when he realised his glass was empty so he refilled it as before – £29. He felt warm and contented and pleased with himself and tired. *As tired as a newt*, he thought. He took his phone out of his pocket and texted Lucy just two words, 'All sorted', then he went to bed dreaming of screenplays and camera shots for *The Great Higgsy Bomb Plot of 2021* and wondering how much it would cost to get Lars Mikkelsen for the role of DS Higgs.

68

It had been ten minutes since the alarm first rang and no explosion had taken place. The light from the kitchen lit up Ken Higgs's back garden and he could see the biscuit tin and hear that it was still ticking. It was a reasonable sized garden and he knew at the far end there was a heavy-duty galvanised wheelbarrow. He opened the back door again and taking the widest path around the biscuit tin ran to get the wheelbarrow. He wheeled it back and upended it over the biscuit tin, covering it completely. Ken Higgs came back indoors. He needed to report this immediately. He would ask Superintendent Andrew Richardson's advice. He would know what best to do. It was late but he knew Richardson would still be working. Higgs felt it would be good to be able to say that he had sorted out the photographic evidence of Lucy visiting Raymond, so he decided to download it to disc. He removed the protective cricket gear and went through to the computer room. Jiggling the mouse, much as Brian had done, he brought the computer screen to life and was presented with Humphrey Rutherford's warning. It shook him, and the implications of the message got his mind racing. The one good thing to read was 'the next bomb will be real'. Being the reasonable detective that he was, Higgs felt it safe to infer that the bomb in the garden was, therefore, a dummy, and purely left there to scare him, which it had. He continued to detect.

If you fail to do any of these three things I will know. All three of those things would have to be done at the station, therefore to know if these things had been done, the writer of the warning, whoever it was, would also have to be at the station. So, the murderer could be a copper?

Whoever had written the message had also come across as being annoyed that the focus wasn't purely on him, and that time was being wasted on DCI Webster and Brian Rayment. It followed the classic egotistical behaviour of serial killers. He desperately needed to make contact with Richardson, but there were a lot of extra things to consider now. Was his phone tapped? Was Richardson's office bugged? How did he get into the house? There was no sign of forced entry. Could this Humphrey Bogart get into his house again? A few minutes later, Higgs was going through a stack of cardboard boxes under the stairs, looking for an avocado-coloured landline handset. He found it quickly, unplugged the existing handset, replaced it with the old avocado one and dialled Superintendent Andrew Richardson's private number. Richardson answered on the third ring.

'Hello, who's this?' Richardson didn't bother giving his whole name and title. Anyone phoning him up at this time of night on his private number would know exactly who he was.

'It's me, sir. Ken Higgs. There's been a development. Someone's broken into my house and threatened me. I think it could be one of us.'

'One of us?' repeated Richardson

'Yes sir! A police officer. I'm calling from an old phone. I can tell you more tomorrow, but I think we should lay off Lucy Webster and Mr Rayment.'

'Why do you say that, Higgs?'

'I'm concerned about your office or phone being tapped, sir. Do you mind if we leave it until tomorrow? I'll tell you everything then.'

'OK, Higgs. But still bring in the evidence you have on Lucy.'

'Yes, sir. And I'll be in earlier than our twelve appointment.'

'Are you sure you're OK, Higgs? Do you want me to send someone round?'

'No thank you, sir. I'm fine. It's all under control. Have a good night. See you tomorrow.'

When he got back to the house he went outside, lifted the wheelbarrow and had a look at the so-called bomb. He thought it looked like a movie prop. Quite convincing but clearly nothing active in it. Having spoken to Superintendent Richardson, Higgs felt calmer and a little more in control. That particular feeling was soon blown out of the water when he went to his computer and opened up his recent file on Lucy and Rayment.

Higgs spent the rest of the evening, and much of the night, thinking about and considering every person he worked with at the station. Could Lucy Webster have had anything to do with the breaking-in and the 'bomb'? It was quite absurd. For a start she'd been sent home and told to stay there, and secondly, whatever he thought of her, she was a good detective and a quite high ranking one at that. He thought about Brian Rayment. As far as he could tell from his one meeting with him, the man was a nutcase and hardly capable of constructing a convincing-sounding sentence let alone a convincing-looking bomb. Also,

Rayment had no clue of where he lived and even if he had managed to discover that, he had no possible means of making an unforced entry. The idea was unworkable. Could Webster and Rayment have been working together? On so many levels this idea was laughable and yet he was sure there was something going on between them. Despite it now being a folder full of pictures of men's bottoms, or to be more accurate, lots of the same picture of one man's bottom, Higgs had definitely taken a series of photographs of the two of them together. He turned to the other officers regularly working at the station. His analysis of them, like his sleep, was fitful. At 4:30 in the morning, he realised he must have dropped off for a while and quite deeply, as his wife was back home and asleep in bed next to him and he'd heard nothing. He was back awake now though and turned his thoughts to what he would say to Superintendent Richardson – how much he would say and how much he would leave out. His main concern was that Richardson would still want to pursue the Webster and Rayment angle. Deep down, Higgs knew only too well there was no angle with DCI Webster. He was jealous of her. He didn't like her because she had been more successful than he had, and so he tried to drop her in it. In the small dark hours of the morning, trying to sleep in this house, recently broken into by a mass murderer, he now hated himself for it, but he had wanted her to fail. The terrible thing to admit was that he would have enjoyed her failure – what is it the Germans call it? Schadenfreude.

69

Lucy too was having a similar struggle getting to sleep. Her active mind had kept her in that neither-one-thing-nor-the-other state between waking and sleeping. She was just starting to favour the sleeping side when she heard the buzz of her phone vibrating on her bedside cabinet, notifying her of an incoming text. This immediately hauled her right back to waking mode. It was from Brian.

'All sorted.' Whaat? Although this was potentially good news, as with just about all communication involving Brian Rayment, it immediately raised a lot more questions than it answered. It was too late to call him back and get involved with a conversation, or even a question and answer session. Mentally she wasn't up to it and she was also still concerned about any tracking or tapping of phones that may have been set in place. The text, however, did ensure that Lucy wouldn't get much sleep for the rest of the night.

At 10:20 in the morning, her phone rang, not so much waking her up as sharpening her focus. It was Superintendent Richardson.

'Good morning, Lucy. All sorted! I thought you'd like to hear. DS Higgs has assured me that he made an error and there are no complaints or questions about your conduct. I know he's keen to apologise to you. Given that I sent you home unnecessarily and, as it would appear, unfairly, if you want to take the rest of the day off please feel free to do so. However, we could do with you in here if you'd rather get back to work. I'll leave it entirely to you. Is there anything you want to ask me, anything I can help you with?'

'No, sir, thank you very much for calling – I appreciate it. I'll be in about an hour.'

'Thanks very much, Lucy. Come and see me when you arrive at the station. Goodbye.'

'All sorted?' Was this sheer coincidence? Richardson had used exactly the same phrase that Brian had texted. While she got washed and dressed and ready to go back into work Lucy weighed up the possibilities of what Brian could have done. She was trying to fathom what circumstances would need to occur in order that Brian could cause a police officer to make a complete u-turn. She even considered the possibility that there was something supernatural at work. Did Brian have some telepathic or hypnotic power over people, or maybe he genuinely was a master criminal who could gain access to anywhere and threaten blackmail or get rid of anyone who got in his way? Of these two outrageous ideas, amazingly, it was the supernatural one that seemed the more likely. On more than one occasion Lucy had felt that Brian had some kind of hold over her, or that he was reading her mind or even influencing her thought. Several times she had found herself thinking thoughts that surprised her, thoughts that she never thought she would have. She recalled that recently she had experienced a change in her emotional response to Brian. She had been consciously aware of the shift from being irritated by him, to finding him quite endearing. Then there was one of the first meetings she had at Rayment's place with inspector Dew – 'Dew Drop' as Brian called him. Brian had invited her out for a meal. He had invited out for a meal one of the two police officers interviewing him about three murders. She clearly remembered at the time being amused by the ridiculous suggestion. She also recalled that there was a spell of about twenty seconds where she went blank and then surprised all three of them, none more than herself, by accepting the offer.

She arrived at the station at 11:45 and headed into the main incident room. As she walked in, Superintendent Richardson caught her eye and motioned for her to come into his office. He got straight on the internal phone and called DS Higgs to his office as well. When all three of them were in there he handed over to Higgs. Higgs appeared very nervous.

'Good morning, ma'am. I've got a big apology to make.' He'd been rehearsing this throughout a lot of the night. 'I was fed some information that seemed to implicate you in some inappropriate conduct. I've since discovered that it was sent to me by the probable garage murderer – you know, the Bogart person. It now appears it was designed to implicate me as a misinformed troublemaker, to drive a wedge into the investigation team and so get us all doubting and questioning each other. An attempt to lower morale. I've also received a threat to my life and my house was broken into. But again I apologise to you, ma'am, for my misguided actions and for doubting or questioning your conduct. And … I know this is … well … a bit strange, but I'd like you to have this – by way of an apology.' He handed Lucy an envelope. She opened it and took out what looked like a birthday card. On the front of the card was a cartoon hand holding a huge bunch of flowers and above it the word 'SORRY'. Inside the card printed in blue cartoon script were the lines –

Forgive me all my foolishness
And things that I got wrong
You are right as usual
And you have been all along.

Higgs had finished the card in his own hand: 'Please accept the enclosed as part apology, part peace offering and part gesture of goodwill. Have a meal out on me – sincerely sorry – Ken Higgs.'

There were five £10 notes enclosed.

She started to try and hand it back but Higgs put both his hands up waving them and shaking his head.

'Definitely not!' he said as he walked away from her. 'All sorted.'

What have you done, Brian Rayment? How have you managed to get this all sorted? With this the third 'all sorted' she knew now, without a shadow of a doubt, that this was Brian's doing. The rest of the day at the station everyone was nice to her and that was weird. They were never nice to her. Officers came up and asked her advice and opinion. They complimented her on her handling of the cases. They included her in their coffee round but none of this felt like a sincere niceness. It was as if they'd all just learnt she'd been attacked and molested so couldn't be nasty to her anymore. In a strange way, the niceness was even worse than the nastiness. At least the nastiness was a genuine emotion. They did feel that way and they were showing their true feelings.

70

Unlike DS Ken Higgs and DCI Lucy Webster, Brian Raymond had slept very well. He awoke refreshed and in a very good mood. He stretched and farted twice in bed. The first one was loud, very short and quite high pitched, how the queen would break wind if she was here, he thought. Then he revised the thought. No! It's how the queen would break wind wherever she was. The second one couldn't have been more different, being as it was, a quiet long-drawn-out note which tailed off and dropped to become a flattened version of that note in the last moments of the emission. Now who would that be? he thought. Boris Johnson. Again revision. Boris Johnson as he's talking in the House of Commons. Brian would always try and match a celebrity with his farts. Not only the celebrity but the situation in which that celebrity could have produced such a fart. Elton John in a tea shop drinking hot tea. The Jackson 5 on bicycles. He never found the smell side of things in the least bit interesting or funny. It was all about the sound, but there was certainly a lot of mileage to be had from that. As he got up he could feel there was more to come. This could be an opportunity had been waiting for. He ran downstairs to his answer phone and tried to remember how to record a new greeting message. After a couple of practice goes it all came back to him. It was now a waiting game. He would have one shot at this so would have to speak clearly and get his wording right first time. Brian also considered what voice to use. He was very gifted with accents and dialects and was a competent impressionist. While he sat by the telephone awaiting the approaching storm, so to speak, he practised his message in a variety of different voices. Welsh, specifically Cardiff, Geordie, Cockney, Billy Connolly, French, Ringo Starr, Australian, Russian, Bristol, Ken Hom the chef. 'Silly arse,' he told himself. Most people have never heard of him and those who have wouldn't have a clue what he spoke like. He plumped for BBC English – a BBC television presenter from the 1960s. He tried at the voice again, 'Good evening, ladies and gentlemen.' Whenever Brian was in a position of making a public speech or important announcement to a group of people, he would almost invariably start with 'good evening, ladies and gentlemen' whatever time of day. He was once invited into the local sixth form girls college to give a talk on the importance of the sciences in general, and chemistry in particular, for anyone interested in following a career in medicine, specifically pharmacy. At 10:30 in the morning, addressing the sixty college girls, he started with, 'Good evening, ladies and gentlemen.' It was no great surprise that this led to mass sniggering in the ranks. Thinking on his feet and improvising as he liked to do, Brian pretended it had all been an intentional gag.

'No, no, but seriously folks,' he continued, still mentally in open mic night.

'I meant, of course, good morning, boys and girls.' This second faux pas was going to make the lecture difficult to retrieve. He had one last crack at it, still trying to pass it all off as being a joke.

'Good morning, girls and more girls.' A chewed up paper spitball hit him on the lapel of his dark cotton jacket and stayed there. The two members of staff present looked at each other and gave a subtle raised eyebrow expression that DCI Webster and DS Higgs would make when interviewing Bryan years later. Brian bashed on regardless with the hour-long lecture and was starting to claw back some attention, having brought up the subject of drug culture. He now had three spitballs on the front of his jacket and several more on the back from when he had turned to use the blackboard. One girl was interested enough to raise a hand and ask a question. Unfortunately for Brian, she had a thick Glaswegian accent. Unfortunate because it was a situation beyond Brian's control. He would now be obliged to answer in the same thick Glaswegian accent. It wasn't something he had a choice in, it was going to happen. The affliction had landed Brian in trouble on countless occasions, appearing as it usually did, that Brian was taking the proverbial.

'Well now, geddles, this is basically a thurrud wuddled prroblem.'

'Mr Rayment!' from one of the members of staff, the fat one who looked like Oliver Hardy – all fat ones had a little bit of Oliver Hardy in them, he thought. As Brian could hear 'The Cuckoo Song', Stan and Ollie's theme tune, she was giving him the start of one of Hardy's exasperated looks to the camera.

Brian was never invited back. This pleased both the staff and Brian, but quite a few of the girls were disappointed.

Brian could feel and hear the distant rumble of the approaching storm. He wondered whether to help things along with a hot beverage. This seemed like an excellent idea so he made his way through to the kitchen and flicked the kettle on. Almost immediately he had to abandon it and head back to the answerphone. Nearly there! He needed to get cracking now! Ridley Scott had waited three years for this moment of serendipity for this one scene. The most important scene of Brian's life. The film had already cost billions. This is the last shot – no extra takes. Brian undid his trousers and let them slip down to his ankles. He pressed record. LIGHTS! CAMERA! Aaaaaaand ACTION!

'Good evening, ladies and gentlemen, and welcome to Communication Matters, the weekly BBC programme that answers all your questions. Your usual presenter, Brian K Rayment, cannot be with us tonight, but he will personally answer all your questions on his return. Please leave your question for Brian after the tone.' Brian pulled his pants down and squatted naked, all in one movement directly over the microphone, and let rip. It was wonderful! It kicked in like an outboard motor being started and then settled to a constant sonorous buzz saw tone. After three seconds, Brian gave a last little bit of extra effort and created the sound of a motorbike revving before it puttered to a stop. There was a brief pause before he was able to squeeze out a last one of his short, sharp, loud queen specials which had the feel of an audio exclamation mark.

71

Lucy needed to speak to Brian and try to get some handle on what he'd done to get things 'all sorted'! She took herself to the staff canteen and with a coffee sat down at the far end on her own.

She took her phone and opened up the contacts folder. As she was scrolling down to the 'P's – 'Q's – 'R's – the phone rang. It was, of course, Brian. She got in first.

'How did you do it, Brian? It's all sorted, like you said. What did you do?'

'Aaah, that would be telling,' he said. ' Let's just say I'm your fairy godmother.' That didn't seem to sound right. 'I'm your Fairy Godfather,' he tried correcting himself, instantly getting a picture of Don Corleone in a small white ballet outfit with wings and a wand. Marlon Brando as the Don was saying with a pronounced lisp, 'Your with ith my command. I thall make you an offer you can't refuthe – don't ever croth the family again.'

'Hello, Brian, are you still there?'

'Yeth – yes – sorry – I mean thorry – no I mean sorry, I was miles away,' he said trying to shake himself out of the daydream. 'I just called to find out how it went. Have they dropped the inquiry?'

'Yes, they have. Everyone's being nice to me. Getting me

coffee from the machine, calling me "boss" It's horrible'

'Yes, sounds dreadful,' agreed Brian without a trace of sarcasm, loathing as he did both coffee from machines and Bruce Springsteen.

'Police officers are all such a funny questionable back-stabbing lot. Most of them aren't what they seem at all.'

'Am I what I seem? At all? asked Brian. Lucy considered this for some moments.

'Yes, you are,' she said. 'I think you're exactly what you seem.' Brian, being Brian, saw no other way to interpret this than the ultimate compliment.

'What a lovely thing to say. That's possibly the nicest thing anyone has ever said to me. Thank you so much, Lucy, or should I call you CID Webster – I mean DCI Webster – now you're at work at the police office?'

'Station.'

'Yes, police station.'

Again Lucy experienced the inexplicable excitement, for it was excitement, at having another of these strange free-wheeling conversations with Brian Rayment. There was an innocence and an honesty and a freedom of thought about the things that Brian said. Or maybe there was no thought at all, perhaps that was it. He seemed to speak as soon as the words entered his head with neither regard nor disregard to their effect on the people to whom he was speaking. She was certain he wasn't intentionally malicious nor was he intentionally complementary: he just delivered the words.

'Did I sound gay just now when I accidentally lisped?' he suddenly asked. She was tempted to quiz him on how he could accidentally lisp but thought better of it.

'No, I don't think so. I don't think it means you're gay if you happen to lisp. There are plenty of gay people who don't lisp, Brian.'

'Oh no. I only asked for future reference. I didn't mind being gay, I mean I wouldn't mind being gay. I don't mean that I've always fancied having a go at being gay, I mean I've got nothing against being gay – I haven't, honestly. My uncle was a latent homosexual.' He went quiet for a moment, thinking. *Or was it a blatant homosexual?* he wondered to himself. 'I also had a close friend who taught with me at the art college. He told me on my first day there that he was a practising homosexual – not that he ever needed a lot of practice by all accounts.' Brian was on a roll now and was just pausing for the occasional breath. 'When do you reckon the word "gay" stopped meaning happy and cheerful and exuberant and started to mean homosexual? I mean it obviously didn't happen overnight, say on the fifteenth of September 1961 for example.'

A 1960s newsreader: 'And finally, at exactly midnight tonight, the word "gay" shall cease to mean happy and cheerful and exuberant, and shall instead mean homosexual.'

'There would have been a transition period where it could have meant either. When Gilbert O'Sullivan said he was cheerful bright and gay in "Alone Again Naturally", I don't think he meant that he was cheerful bright and homosexual – even if he was wearing a schoolboy outfit. What do you think, Lucy?'

'Well it's a fascinating topic, Brian. I can tell you've given it a lot of—'

'Also there's the word "straight". It's used now as if it's the opposite side of gay, the back side of gay if you like. Who gets to decide these things? It can't be very nice for gays, can it?

Downright offensive really. Straight isn't the back side of gay, straight is the back side of bent, so that's a pretty unpleasant implication, isn't it? I'm sure it would've upset my uncle. "Good God above," he would've said. Though I suppose it's possible to have words with two different back sides so to speak. Take the word "old". The opposite of old could be "new" or "young". Do you think that means "new" equals "young"? I mean you could have a new girlfriend but she could be as old as your gran, couldn't she?' Brian took a moment out trying to imagine life with a girlfriend who was old as his gran. He struggled with it, and broke into a bit of a sweat, as he couldn't shake off the image of the girlfriend actually being his gran.

Lucy took the moment while Brian was off on this disturbing little exploratory ramble to try and find an opening back into the conversation – but it was pointless.

'Did your uncle talk much ab—'

'BLT. Have you heard about that?' It was one of the few sets of initials that Brian understood. He continued, 'Bacon, lettuce and tomato, that's a good traditional sandwich. Now I'm not entirely sure of the details, but I think the gay community has created a kind of extended bigger improved sandwich by adding other ingredients. They seem to have this one called an LGBTQ plus. Lettuce, of course, G? What do reckon? Grapes? Bacon and tomato, as usual, Q? Quarter pounder? and the plus? Plus any relish I suppose. Doesn't sound bad, does it? I'm not too sure about the grapes though, a bit of

cheese would be better. Maybe it's "G" for gouda or gruyere or

gorgonzola. That's more like it. Yes, I think these gays are onto a winner with

that LGBTQ+ sandwich.'

72

While Brian had been updating his answerphone message, DS Higgs was updating Superintendent Andrew Richardson on his u-turn regarding inappropriate meetings between Brian and DCI Webster.

Higgs had chatted to his wife over breakfast, playing down last night's break-in. He didn't mention the bomb or the death threat or the folder of his surveillance photographs that had all mysteriously become photographs of a horrible looking bottom. He told her someone had broken into the house, but as far as he could tell, nothing had been stolen. So not a break-in as no doors or windows appeared to be damaged or forced, but in legal terms, still breaking and entering – even without the 'breaking'.

'Oh silly man, didn't he put the key back?' asked Marjorie. 'He didn't sound at all well. I don't think he should have been at work. I think he's probably caught the pandemic.'

'What you talking about, love? Who didn't put the key back?'

'Your super.'

'You're not so bad yourself.' Despite being alarmed at Marjorie's response, Ken Higgs couldn't resist entering into the oft-repeated in-joke. 'But who didn't put the key back?' he finished the gag.

'Superintendent Andrew Richardson. He phoned up yesterday and wanted to leave some important file for you. He was ever so rough – it didn't sound like him.'

'It wasn't him.'

'Course it was!

'It wasn't him. It was someone pretending to be him. It was the intruder pretending to be him, and you told him to use our spare key and where we kept it.'

'Don't be daft, Ken. How would an intruder know our number? We're ex-directory, aren't we? And we don't give our home number out to anyone except your work friends. It's only the police and my mum and dad who know our number.' She did have a point. 'And Mum and Dad know where we keep the spare key anyway,' she added in case he'd thought her parents could be involved.

This was all completely true. They had been obsessively careful with the home phone number. Each had their own personal phone for daily communications and friends but there were fewer than twenty people who had been given their home number, Andrew Richardson among them. All those people, police officers themselves apart from her parents, had understood that home numbers of officers are never passed on by second parties. It was at first advice, and then a directive from the top brass, as a matter of security for police officers and their families.

Marjorie's parents always phoned during the day on Wednesdays and Fridays, Marjorie's days off. The rare evening calls would only ever have been from Ken's police colleagues. It was entirely reasonable that Marjorie should accept that it was Superintendent Andrew Richardson with whom she'd spoken.

In one aspect he was reassured by this knowledge, but at the same time, it more or less confirmed that it must be a police colleague who called Marjorie pretending to be Superintendent Richardson. Following this line of thought, Higgs could only conclude that the intruder, and hence the garage murderer, had to be someone at the station who was also on his home phone list of contacts. By cross-referencing he was able to whittle down his phone contacts from twenty-four to seventeen. Seven of the numbers belonged to work associates from other forces, towns and cities and with whom he had little contact. None of these seven had ever even been to the Bath station. He was able to further eliminate six more names. Four worked in the forensic department and never set foot outside their own lab, and two were based in the stores and evidence rooms. None of these six would have any knowledge of DCI Webster's movements or any awareness of or interest in Brian Rayment. Higgs felt certain that whoever made the call to his wife was indeed a male, which enabled him to cross off the four remaining female officers on his phone contact list. This finally left Higgs with the conviction that his intruder was one of seven colleagues he saw on a daily basis and who, if the warning on his computer was to be taken seriously, he assumed to be the garage murderer. Consequently, he was disinclined to reveal anything to anyone.

73

Brian had an important and busy morning lined up. Having just re-recorded his answerphone message he needed to check it to test the full effect, to see how it sounded in real life. He had several other things to check as well. It was important to get his priorities in order. First thing's first, he needed his phone. As usual, Brian had set it charging overnight and now the battery symbol flashed a full 100 per cent. He opened up the phone's video folder to make his early morning check of the three video passes of Lucy asleep in his spare bed. Thankfully they were all fine – none missing, no deterioration, all present and correct. He felt safe now closing the folder until his early evening check. Brian had also made a mental note to have a closer look at all the other names and phone numbers listed in Lucy's notebook. All his images, including the original photographs of her notebook, had mysteriously disappeared when the radiator had leaked and his phone had ended up submerged. However, he had already copied down the numbers and her notes exactly as they appeared in her book. He wanted to see if there was a mobile number for Ken Higgs and also a number for Superintendent Richardson. He looked at the original notes he made and saw that only the home number was listed for Higgsy. He copied this down again on a plain pale yellow Post-it

so he'd have it to hand, along with Richardson's only number –
a mobile. He took the opportunity to scan through all the other
names, numbers and notes. Right! All his checking was up to
date – he needed to go and get copies of his two new bunches
of keys. He drove into town and then headed once again for the
cobblers, and once again he could feel himself getting worked
up over the fact that cobblers seemed to be the only people who
could cut keys. Analysing it he realised the thing that jarred
with him was that cobbling was quite a crude brutal sort of
job involving pounding hammers, big pots of glue applied with
Walt Disney cartoon brushes, coarse grinding machines, sharp
paring knives and hefty leather stitching machines. Key cutting
on the other hand was a small scale precision job. It seemed to
Brian akin to a butcher having a weekend job performing laser
eye surgery.

On the two bunches, there were nine keys altogether, but
two were duplicates of the car keys. Each of the bunches of keys
used a small carabiner, rather than a traditional keyring. This
made it very easy to slide all the keys off, once the carabiner
had been unscrewed. Brian thought this was an excellent
invention and made his mind up to steal one of the carabiners
and replace it with a regular keyring before he returned the
keys. Increasingly theft was becoming more and more a part
of his daily life. He had found that being a triple murderer
was quite liberating and opened up many possibilities of life-
improving criminal activity, that would have been unthinkable
in his pre-murder days. Last night to while away a few minutes,
he went through all his criminal activity since the murders. So
far he'd chalked up arson, theft, petty larceny and breaking and
entering. The idea of trying grand larceny rather appealed to

him and he added it to his mental 'things-to-do' list.

He reached the cobblers with the keys all removed and he placed them on the counter. I would just like one of each of these please. The cobbler/key-cutter looked at them and moved them around the counter with his forefinger.

'Can't do this one,' he said, flicking out one of the car keys. 'You'll need to get a code from the garage and order one from them. Or this one! No idea what this is. Never seen one like that before. I haven't got a blank remotely like that.'

'That's probably the one for the cells,' said Bryan before he could stop himself.

'Eh?' said the cobbler.

'It'll be the one for the safe where we all keep our cell phones overnight. Every night, the whole family, all of us, put our cell phones in a little safe to keep them … safe.'

Oh nicely done again, Brian, thought Brian.

Now he had his own near-complete set of keys he needed to return the two original bunches, each now using the large traditional keyrings he'd just purchased, as quickly as possible – hopefully before they were missed. He didn't have time to wait for Marjorie to go out again. It could be days, but also he couldn't let Marjorie see him or hear him. He must give no chance of her describing him or recognising his voice. He needed to go back home to prepare a few things for the key drop off at Marjorie's. Brian had long been aware that he was an inventive and supreme master of disguise, so he enjoyed creating a new look for returning the keys to Marjorie. Twenty-five minutes later he was knocking on her front door. Although it was a cold day the bandages were keeping him nice and warm.

74

Marjorie opened the door and just stared at the figure in front of her. Brian was wearing most of his clothes, one on top of the other, which effectively distorted his true body shape and rendered him huge. A pair of pyjamas, being the outermost garments, were pulled tight and bulging over all the layers of shirts pullovers and trousers. His hands, arms and head he had completely bound in white crepe bandages. In front of him, he was holding, with both bandaged hands, an A3 flip chart pad on which was written 'Hello. I'm deaf and dumb and injured.' He flipped over a sheet like in the Bob Dylan video. On the next page was written, 'Could you please spare a penny for a crust of bread?' he looked as if he had escaped from an intensive care unit or possibly a lunatic asylum. Imagining how the conversation was likely to go, Brian had tried to predict what Marjorie's first reaction to him would be. His plan had been to have a cleverly prepared and appropriate response written out on the next sheet of his flip chart. Having run through several possible, likely opening lines from Marjorie – are you alright? do I know you? what seems to be the problem? – he was realising that this was one of those situations that could easily backfire on him. The chances of him producing a suitable response were slim, to say the least. It wasn't a one-answer-suits-all situation. The more likely outcome would be an absurd response leading to a surreal conversation. In Brian's experience, surreal conversations were things in which most people weren't comfortable. If he did manage by some fluke to pull off the near-impossible and give a perfectly anticipated answer on his next sheet, it would look like he was performing, door-to-door, some sort of deaf and dumb mind-reading magic act. Not the best approach for remaining unnoticed and unmemorable. His final plan was to follow up his two-sheet-intro with some improvisation. He had with him a thick black felt pen with which he could write responses or further questions as he thought of them.

Marjorie spoke for the first time, 'Are you hungry? Let me make you a sandwich and a drink.'

Brian hadn't expected this, but now he thought about it and it was on the table, he quite fancied a sandwich. So that he'd be able to respond to this without talking, he needed the felt-tipped pen he'd put in his trouser pocket. He encountered an unforeseen problem. Which pair of trousers? He was wearing six pairs all with pockets. Brian thrust both bandaged hands down his pyjama bottoms and began to rummage around. Marjorie was transfixed by the disturbing apparition before her as Brian's hands were creating obscene and unhealthy looking lumps and movements inside his pyjamas. He finally managed to extract his felt pen and write, 'Thanks very much,' before he realised that accepting a sandwich would spin out the meeting, so he continued writing, 'but I've already eaten a huge meal – I'm full up.'

Marjorie was still in a bit of a daze from Brian's pen-search and asked with a distant distracted air, 'Why were you asking for a penny for a crust of bread?' which was not an unreasonable question in the circumstances.

Brian wrote on the next sheet, 'In case I become hungry.' Marjorie was trying to equate this with the initial deaf and dumb claim.

'Did you hear what I said?' she asked. This sounded to Brian reminiscent of a frequent childhood reprimand. 'I told you to stop going cross-eyed, Brian. Did you hear what I said?' The memory kicked him into action.

'Yes of course I heard you,' he answered in a heavily muffled voice.

'You don't seem very deaf,' said Marjorie, 'or dumb.'

Keeping silent, and back in dumb mode, he looked around with a puzzled expression as if he'd heard some vague distance sound and was trying to locate the source. Although it was a good performance, Marjorie didn't see any of it, of course, thanks to the bandages entirely covering Brian's head. This had all taken a funny turn. He needed to cut to the chase. Still holding the pen he flipped to the next page and wrote, 'I only stopped here to tell you there are bunches of keys by your car on the driveway.' He pointed to the keys he had dropped by the car earlier, just before he knocked on the door. He continued on the next sheet, 'Be a shame if your car was stolen. Hubby wouldn't like that. Ha-ha-ha.' He was on a bit of a roll and Brian didn't realise just how brilliant this last line was. It was the one thing that stopped Marjorie from ever telling Ken about this meeting with him.

Marjorie called out, 'Thank you for that,' picked up the keys and started back to the house. She paused and turned to Brian again, 'I do appreciate it. Thank you again, good luck to you, whoever you are. Goodbye.' She went straight to the phone table to return the keys where they belonged, never to mention them or understand how they got outside in the driveway. She spent a long time thinking about the incident and the strange heavily padded and bandaged man in pyjamas claiming to be deaf and dumb. How fortuitous that he should call. She knew how angry Ken would have been with her. What if he'd come home and seen the keys himself? She still felt guilty and bad about yesterday's break-in, even though they both knew it wasn't her fault. Ken Higgs had not seen the keys, though, and he was far more concerned about the police colleague who was possibly at fault for the three Garage Murders.

75

Ken Higgs arrived at the station anxious and wary. He looked around the squad room, checking his list and saw that all seven of his final list of break-in suspects were in today. Since his morning discussion with Marjorie, he had been reassessing these seven. For a variety of reasons and a healthy dose of gut feeling, he was narrowing it down and assuming it to be one of the Peters. Gun to his head he would have said Peter White. Superintendent Richardson put his head around the door and said to him, 'Would you like to come in, Ken.'

Ken nodded and made his way to Richardson's office. Peter White was already there looking his usual embarrassed self. He knew it. This is it! It was Peter White! The super was on to him too and this was going to be the big reveal.

'Peter's got some news that will shed an entirely different light on the whole matter of the Garage Murders,' said Superintendent Richardson. Peter White looked even more embarrassed and like he had something he wanted to get off his chest. This was going to be good. This was going to be special.

'Over to you, Peter,' said Richardson.

'I took a phone call here this morning, as soon as I got in, at about eight just gone.'

Hello, where is this going? thought Higgs.

'It was from Jonathan, the son of Rose and Len, the other two who were killed at the same time as the Garage Murders. He told me he'd been cleaning out his parent's house, going through all their things, and he came across a camera.'

'What sort of camera?' asked Higgs.

'Well that's the whole point,' continued White, 'it was a small security camera. Jonathan had been on to his parents to take security at their house more seriously, and last Christmas had bought them a small CCTV camera. He was convinced that they had opened it and just put it away in a cupboard. He found it last night, very well concealed in amongst some books and ornaments on a shelf. It was set to wide-angle to give the maximum possible view of the main room. Very professionally done. Looks like they got someone in the know to set it up for them. They'd been using it every day, setting it every evening when they went to bed, quite early, and timed to stop at nine in the morning. A twelve-hour recording every night. The last time it recorded was on the day we assumed they went missing.'

'Did it record anything of interest?' Higgs asked.

'Yes, I think you could say that,' answered White. 'It showed both of them being murdered.' In terms of statements to stop shows, it would take some beating. There was a complete temporary silence. It was like the moment a car crash is inevitable. The speeding car has left the road and is in the air and it goes quiet. It stays silent for what seems too long and then all the noise happens at once and gathers its own momentum. After the brief silence, Higgs and Richardson produced all the noise. They couldn't get the questions out fast enough. It was clear that, although Richardson had undoubtedly heard about the camera being found, he had no idea of White's devastating news. When the two of them had run out of questions and before White could properly answer any of them, Superintendent Richardson said, 'Hold on, White, everyone needs to hear this.' He had an intercom microphone on his desk which he seldom used. The last time was in the summer when there was a small fire in one of the storerooms that was easily under control but necessitated the evacuation of the building until it had been checked. Health and safety. Richardson used the intercom now.

'Everyone in the main incident room immediately.'

Within minutes the incident room was full.

Nobody knew what to expect. It could be news breaking of a new case or an important update on an existing case. It could be news of a misconduct or inappropriate procedures from one or more officers. It could be notice that Prince Charles was going to drop in on them this afternoon. Lucy was still edgy and was convinced it was going to be more suggestions of misconduct about her. The atmosphere around her had remained fake. It was an awful and unnatural environment to be working in. PC White took the floor. Without any introduction or preamble, he started.

'I took a phone call here this morning which resulted in a major development in the so-called "garage murders and related cases". The call was from Jonathan Gray, the son of the murdered couple Len and Rose. While clearing out his parents home, Jonathan discovered they had been using a CCTV camera for twelve hours each night. The camera was in operation on the night it is assumed they went missing. Their murders and murderers are caught on the film.' As earlier, the very brief silence after the revelation was broken by noisy reaction from the assembled squad. It was rare that White had centre stage in anything, and he was enjoying his moment and was letting the gathering take its time to digest the full implication of his announcement, and to realise that there was even more exciting news to come – who was it? There was even the start of a smile appearing on White's face.

'OK, White, get on with it. Who was it? What was on the video?' said Richardson.

'It was all three of the garage victims, sir.' Again the noise broke out and again White enjoyed the reaction.

'OK! OK! Quiet! Let him speak or we'll never get to hear it.'

'At 11.43 p.m. three masked intruders come into shot, two smallish males and one fat female. Large female. Apparently, they seemed to be quite active, but there's no sound of course. At 11.47,' said White, looking at his notebook, 'Len and Rose enter the room in their nightclothes and the three intruders grab them and shake them. It appears they are shouting at them. Len leaves the room and Rose is obviously distressed and then she collapses. Len returns with a heavy-looking box. He sees Rose and drops the box, running to her. He spends a few moments checking on her then flies into a frenzy and launches himself at one of the intruders – Tony Bartlock as we find out soon. Len has what looks like a bread knife with him and he's attacking Bartlock with it, and appears to be getting the better of him. The large woman – who turns out to be Marlina Bartlock – grabs Len from behind, upends him and pins him to the floor. The film shows that Len is screaming and shouting. Rose has come round and is also crying or shouting. Tony takes out a gun and fires two shots at Len and Len is still. Bartlock has just killed Len and is standing staring at him. The second intruder snatches the gun from Tony's hand, turns and immediately fires a third shot at Rose. The intruder – Stuart McGregor – has just killed Rose. The time reads 12.01.' This time the whole room remained silent. White continued to give further details of how the three removed their masks, showing clearly their identities, and then over the course of the next hour move the bodies out of shot, presumably out of the building into the car in which they were eventually discovered.

76

PC White's devastating presentation immediately put quite a different slant on the two ongoing investigations. Although related, the murders were being treated as two separate cases: the murders of Rose and Len and the Garage Murders. Now after just one phone call from Jonathan, the first investigation had been solved and the killers were found to be the victims from the second investigation. Although the murder of the three killers remained unsolved, the subsequent interest and urgency in the case plummeted. There was a general feeling amongst all the officers working on the case that it was a form of poetic justice. Fifty years ago they would have been hanged anyway. None of the three had any relatives or friends urging the police to crack on with the investigation and bring it to a conclusion. There was an overall air of relief at the probable slowing down and eventual withdrawing from an investigation that was going nowhere. A public display of continuation had to be maintained. Meetings would be arranged, decisions would be arrived at, about all manner of related things. How much should be revealed to the press, of the phone call and CCTV footage? Was there any advantage in releasing that information at all? Should the Garage Murder investigation case be put on hold? What purpose did it serve the public or the police to continue with the expense and ill-affordable man-hours in an investigation that no one was interested in or bothered about? There would undoubtedly be the claims of a serial killer still on the loose, but despite it being a multiple murder case, everything pointed to it being a one-off incident and not the start of a serial killing spree. It was almost certainly related to the murders caught on CCTV and perpetrated by the Garage Murder victims themselves. Whatever course the investigation now took, there were still a few loose ends to tie up. The CCTV footage would have to be reviewed and written up, as would Jonathan's phone call. Jonathan, having the strongest motive, would need to be re-interviewed, though everyone was certain he had nothing to do with the bizarre surreal events that took place in the garage. Friends, relatives and other neighbours of Rose and Len would be questioned again, being the next most likely, though still unlikely suspects. These formalities would be dealt with over the next couple of days and then the presumption was that the case would slowly make its way into the cold case files and eventually the police history books.

There was an overall air of anti-climax for the rest of the day. For the last four weeks, the entire squad had worked long relentless and tedious, but ultimately unproductive, hours. Now the scale and irrefutable nature of the evidence just dropped in their collective lap had left them feeling almost cheated. As a result of this one phone call, everyone's time spent and hard work had just become irrelevant.

During the next two days, the station slipped back into its pre-Garage-Murder routines. Some officers just enjoyed a few more relaxed days, others felt the stress and frustration of being pipped at the post. For those officers, it was something akin to a stand-up comedian expertly crafting and building up a story only to have, at the last minute, a random member of the audience shout out the punchline.

Lucy was all at sea, drifting, and by the Wednesday evening was at the end of her tether. She succumbed to increasingly frequent thoughts of Brian, and without considering the consequences called him.

'Hello, Brian. It's DCI W … sorry it's Lucy.'

'Hello, Lucy. How lovely to hear from you, how you doing?'

'Not very well. I wondered if you fancied a drink tonight? I wanted to get your opinion on something.'

'My opinion of a drink?' Lucy head already discovered it was best not to be too easily lead down these tracks. She ignored the question

'I've got a big decision to make and I'd like your view on it. I thought you'd be just the person to offer a different view of things.' Brian had already taken a very different view of the situation. He was convinced once again that Lucy was about to bring up the subject of marriage or propose to him.

'Oh good-O,' he said. 'Where shall we meet?'

'Not the Marlborough!' she said definitely. 'How about the Star – say eight? You may want to give my decision – my dilemma – some thought before we meet tonight. I'd appreciate it if you did.'

'I've already been giving it a lot of thought and I think I can safely say that the answer is "I do". Or possibly "I will", depending on how you phrase it.'

'I haven't even mentioned the problem to you yet, Brian.'

Brian smiled to himself and said, 'I think we both know exactly what your big …'

'I've handed in my notice, Brian.'

'You what?' said Brian, stunned and shocked at both what she was saying and what she wasn't saying.

'I gave written notice to my superintendent but he said he wouldn't open it for forty-eight hours. He said I should think carefully about what I was giving up. If I change my mind I can ask for it back anytime within the next two days and nothing more will be said about it. If I'm insistent on going through with it, I can either work a month's notice and have a big leaving-do at the end of it – or leave straight away. So, that's why I'd like to meet tonight. I really would welcome your thoughts. Shall we agree, eight at the Star then?'

'I'll see you there. I'll wear my Ted Bundy outfit.' It was another of those sentences he meant to think rather than say out loud.

77

Two days earlier, and for the first time since the Garage Murders, Brian found himself in the same charity shop where he'd bought the Humphrey Rutherford felt hat. This time he had with him a very specific shopping list. He had assumed he would need to troll around all the charity shops in town, but it was not the case. As it turned out, he got fixed up with the four items on his list, all in this same shop and all for under £14. He'd found a wig, more blonde and more curly than he would have liked – a bit too Harpo Marxy – but it would do the job. A regular checked peaked cap, a large pair of gents trousers and a small pair of size 7 gents shoes with a heavy tread. He was about to take on the role of Brian Holmes, long lost younger brother of Sherlock and Mycroft, with the same uncanny gift for disguise, but operating on the other side of the law.

'Holmes! Stand up! I didn't see you at the lecture on camouflage and disguise this morning!'

'Thank you very much, sir.'

When he got the items home, he quickly got involved with the adjustment and fine-tuning of the disguise. He put the blonde curly wig on and set about it with some hefty industrial quality scissors. He removed most of the curls until he was left with a short, shaggy, rough-cropped version. With the cap on top, it worked perfectly to change the outline and shape of his head. The trousers were fine as they were. The biggest change required was with the shoes. Using a combination of the scissors, a chisel and a kitchen knife, he removed the uppers of the shoes as best he could, effectively leaving just about an inch worth of the heavily-treaded soles. Using a contact adhesive, he stuck these roughly-hewn soles onto the worn-out soles of an old pair of his own shoes that were almost ready for the bin. While he waited for it to get dark and for Marjorie to go out, he bagged up a few more items that he needed for this evening's work. Just before he set off, he securely tied some knives and forks vertically all around his knees to change the whole character of his walk. For further impedance, he wanted to put something uncomfortable in his shoes. Nothing came to hand apart from some drawing pins, which he felt would make walking impossible rather than difficult. Earlier that day he'd sat on a pair of pound shop glasses and broken them. He took the two halves and further broke them into several pieces and put the pieces inside his shoes. He knew from experience that the plastic glasses broke very easily. With the latex gloves on he was ready. At 8.00, exactly a week after the great letter-bomb plot, an old man wincing in pain, and with obvious great difficulty walking, made his way gingerly and stiff-legged along the road and into the Higgs's driveway. His key was already in his hand and he used it to go in through the front door. He was much more focused and had planned this evening far better than he had last week's escapade, which had been largely a sequence of spur-of-the-moment which-would-you-rathers. He now knew the layout of the place well and had a few specific tasks to complete – things to steal may be a more truthful way of looking at it. As he had done a week ago, he put on the kitchen light. This was plenty to light up the whole house, so he went upstairs, which was far from easy. He found the master bedroom without much trouble, and went straight to the cupboards. The right-hand one was Marjorie's, so he went to the left. His first thought was what a terrible selection of clothes Higgs had, and he had to tell himself to keep focused. There was another cupboard in the room next door, which he assumed was the spare bedroom. He opened the cupboard and saw hanging at the back, behind some winter coats, were two police uniforms. One looked in better condition, and although Brian was no expert, it appeared to hold a higher rank than the other. Brian took it and put it in a large Iceland bag. On a high shelf above the hanging clothes were two police hats. Brian took them both. Going downstairs was a great deal quicker but more painful. He slipped at the top and juddered his way down on his back. When his feet hit the floor the cutlery gouged into his knees. He took it in what would have been his stride, but was now more of a Douglas Bader waddle. It was method acting and would make for a more convincing performance. If Robert De Niro could put on sixty pounds to take on the role of Jake La Motta, he could certainly gouge his knees with cutlery for this role of 'crippled old burglar'. When he was here a week ago, looking through the files on Ken Higgs computer, he came across a file marked 'SAFE'. it was one of the few files he opened up to look at. There was just one cryptic line written in the file.

Brian had brought a copy of this with him. As soon as he had decided on making this second break-in, he had been trying to decipher the line: 'comb 607686 A Christmas Carol – Pickwick Papers.'

Was it in code? Probably not, he thought. He reasoned

that Higgsy wouldn't be expecting strangers to trawl through his computer files, which meant the note was just for him. Why would he need to write a note for himself? To help him remember.

A Christmas Carol, Pickwick Papers were classic books by Charles Dickens. Where would he find them? Bookshelf.

The computer room had no light switched on but was bathed in the borrowed light from the kitchen. It was enough to see the far wall, which he recalled from his bomb visit. It was a wall of books. Eight shelves full of books from floor to ceiling. He went to it and tried to read the spines but it was too dingy. He switched on the baby spot by the computer and angled it to the shelves, lighting them enough to now make the titles readable. There were a lot of books but it took very little time to spot a row of identical, faded, red books. They were the only 'set' as such. He assumed it was a budget edition, probably from Reader's Digest, of the complete works of Charles Dickens. Brian moved in closer to read the titles and saw that they appeared to be in no particular order – certainly not alphabetical, neither were they chronological. Somewhere deep in his past he had filed away that the Pickwick Papers was Charles Dickens' first novel. It was the twelfth one along in the way this set had been arranged. A Christmas Carol was the third book. He was pinning all his hopes on the solution to the code being in, or with, these two books. An extra sheet of instructions – words underlined. Using his forefinger, he tried hooking out a Christmas Carol. It didn't budge, something was holding it back. He tried the same thing again but pulling harder. The book started to move but bringing with it Martin Chuzzlewit and Nicholas Nickleby. They were attached. There was a solid fourteen-inch block of ten Charles Dickens novels solidly glued together, starting and ending with a Christmas Carol and the Pickwick Papers. Brian removed the block of books and could then see that they were not books at all. It was a fake unit, whose sole purpose was to disguise what was behind it: a Burton Eurovault Aver S24E digital home safe. There was a digital keypad, very much like that of a mobile phone, with a small two-inch lever to the left of it. Brian flattened out the piece of paper with the combination number written on it. He spoke the six-digit number out loud as he pressed the appropriate numbers on the keypad.

'Six-zero-seven-six-eight-six.'

He tried to turn the lever clockwise, but met resistance and nothing happened. He repeated the sequence and tried turning the lever anticlockwise this time. Still, nothing happened. Still immovable. He felt a rush of disappointment course through him. Having found the safe via the books comparatively quickly and easily, it just served to heighten the let-down of the six-digit code not working. Backwards! He went through the procedure twice more entering the six-digit number in reverse, trying the lever once anticlockwise once clockwise. Still no luck. He moved in close and studied the keypad. There were twelve buttons. The numerals from 0 to 9, a button with a green circle on it and a twelfth button with the universal power symbol. Above the buttons was a small LED display screen. He pressed the power button which lit up red. The display screen was also lit but with a dim white light. There were three beeps like the end of a microwave cycle. After a few seconds, a rolling message appeared on the display screen: *'ENTER THE SIX-DIGIT SECURITY NUMBER'*. Reverting to the original number, once again he spoke it out loud as he pressed the buttons. As he pressed the final '6' button there was a single longer beep and the button with the green circle lit up. The rolling screen rolled out a new message – **PRESS THE GREEN BUTTON AND TURN THE LEVER ANTICLOCKWISE TO OPEN THE SAFE.** Brian followed the instructions and opened the safe.

78

Immediately he saw there were things of great interest to him. At the front of the safe were four taped stacks of banknotes, each about a centimetre deep. They were all £20 notes – fifty of them in each bundle. He took the £4,000 out of the safe and put it in another of the several plastic shopping bags he'd brought. Having removed the stacks of notes, he could now see a fairly large, clear, plastic kitchen storage box. He took that out and unclipped the lid. He heard Ennio Morricone playing the theme tune of *The Good, the Bad and the Ugly*. Finding the treasure. He was the Good, Higgsy was the Bad and … he supposed Marjorie could be the Ugly. The storage box was full of treasure. It was full with many items of jewellery and gold from a bygone age. He put his hand in and moved the items around, giving himself a better look at the haul. There were at least six gold rings of various sizes and thicknesses, and some large, ugly, hefty looking brooches which also appeared to be gold. There was a thick rope of pearls and several sets of diamond earrings. None of it looked very attractive, but all of it looked very valuable. It was extraordinarily exciting, which caused Brian to break wind.

Screwing up his nose and mouth in the classic 'disgust' face, he fanned the air with his hand, dispersing the richer-than-usual mix and feeling glad that he'd released it in Higgsy's house and not his own. Still holding his breath he put the storage box of jewellery into the bag. He reached into the safe where there were just two items left. He pulled out a stiff brown manila envelope, which was wedged full with documents and papers. They were too tightly packed in to remove easily. *You need a bigger envelope here, Higgsy, tight git.* He shook the items out onto the floor in front of the bookshelves. Oh yes! There was some very useful stuff here. Passports for Ken and Marjorie – driving licences for both of them along with car documents showing that Marjorie's Prelude was in Ken's name. There were several police ID cards, obviously representing a considerable passage of time, judging by the photographs. The earlier ones, showing a younger Ken Higgs, had photo-booth type pictures stuck on – the later ones, more of a plastic credit card type, had a scanned-in photo. Brian didn't bother forcing all these items back in the small envelope but just emptied the lot into the shopping bag that was filling up very nicely. The last item in the safe was a dark wooden box about the size of a shoebox but only three inches high. It had two brass clips and a leather handle on the front. On the top of the box in gold paint was printed Detective Chief Inspector Ronald Higgs.

Brian opened the box and saw the photograph first. There were several newspaper cuttings, certificates and papers, but uppermost was the photograph of DCI Ronald Higgs. He was in a police uniform but it wasn't a formal shot. DCI Higgs was smiling and appeared to be larking around holding a gun very much in a James Bond pose with folded arms. It was a colour photograph and the slight blue tinge gave it the feel of a picture from the 1950s or 60s. On the back was written 'Ron with his new gun. New Cross London March 1953.' There were two newspaper cuttings from 1952 about the Derek Bentley 'Let him have it' murder case.

There was an official letter to DCI Ronald Higgs telling him that, following the Bentley case, he had been chosen to become one of the several hundred armed officers. After the 1952 Derek Bentley case, in which a constable was shot dead and a sergeant severely wounded, the issue of routine arming in Great Britain was raised. As a result, around seventeen per cent of officers in London became authorised to carry firearms. It would appear that DCI Ronald Higgs was one of those.

Under the photograph, letter and newspaper cuttings was the gun itself. There were also two brass clips each holding six rounds. The gun looked pristine and unused. It was the sheer coincidence that was the main element here. Brian had only ever rummaged through another person's private belongings on two occasions, both of these since the liberating action of the murders allowed him to do so. On each of these occasions, he'd uncovered a gun. Was having a gun stashed away more common than he'd imagined? Maybe it was a very frequent addition to most people's cupboards, but just one that wasn't talked about. He started to formulate the idea of doing a bit of research on the subject. If he chose 100 houses at random – it would have to be a good cross-section of the community – and then broke into them one by one, so that he could explore the contents of their cupboards and the secrets of their pasts, it would give him a good working percentage of gun hiders. It would make an interesting and worthwhile future project and would be more to file under 'time well spent'.

He put the gun and cartridges in the bag with the other items. The excitement of it all made Brian want to fart again.

He considered unloading as much of the dirty wind as possible into the safe and then shutting the door and sealing it in the airtight box. Both the good thing and the bad thing about this idea was that the whole payoff was in the imagined re-opening of the safe. He wouldn't get to witness it, but the idea still appealed. The deciding factor turned out to be one of logistics. To manoeuvre himself into the necessary delivery position would require the removal of the knee cutlery and also the excruciatingly painful footwear – there wasn't time. He closed the safe and put the block of Dickens back.

It was time to make his exit, and his entrance as it happened. Checking the roll of duct tape and the centre punch he'd brought, Brian went out of the kitchen into the back yard and looked back into the large open-plan room he'd come from. Using nearly half the roll of tape, he covered the back window in it and pressed it down well. He held the centre punch hard against the taped glass and pulled the trigger. He could feel the glass go and saw the tape get pulled in as the window sagged and collapsed. He pushed it all into the room, largely in one taped-together crumpling sheet. A few small splinters and shards escaped, but as breaking large windows go, it was neat. With his small soled shoes, he walked and jumped about in the wet mud in the back yard leaving several good clear impressions of the tread just outside the window and several good clear impressions of the broken pound shop glasses in his feet. He climbed back into the house careful to leave more muddy prints on the floor. As soon as he was in the house he went back to the kitchen door, locked it and turned out the lights. With his two bags of spoils, he made his way through the house and left by the front door.

79

Two days later, on the evening of Lucy's phone call to Brian, they met for a drink at the Star as arranged.

'Well, which would you rather?' asked Brian.

'You often say that don't you?' said Lucy. 'It seems to be some sort of default statement for you.'

'The thing is,' said Brian, 'our whole lives are constructed of "which-would-you-rathers". Some are very small but others are huge.' Lucy had adopted the expression that Brian was very familiar with. It was a cross between bewilderment and irritation. Whenever Brian had a conversation of any length it was never too long before the expression appeared in some form or another. He started to explain. 'From the minute you wake up – from the minute you are conscious, you are making decisions, and all those decisions boil down to "which would you rather?" For example, which would you rather, lay in bed for an extra five minutes feeling slightly uncomfortable, or get up straight away and use the loo? Would you rather make a cup of tea before you get dressed or after you get dressed? Would you rather have that tea in a cup or a mug? Would you rather have the first sip straight away or wait for a few minutes? A lot of these decisions are made instantaneously and subconsciously because of your experience and their familiarity. When I was at art college some friends and I often played a game we created called "Which Would You Rather?" that's where it started really. The poser of the question would have to come up with a specific and difficult dilemma for the posee to answer.' Was there such a word as posee? He wished he hadn't used it. Saying 'posee' made him sound a bit pretentious, a bit of a poser. Then he remembered that he was in the middle of explaining that he and his friends had been posers – of questions.

Having sorted that out Brian continued. 'It started with fairly regular dilemmas. For example, which would you rather, eat fish and chips every day for the next six-months, or never eat fish and chips again? Or which would you rather, lose a twenty pound note or lose the book you're reading? This model quickly progressed to a much more interesting and humorous version using the unexpected juxtaposition principle. Which would you rather, be punched in the face once by Michael Aspel or go and scratch your car door with a screwdriver? Or maybe, which would you rather, drink and eat only milk and potatoes for a year or walk to John O'Groats starting right now without putting a coat on? It was not long before even this was not quite enough for us. I'm sure there is still a handful of ex-art college students who still play the final version of the game which evolved over several months. The game became absurd, surreal and complex with multifaceted dilemmas. As it moved into this phase we created such classics as – which would you rather, scuff the toes of every pair of shoes you own on the pavement and then drop a breeze block onto your bare feet from a height of four feet, or pay a tramp fifty pounds to come and smash up your kitchen and then a further ten pounds each week to come and have diarrhoea on your front path? And –

which would you rather, keep six pounds of unwashed potatoes down your underpants for the next four years, never giving any excuse or explanation for it, or change your name to Margaret Thatcher and have hiccups for six months while every seventh word you say is Acker, as in Acker Bilk?' Brian often wondered, far more frequently than you might imagine, Acker Bilk as a little boy. He would picture the other local children knocking on Mrs Bilk's door saying, 'Can Acker come out to play?' When he pictured Acker Bilk as a little boy it was quite a horrific image, generally of a five-year old schoolboy's body with the bearded and bowler-hatted head of the adult Acker.

'I've never known any other Ackers, have you?'

Lucy shook her head. She'd never known any other Ackers. She'd also never known any other Brian Rayments.

80

'Where it does come in handy is helping you make decisions,' he said.

'How do you mean?' asked Lucy.

'Just give me an example of a tricky decision you have to make and I'll explain it to you.'

'OK then! Should I shoot all my colleagues at work or not?'

'Alright alright, let's rephrase this. Which would you rather, kill all your colleagues and have them out of the way forever, but have to pay the consequences of a long extended court case and almost certainly end up with a long prison sentence, or don't kill them and still have to have them around …'

'Brian – Brian – I wasn't serious!' she interrupted.

'Well it sounds pretty damned serious to me,' he said, 'killing a whole squad room of police people in cold or even hot blood has got to be an extremely serious offence.'

'Oh, Brian! For goodness sake! I just said that because I hate the place and the people so much. Now I've come to understand that, I can hardly bear to set foot in the place. That's why I've handed in my notice. Like I said, my superintendent said he wouldn't open it for forty-eight hours. I'm supposed to be thinking carefully about what I'm giving up. I've got two days to make a decision. If I go through with it, I can either work a month's notice and have a proper leaving-do, or leave straight away. Seven months ago when a detective sergeant left, with ten years service, her leaving-do lasted under twenty minutes. They gave her a bunch of flowers and a microwave … from Tesco's,' she added scornfully. 'I've no idea what to do – but strangely I did want to talk to you.'

'Well, I think Tesco's microwaves are supposed to be pretty good. My auntie had a stainless steel one.'

'Not about the microwave, Brian, about the situation in general. What am I supposed to do? What should I do? What do I want to do?'

Brian went quiet and was obviously giving the questions his full consideration. Eventually, he spoke.

'Lucy – I'm going to do something I've never done before in my life,' he said solemnly. 'I'm going to give you a three-pronged which-would-you-rather. This will be a difficult one, but it will help you to see things clearly and make the right decision as to the best course of action. Here it is then.

Which would you rather, (A) Withdraw your letter of resignation and continue to be a detective chief inspector, where you have a good and guaranteed income, but where you will have to spend your days in and amongst people you don't like, in an atmosphere you detest. (B) Let the letter of resignation stand. Work out your month's notice and then pick up a free bunch of flowers and a Tesco microwave at the end of it, and from that point on be free to follow whatever future career you choose. Or (C) …' He appeared to waver a bit, taking in a few deep breaths.

Lucy looked at him. He was so earnest. He was genuinely trying to give her the very best advice and help that he could.

He was giving her this unique version of his own particular brand of creative thinking, crafted through years of striving to cope in a world that was reluctant to accept him. She felt an odd mix of emotions. There was sadness for him. The struggles he had endured, which in turn had alienated him from society but at the same time strengthened him against it, made her want to hug him. Looking at him there was happiness within her and a feel-good glow that someone would put so much into answering what to most people would be a hypothetical question. He continued in a rush.

'Or (C) throw your job in now, leave straight away and come with me on an adventure. You'd have to act immediately because I'm leaving tomorrow. We could be like Bonnie and Clyde, Robin Hood and Maid Marion, Butch and Sundance, the Lone Ranger and Tonto.' Brian was talking fast, trying to get it all out before Lucy could object or interrupt. 'You won't ever have to see or mix with those people who upset you. You won't have any guaranteed income of course, but you'll have me. We'll have each other and we'll have the adventure of a lifetime and go where our hearts lead us. We can travel on a whim and a prayer. Whaddya reckon?'

Lucy didn't say anything. Brian started up again, full speed ahead.

'We could find ways to make money – buying and selling stuff, robbing banks. When I said about Bonnie and Clyde, Robin Hood and Maid Marion, and Butch and Sundance and the Lone Ranger and Tonto, you haven't got to choose one of those to be. You could be a mix. We could both be a mix or you could be one of them and I could be a mix or, for example, you might be Butch Marion or Bonnie Kid, whereas

I might be completely Tonto.' Lucy wasn't sure if he said these things intentionally or whether they were the ramblings of an innocent. If he said them on purpose it was quite clever, if not then it was quite endearing. Either way, she liked it. She looked at him again and there was a slightly frightened look to his earnestness, as if he was concerned that he might have overdone something and that she was about to walk out of his life. He looked entirely vulnerable. She reached up put her hands behind his head and pulled him towards her.

'Come here,' she said and kissed him. They stayed in the embrace for quite a time. The embarrassment of facing each other afterwards keeping them there as much as the passion. Finally, she eased him away and looked into his eyes. 'C,' she said.

'See what?' he whispered hoarsely

'C. I choose C.'

'Thank God for that – thank Sinatra, I mean.' Lucy didn't ask. 'We leave tomorrow. I've got tickets for the Orient Express. A five-day trip taking in Paris and Venice. We set off from London tomorrow.'

'You've already got tickets?' said Lucy unbelieving.

'Yes – a bit of a gamble I know, but I just had to put faith in my ability to present a which-would-you-rather in an irresistible way. I have had a lot of practice.'

They arranged to meet the following morning at Brian's house at 9:30. Lucy went home and packed a few things and then phoned Superintendent Andrew Richardson to tell him she wouldn't be coming in anymore, so he could open the letter anytime he wanted. While she was packing and making the call, Brian was loading his suitcase with disguises, including

Higgsy's police uniforms, passports, ID and of course the gun. He'd also packed the cash and the plastic box of vintage jewellery

'What made you choose the Orient Express?' asked Lucy.

'I just thought we could maybe spend a year travelling around by train. I don't mean one long train trip that lasts a year. We could stop off at different places and have a look around a bit. I thought it would be an exciting start though, Bonnie and Clyde in the Orient Express – if that's not a recipe for murder I don't know what is.'

'I've left the service now, Brian, so I want nothing more to do with murder – if that's OK with you.'

A few miles further on and Lucy said to Brian, 'You do know what happened to Bonnie and Clyde don't you?'

'Yes I certainly do,' said Brian, who had researched the two outlaws to point of near obsession. 'Here's a question,' he said. 'Who do you think had more bullets in them in the end – Bonnie and Clyde or the three Garage Murder victims?' For nearly a minute, Lucy looked at him then straight ahead, then back at him.

'How do you know the garage victims were riddled with bullets?' said Lucy. 'That information was never released.' Brian carried on driving, watching the road, just carried on driving.

Eventually - 'In that case, it's probably a good job you're not a police officer.'

Graeme Puckett graduated from Bath Academy of Art, worked at Butlins for a season as a portrait artist, and subsequently as a freelance illustrator and corporate caricaturist for 25 years. Graeme's work frequently appeared in T.V. Times, Woman's Realm, Knave, Fiesta and the like.

In the 90s, Graeme changed course, when he and his partner Ann started swing dancing and discovered they were good at it. After 18 months, they became UK champions and went on to win many more national swing dance awards. As Hoppin' Mad, they've continued teaching and performing Lindy Hop all over the world, and run regular weekly classes in Bath and Bristol. They were the dance consultants for the film *Chicken Run*, which they watch every Christmas, to see their names in the closing credits. Graeme and Ann have appeared swing dancing on numerous TV shows, most recently the Netflix award-winning series *Sex Education*.

During the pandemic lockdown, when partner-dancing ground to a halt, Graeme kept in touch with his friends by writing to them. By the third or fourth letters, reading between the lines he was no longer receiving, he suspected his friends were feeling pressured by the obligation to reply. To salvage what friendships he had left, he just started writing for himself. This is it.

Graeme lives in Bath with his partner Ann and their two children, Badger and Little Bear, who, like Graeme, are both short-haired domestics.

If ever you are in Bath or Bristol, Graeme and Ann would love to see you at their swing dance classes.
www.hoppinmad.co.uk